THE BRIGHOLD

Phil Arnold

Trafford
PUBLISHING™

Also by Phil Arnold: *Seven Holes in England*

Order this book online at www.trafford.com/07-1557
or email orders@trafford.com

Most Trafford titles are also available at major online book retailers.

© Copyright 2007 Phil Arnold.
All rights reserved. No part of this publication may be reproduced, stored in a retrieval
system, or transmitted, in any form or by any means, electronic, mechanical, photocopying,
recording, or otherwise, without the written prior permission of the author.

Note for Librarians: A cataloguing record for this book is available from Library
and Archives Canada at www.collectionscanada.ca/amicus/index-e.html

Printed in Victoria, BC, Canada.

ISBN: 978-1-4251-3879-0

*We at Trafford believe that it is the responsibility of us all, as both individuals
and corporations, to make choices that are environmentally and socially sound.
You, in turn, are supporting this responsible conduct each time you purchase a
Trafford book, or make use of our publishing services. To find out how you are
helping, please visit www.trafford.com/responsiblepublishing.html*

*Our mission is to efficiently provide the world's finest, most comprehensive
book publishing service, enabling every author to experience success.
To find out how to publish your book, your way, and have it available
worldwide, visit us online at www.trafford.com/10510*

 www.trafford.com

North America & international
tollfree: 1 888 232 4444 (USA & Canada)
phone: 250 383 6864 ♦ fax: 250 383 6804 ♦ email: info@trafford.com

The United Kingdom & Europe
phone: +44 (0)1865 722 113 ♦ local rate: 0845 230 9601
facsimile: +44 (0)1865 722 868 ♦ email: info.uk@trafford.com

10 9 8 7 6 5 4 3 2 1

CHAPTER ONE

In the 'tween light clutch of an early spring morning, while the gentle mist still lay close to the ground, just as the fresh dripping dew fell sylph-like upon the clammy earth and percolated the moist surface into wet diffused skeins of translucent stringy mud, George Ward, the county gravedigger blew out the stump of the candle lighting his tiny kitchen and let himself out through the back doorway. Outside, he carefully selected one of a pair of well-used greased shovels and, swinging the long ash handle over one spare shoulder, strode up the cracked garden path and let himself out through a dilapidated front gate.

The narrow country lane twisted away from the cottage, stretching out like a flattened snake up the tree-lined hill and out of sight behind an outcrop of buttressing sandstone. With his lips pursed in a tuneless whistle he passed the dark hulk of Mayfly Cottage, silent and gloomy in the still atmosphere, the mist-slated roof still shiny from the previous night's shower of rain. The hedges encircling the cottage were high and imposing, giving the place the aspect of sadness and neglect.

In the early morning silence the gravedigger's iron-tipped boots rang loudly on the loose stones of the lane, startling a crowd of crows that were picking at the dead body of a rabbit lying in the road. With one concerted flurry they shot into the air and winged to a line of tall poplar trees bordering the lane. George knocked the carcass aside with a swift kick and shook the shovel in the direction of the birds that just answered his gesture with concerted cries of alarm. Transferring the shovel to the other shoulder, he strode into a weak morning mist, leaving the crows to hop down to the dead body again and return to the feast.

The rusted iron gates of the village cemetery loomed up before him and at his touch opened with a squeal of unoiled hinges. The tall black iron gates with the county crest of a winged angel praying with uplifted eyes and hands, creaked shut after him as he trod on the rough cinder path edging a long row of leaning gravestones. In the quiet of the morning his footfalls echoed through the small graveyard and reverberated off a roughly constructed slab stone wall running the boundary line of the cemetery. A wooden tool shed loomed up before him and, selecting a large metal key from a key ring holding several others, he lifted a rusted padlock and thrust the big key into it. Spots of dew dripped from the lock and he brushed them away, turning the key with a practised snap of the wrist. The lock sprung open and the door swung inwards.

George stamped off the clinging clinker from his boots and entered the shed. Inside were housed a wooden wheelbarrow, a pickaxe, a long-handled rake, another shovel and a small collection of clay pots. Dropping the shovel and the pick into the barrow, he gripped the long wooden shafts, straightened up and backed out of the shed. The barrow wheel sprang into life and with a small squeal of protest turned and bumped over the wooden threshold. The gravedigger steered the barrow towards a pile of freshly dug earth sited between weather-beaten gravestone slabs and, skirting the soil heaps and stones, dropped the wheelbarrow with a thump at the side of the half-dug grave.

The metal pickaxe and the steel blades of the tools crashed together as he threw them into the hole, bringing down an avalanche of soil as they thudded to the bottom. There was a bigger earth fall when his boots scrambled down the sides and landed in a shower of falling soil and gravel beside the implements lying on the earthen floor.

The morning advanced and the grave sunk deeper. The sharp point of the pickaxe tore at the dark earth, driving down six inches with every forceful swing of George's sinewy arms.

Later the morning mist lifted and a weak sun probed into the graveyard, its rays striking the fabric of the gravedigger's coarse woollen shirt, the perspiration from his working body having formed patches of sweat on the arch of his back and at the armpits.

After a while he stopped to wipe a sweat drip from the end of his nose and licked a pair of dry lips. He reckoned he had dug out three feet or more and, judging by the amount of freshly dug loose soil mounting up at the graveside, it was almost deep enough. Another foot will do it, he decided mentally, and reached for the pick again. Breathing in a deep lungful of air he lifted the heavy tool high into the air and brought it down with some force, biting into the earth, only this time it kept on going until the ash handle of the pick met the ground and brought it up short. George struggled to free it, but only managed to push the tool deeper into the void. He swore to himself, trying to wrench it free. It seemed to be held by something just below the surface of the ground.

Throughout the years digging holes in the cemetery, George had often found an old grave, and if the owner of the plot could not be traced the remains were removed to another site where they were reburied. George shook his head and slowly scraped the loose soil away with the shovel to reveal the wooden remains of a coffin. Little by little the whitened bones of the long dead occupant were uncovered until he was able to pull them into position beside him. He halted to cuff the sweat from his sharp nose and began the work of removing the pieces of wood from the newly uncovered grave. Rotten wood, heavy with the musty tang of rank decomposition, fell apart in his hands, and all about him was the rancid air of utter decay, which joined in the influx of every laboured breath he drew in, and in doing so penetrated deep into his lungs.

The depth of the hole and the lack of air at the bottom of the pit seemed to make the smell worse. He straightened his back, looked down and was astonished to see the coffin remains slowly subside and fall away, leaving a broad hole about five feet square, from which a mass of yellow was rising. As he watched, the dust swirled up into the pit and rose above his knees, where it stayed, emitting a horrible smell. The gravedigger gazed open-mouthed at the venomous issue and suddenly seemed to awaken from a stupor with a yell of fright, trying to distance himself from the fetid rank

6

smell rising up from the cloud.

The dust climbed higher up his body and he put out a hand to ward it off. His hand waved through the cloud and a queer tingling swept through his fingers; a cold clammy touch that started at his fingertips and, like a crawling spider, progressed to his palms and then his wrists. Quickly he snatched his hands away and rubbed them on the coarse surface of his mud-encrusted corduroy trousers. The cloud swirled and soon fiddled and probed at his nostrils, prying with icy fingers at his tightened lips, resting like a festering sore on the skin of his face. Beneath his feet the ground continued to open up. The hole widened, spewing yellow dust that boiled upwards. With staring eyes he tried to see into the hole, but all he saw was the rising yellow dust streaming out, reaching out for him.

With an agonising scream he tried to scramble up the steep sides of the hole, but only succeeded in bringing down clods of loose earth. In his panic he tore with bleeding fingernails at soil and stones alike, blood dripping from them and mixing with the cloud of yellow dust. The shovel went first, vanishing down into the hole, followed closely by the pickaxe. From his compressed lips a yell of complete agony spilled out. He made one last desperate lunge for the grave top, but he fell just too short. The last vestiges of the grave bottom collapsed under his madly flailing legs and he hurtled into the hole, falling through it into a dark void that held out fiendish hands to encircle and claim him.

Above, the morning held its breath and a sighing wind rippled through the trees, traversing the graveyard and bending the grass blades. The weak sun, heading for its

7

zenith, cast a dark shadow on the new grave—the only witness to see the dust cloud whorls, writhing like a twisted serpent, contract and withdraw into the recesses of the hole. Below, the mad maelstrom of wildly spinning light and dust whirled in a sensation of dizzy gyrations. The added suction, drawing, pulling, demanding and squeezing, plunged ever downwards, compelling and driving deeper into the depths of the abyss.

The body of George Ward, mind numbed by the shock of the descent, hurtled headlong, breathing and choking on the dust storm, drawing in spasmodic lungfuls of the dust and expelling them with heaving retching coughs that threatened to tear his billowing chest apart. With outstretched arms to ward off any passing spurs of rock, he plummeted downwards, sightless and helpless, waiting for the inevitable end of his fall—then it happened.

His falling body was arrested by a sudden immersion into an enveloping carpet of soft material that clung to him as he arrived, breaking his fall. He plunged into it, swimming in it, flailing about with widely thrashing arms and legs, fighting the suffocating blanket that threatened to engulf him. He was then battling for the surface, coughing and gasping, eyes streaming hot tears until his head arose above the surface of the soft carpet. In the half-light seeping down from the hole through which he had plunged, he was able to spit out the yellow dust caking his mouth and, with several snorts of expelled air, clear his clogged nostrils from the embrace of the clinging dust.

Looking around he was able to see that the material that had eased his fall was a great heap of the yellow dust and, as the fine powder began to settle, in the feeble rays of the weak daylight filtering down from above, he was able to make out his surroundings. He was in a large vault, so gloomy it was well nigh impossible to see into the corners. To improve his vision he lifted his shirt tail and used it to clean out the dust from his eye apertures. He then hawked up a large gob of mucous into his mouth and expelled the remains of the dust crunching between his teeth.

Within a few minutes George was able to get a glimpse of the size of the cavern and was surprised to see it was a big arched vault, about forty feet square or more and composed of thick walls that appeared to have been hewn out of solid rock. Looking about him, he suddenly went into a blind panic, wrestled his way out of the dust then stood on a rocky ledge quaking with fear, gazing at the light coming down from above. Out of the corner of his eye he saw the square shape of another mound rising up from the ground and with wildly beating heart he waded through the thick dust and coffin debris to stand at the side of a huge, mouldering wooden coffin. It was supported by a bed of neatly piled rock slabs and looked like it was hundreds of years old.

Momentarily losing interest, his plight came back to him and he began to look for a way out of the cavern. With clumsy feet he inspected the cave for any escape holes, but after a couple of circuits he began to realise it was secure. Standing in the square of light coming from above, he judged the hole to be four feet or more in size and set in the centre of the cavern. This might be the entrance to the tomb, so that could explain why there was no lower door, a new thought that brought a fresh line to his already furrowed brow. George sighed and his gaze wandered to the wooden coffin once more. He then guessed it was some twelve feet in length and three feet in width, but the sheer size of the sarcophagus and the way it was constructed amazed him. The corners were of wrought iron with bands of the same metal running across the box from top to bottom. He gauged the weight to be of half a ton or more.

The worried gravedigger again turned to his person, and a closer inspection of himself revealed a lot of deep scratches on his arms and legs with a really bad cut on his chest where the sharp rocks had caught him. The wound seeped blood, oozing through the thick skin of yellow dust coating his clothes. The red emission had begun to form a thick crust of coagulated blood on his shirt front and flapped from side to side with each movement. On the rudely cut wall behind him, the light from overhead formed a rectangular pattern on the rocks, and the passage of the weak sun crossing the heavens caused it to move in a transitionary sequence as well.

After his initial moment of terror in falling into the hole, he was able to collect his thoughts into an assessment of his plight and, after a cursory longing look at the light source out of reach above him, realised his hopelessness with a feeling of deep despair. He tried shouting at the top of his voice, but gave up after a few minutes. The dust was still in the topmost part of his larynx and the effect of producing loud noises made him subside into bad fits of coughing. He doubted whether he was being heard anyway. The graveyard seldom had visitors and the thickness of the cavern walls combined with the dumbing down of any sound by the dust, seemed to muffle any cries for help he made.

Soon it began to rain. The raindrops dripped down in a

never-ending stream, bringing with them a steady waterfall of muddy brown water that quickly inundated the dust pile transforming it to a yellow quagmire of thick and treacherous ooze. Although the drips quickly saturated his clothing and froze him to the bone, there was a positive factor as well, for it quickly cleared the cavern air of the floating dust motes and in a short while George was able to breathe fresh air once more.

The time dragged into the afternoon and for the umpteenth time he sloshed through the dust-riddled puddles, examining the tomb. He passed by the sarcophagus in his circulations, but only once did he pause to examine it more closely. Through the gloom of the cavern he could only just make out a few legible letters inscribed on one side of the box, but either they were in a foreign language or the progress of time and general decay in the period of incarceration had made them all but unreadable

It was during this time that his gaze had wandered over the wooden coffin, looking for signs of anything to give an insight into to whom the thing belonged or even what is was. From what he could see, apart from these few letters there was nothing, however hard he strained his eyes. He gave up at this juncture and returned to his circuits of the cavern. The rain stopped and the stream falling from the hole in the roof eased to a steady drip. He sat on a dry part of the ground and contemplated his position. I really need a rope to haul myself out of the hole, he mused, but there was no rope. The only things he possessed were the digging tools that had fallen into the hole with him, but of what use were they to him down here?

The tomb was a solid rock cave and, as far as he could

make out, entirely without means of entry or exit, so how had the coffin been brought into here? There was no door, no window, not even a mouse-hole. When he looked up and saw the rectangle of light beaming down on him, the possible solution came to him. Maybe I fell through the door of the tomb. The thought widened and in his imagination he saw the coffin being lowered into the cavern, where it was put into place on the rock table many years past, but how many years past? Perhaps a hundred, no, it's older than that. Possibly five hundred years, maybe even more.

His interest gained ground and he swung around to eye the mound. Perhaps it's valuable. Mummy corpses have been found in different countries of the world and proved to be valuable. He got up and twisted around to view the coffin, instantly regretting the move as the pain from the wound to his chest knifed through him. He fingered the cut tenderly, feeling around to assess the extent of the damage. As far as he was able to ascertain, the cut had stopped bleeding and was forming a big scab on the surf ace of his chest, but he could feel the particles of dust adhering to the coagulated blood so, gritting his teeth together against the expected pain, he brushed them away. The wound instantly hit back at him, so he stopping brushing, just dabbing at the cut instead. He got the cut as clean as he was able with the rank tail of his soiled shirt and tore off a narrow strip of the material to use as a makeshift bandage, in the process twisting his lips in a grimace of pain as he accidentally touched the wound. He managed to tie the ragged wool strip around his breast, finishing with a couple of tightly drawn knots. The other lesions to arms and legs he left alone, although they were smarting badly with the painful prick of the dust in them. Various small bruises and scratches were ignored. He straightened up from his close inspection of his limbs and felt satisfied he had done everything possible to stop any infection from gaining a foothold.

George Ward was an angular man with not an ounce of fat on his bones. The veins stood out on his neck and arms, as it mostly does on all lean men, and his muscles, although small, were whipcord hard and ideally suited to his job of excavating graves. He was fifty years of age and had been a widower for the last ten years. His wife had died after a particularly heavy bout of influenza and for awhile the loneliness of being without her hit him very hard, but gradually her presence faded to a memory and he threw himself into his job with more vigour. He had been employed by the local council ever since he left school, and when he first stepped onto the ground destined to be the village cemetery he had the somewhat dubious distinction of being the first gravedigger to break the virgin soil and dig the first grave. This state of being the only gravedigger had remained so for fifteen years and every cadaver carried into the cemetery was borne there with the certainty of being buried by George Ward. There was no other man to help him with his work. Every shovelful of earth was dug, lifted and piled up by him and when the service given by the local vicar was over, the heaps of chalky soil were painstakingly returned to from whence they had come.

George was a careful man in his appearance, job, reputation, everything. He knew full well his employer, the county council, had its good name to uphold, so his steady employment during these extra good years rested entirely in his hands. He also had a good reputation to maintain, which could not be sustained without him being in good health. That is why he was meticulous in his insistence of treating every injury with extra precaution.

He stamped his boots on the mud-encrusted floor of the cave and looked up at the rectangle. His face blanched with concern when he saw that the light coming through to him was beginning to wane. Night was approaching fast and he faced the prospect of spending the dark hours in the tomb; something he had been dreading. He had no way of knowing what hour it was because the big pocket watch his father had willed him was at the jeweller's being re-equipped with a hairspring after its demise. Within reason he had been able to judge the time by the shadows surrounding him, but that was on the outside. He had a good idea it was after five, but how much after? He shrugged a pair of thin shoulders, thinking that as night was coming it threatened to turn the tomb into something of a black hole. Even now the shadows were thickening as the light waned. He was compelled to think more and more about sharing the tomb with the mysterious coffin only half a dozen paces or so from him. He shrugged again, a little from the cold, but a bit more from the second thought.

George had little fear of the ordinary corpse, he had seen enough of them in his job to start feeling squeamish in the proximity of a human skeleton, but this coffin had an aura about it, something out of the ordinary, and it was making him feel uncomfortable by its presence. There was something peculiar in the feel of the thing, maybe it was too old, or strange in the way it was constructed. Why steel bands on the thick wooden boarding? Was that to keep out marauders or keep the occupant in? He laughed softly to himself and regretted even thinking the thought. Now the thing was beginning to occupy his mind more than it should. His first thoughts must be about getting out of the tomb and not of the mound yonder!

He squatted on a dry patch of rock floor again and tried to think of something else. He felt hungry and thought about the ham bone waiting for him in the larder. A small bakery in the village baked a good loaf of bread and delivered it as well; just the job for a starving man to ease the pangs of hunger. He started up, thinking fast and furious. Of course, the baker! He'll miss me, I'm always at home when he calls. The next thing he'll do is come down to the cemetery and see if I'm all right. This cheered him up considerably and he waited for the baker to make an appearance.

Meanwhile, the evening marched on, the cavern grew black and soon he knew that the baker was not coming. Not today, that was evident, but if he was to hold out until tomorrow he would be missed, and that was a certainty. It was the day that the man who owned the cottage usually called for the weekly rent and if George was missing he generally called at the graveyard for the money. He had only to see the hole and he would rouse up the entire village. The only thing, George thought with deep regret, was that he called at the cottage after visiting a dozen or more of his tenants, so if he was going to discover his misfortune it would be not until after four in the afternoon.

Gloom, thick and impenetrable, descended on him. Here

he was, sitting on a damp floor, surrounded by a suffocating blanket of dark that was so thick you could almost touch it. George licked a pair of dry lips and thought of a cool glass of bitter. The pink and brown tongue circled his mouth, leaving the gleam of fresh spittle in its wake. He tried to put the idea from his mind by concentrating on his surroundings. He looked up at the rectangle quite hard and was surprised to see a solitary star shining through the opening, making the blackness seem not so impenetrable, so much so he could swear he glimpsed the wall opposite him in the starlight. Soon the earth revolved on its axis and the star eventually went out of sight.

The wound in his chest subsided to a dull ache, his head began to droop. The still air in the cave, bereft of motion, effectively induced sleep. He slumbered on, sitting upright on the hard stone floor...

With a start George sat up, ears cocked for the sound that had roused him. It came again; a soft, scratching scraping noise.

CHAPTER TWO

There was a weak moon that night. Scudding through dark silvery rain clouds it jumped in and out of the clouds with darting rapidity. The moonbeams formed a path of brilliance into which Len Denny silently stepped. He was a big man, strong and powerful, equipped with large hands and broad shoulders. He was carrying a large hessian sack with his set of strong fingers wrapped around the neck like a steel band. Carefully he stood still in the moonlight, listening for any alien sound. He appeared satisfied after awhile and swung the sack over a big shoulder before setting off.

Denny had to be careful because the bag contained two cock pheasants, a single partridge and a couple of spring rabbits, and Bennet, the gamekeeper of the Links Green Estate owned by the local squire, was in the vicinity. He smiled and shook his head in disbelief; either he was having extra good luck tonight or the gamekeeper was getting old. The pheasants and the partridge would fetch a good price at the local inn, while the rabbits, tender with youth, would end up in the pot.

His footfalls were soft on the wet grass and he swiftly stooped to push a wire snare into the sodden turf before starting forwards. With his shadow following him he pushed his bulk into a meshing clump of bracken fern growing on the estate boundary fence and, with practised swings of his huge arms, swept the saturated foliage aside. He made the chain-link fence with ear tuned to every sound, stooping to grab and lift a section of the wire away from its wooden supports with powerful muscles and expert fingers. Within minutes he was slipping under it and worming his way to the other side. He straightened up and for a brief moment paused to listen, senses stretched. The noises of the night came to him. A twittering bird overhead, a distant owl's hoot and the solitary bark of a dog from a nearby farm were the only sounds to break the silence.

With silent tread he walked well known paths and soon came to the edge of the wood. He stopped again, listening before breaking cover and stepping onto the surface of the village road. With rubber soled boots he strode away, his breath exuding vapour plumes when his strong legs quickened into a faster gait. Farther along the road the village cemetery came into view and the hushed gardens, with darkened gravestones and skeletal trees, passed by in silent procession. It was almost a nightly march for him. The animal population, especially the rabbit species, was on the increase and the woods were positively bursting at the seams with pheasant and partridge.

Denny's silent steps quickened to pass the cemetery, eager to get to a waiting pint of ale, then his head turned to a see a strange glow in the direction of a recently excavated grave and he muttered to himself.

"Old George is doing a bit of overtime. Odd he is working this late though, and by lamplight too, must be a very important funeral for him to be working at night. Can't hear any noise from the hole, must be deep down."

His footsteps faltered. In the past George Ward had proved to be a willing customer of his, being partial to a bit of tender rabbit meat. Denny pushed open the squealing moonlit gates to the cemetery and crunched his boots on the cinder track that led to the grave with the glow coming from it. As he drew closer the light became more intense. It changed to a green-tinted phosphorescence and bathed the hole and the piled up mountains of chalky soil in an unearthly glow. Seeing this, Denny hesitated and his steps faltered. Countless years of nightly jaunts into the countryside had made him unafraid of the night, but this queer light coming from the hole vaguely disturbed him. He was surrounded by other gravestones that during the day would appear normal and cause him no alarm, but in the chill of a lowering sombre sky with distant storm-flashed lightning forking the horizon and in addition, this strange luminosity shining up from the hole, it stopped him just short of the grave. He eyed the light, squinting in the brightness. Shall I, he thought, shall I just take another two steps? It will bring me up to the edge of the hole and I can see from where this brightness is coming.

As he stared, a gentle cloud of bright yellow dust slowly arose from the foot of the hole and hovered above it, suspended like a large bubble of boiling fog, seething and swelling silently in the luminous glow springing up from underneath the cloud. Denny dropped the sack in fright and stepped back from the hole, uttering a low moan that threatened to strangle in his throat. Through teeth beginning to chatter he raised a big gasp and staggered back, eyes protruding, goggling at the apparition. He was shaking visibly and the sweat began to pimple his brow and shine on his cheeks. Tearing his fascinated gaze from the sight of the cloud he turned tail, leaving the sack where he had dropped it, lying half-open over the edge of the hole, divesting itself of the contents, which fell one after the other into the open mouth of the cavern

In his haste, Denny stumbled over concealed objects and in a blind panic tripped over fallen gravestones and prostrated himself on the cinder path, winded and shaken. For a brief spell he remained there, trembling violently, muttering hysterical cries, while the dust cloud slowly melted into the hole until the only thing remaining was the glow of phosphorous radiating up from the tomb. He managed to regain his feet at last and, with an awkward shambling gait, staggered to the gates. He flung them open wide before lumbering down the road to the village, uttering hoarse terror-stricken yells that roused the domestic population for miles around as he wove from side to side, vanishing into a gathering mist that did little to muffle his cries.

Behind him, the cemetery gates, lying half-open, were reflected in a glow not unlike a sort of malevolent St Elmo's fire, which burned brightly for a instant before being extinguished, leaving the glare over the grave barely able to be seen.

The first the villagers heard of the incident was when the distressed poacher lurched into the taproom of the Red

Cow demanding a drink in a hoarse voice, ashen faced and shaking uncontrollably. His eyes were wild and staring, and it was half an hour before anybody could make any sense out of what he was gibbering. Most of them concluded he was drunk; something for which he was noted. The first anybody had any inkling of what it was all about was when he started mentioning the name of Ward, the gravedigger. This tied up with the disappearance of the man and the fact that he had been missing since early the previous morning. The village policeman got to hear of it and promised to investigate the matter as soon as he was able. The news of the incident reached the ears of a county chemist called Lund, who passed it on to another, a colleague named Meary.

John Meary was a person of some note. He had some knowledge of the black arts, and satanism interested him to such a degree that when he heard of the poacher's story, he hurried post-haste to the village, where he lost no time in seeking him out. Denny let him into his cottage after an assurance that he was there to help him.

The poacher was still agitated and obviously very much affected by his experience. From the start, Meary tried to put him at his ease by assuring him he had only come to hear of the man's experiences and had no interest in bringing any poaching charges against him. Although the poacher was glad to hear of it, he did not seem to be unduly worried by the prospect of court action, rather he seemed to be preoccupied in listening to the other outside noises coming through the thin walls of the building.

Meary studied the character as he tried to settle down into a well-used routine where the one in question would be lulled into giving a good account of themselves, but with Denny it was going to be a hard slog. However, Meary was a man of some resolve and not one to be easily distracted from his work.

"Can you tell me what happened?" he asked, facing the poacher across a sturdily constructed kitchen table. "In your own way, that is. I only want to hear, in your own words, what you actually saw on the night you went into the cemetery."

Denny turned a worried face in his direction.

"I *did* see the dust cloud," he protested. "The others down at the pub said I was drunk." He fixed Meary with a look of utter agony. "I know what I saw that night and it is something I don't want to see again. It's all right for them, they weren't there to see what I saw." He turned plaintive eyes on Meary, saying, "You've got to believe me if we are to continue this inquiry."

Meary nodded in quick succession to reassure him and went on.

"In your own words please, Mr Denny."

Denny swallowed a large lump in his throat and looked at the man opposite.

"I was just going to see Ward about whether he wanted some rabbits," he said, with a beseeching look. "He had had some before, so I knew he was a likely customer." He swallowed again before continuing." When I got to the graveyard gate there was this light coming from the hole and I thought it was George doing a bit of overtime. I'd almost reached the hole itself when this bank of yellow dust appeared and stood there over the grave as if it was staring at me. Underneath the dust, this queer light was coming from the hole and the dust rested on the top, hovering just about five feet in the air."

He paused for breath and stared at Meary, who was writing furiously in a thick page jotter. Meary looked up, caught his eye and smiled.

"Don't mind me writing it all down," he said, tapping the notebook with the pencil end. "And what happened then when you saw the cloud?"

Denny rubbed a gnarled hand over an emergent beard. He was still agitated with the recent events, but felt the better for the unburdening of his troubled mind. He swept the kitchen with a quick look and returned to the story.

"I was terrified then. Imagine being in a graveyard an' seeing this thing rise up before you. It was mind-boggling I can tell you."

He finished with a sniff, and waited as Meary added a full stop.

"And then?" Meary questioned, pencil poised above the notebook.

"I just ran! I was in a blind panic an' I got out of there fast as I could. I remember being tripped by what looked like a gravestone an' I went sprawling. I cut my knees to the bone on the cinder path, but felt nothing. I went through the gate like a greyhound an' didn't stop running until I reached the pub."

"Did you see anyone else in the brief couple of minutes you had on the edge of the hole?"

Denny turned quizzical eyes on him.

"Like what?" he questioned.

Meary laid the pencil on the scrubbed surface of the table.

"Well, George Ward for instance. Did you see anything in or around the grave?"

Denny had a thick shock of dark brown hair that hung forwards, and this hairstyle bobbed with the vehemence of his denial.

"Nary a sight," he said, looking up at Meary. "If George was around there I would've seen him. I never heard no sound, only saw what I saw."

Meary chewed his lip as his hand flew over the jotter, rapidly recording every detail.

"Tell me," he said as he paused, "this gravedigger, did he ever see anything like this before? I mean did he mention whether he'd seen this phenomenon before?"

Denny was shaking his head even while the question was being posed.

"Not George. If he had seen it before he would have said so. George was as solid as a barn door. I know 'cause I've been questioned with him and he would have told me."

"Has anybody visited the grave site since this occurrence?"

"The police, and one or two officials."

"And what did they find?"

"Nothing, nothing except a deep hole that they say was a disused well someone dug in the past. George must have uncovered it when he was digging."

"And how do you account for George Ward's disappearance?"

"I can't, the earth must have just swallowed him up."

"Perhaps he fell down the well."

"Maybe he did, but he didn't answer when he was called."

"He could be unconscious or dead."

Denny expelled a gust of hot air at this suggestion.

"From what I've heard they lowered a light into the hole and there was nobody in sight, so they assumed he wasn't there."

"What do the police say about the affair?"

"Not a lot. They say they got better things to do with their time instead of chasing a missing gravedigger."

Meary cleared his throat with a gentle cough. He was a sallow faced man and the effort coloured his cheeks.

"Well, I suppose I will have to be satisfied with your account, Mr Denny. It's queer though that George Ward has not been seen since that day." He sighed and closed the notebook. "I'm thinking of examining the grave and all it contains. I'm also thinking of organising a search of the cemetery. I shall apply to the council for permission to examine the grave." He got to his feet and regarded the other man. "I wouldn't worry too much about what you saw. It could easily have been induced by some form of hypnotism."

Denny's head jerked up when he heard this.

"So you think it is all an illusion, do you?" he grated, fixing Meary with a hard stare.

Meary returned his look and slowly shook his head.

"No, I don't Mr Denny to be honest with you. I said it *could* have been mesmerism, but it is extremely unlikely."

"This search you speak of, Mr Meary, will it include me?"

Sweat was beginning to form on Denny's face and there was a trace of anxiety in his voice. Meary smiled again and slid the notebook into the side pocket of his suede jacket.

"Let me put your mind at rest, Denny. What I intend to do can be very dangerous to an inexperienced person and not recommended. I have other people ready to come at my call, and when they do come they will bring a lot of expertise with them. If it is what I think it is we are treading on very perilous ground and it is not for the unwary."

"You sound like there is a ghost down in the grave."

"It might well be a manifestation of one. We will have to wait and see, won't we?"

Later on when Meary was striding through the village he had a chance to study the neighbourhood. It was a typical village of the period, with a post office in a central parade of five shops beside a tree-lined park. He stopped at a newsagent's shop and bought a national newspaper. He picked out a wooden seat from a pair of cast iron supported benches at the edge of the park and was soon immersed in world news.

After about an hour he took out a heavy silver watch and studied it for awhile before pocketing it and crossing the street to the post office. Once inside he was directed to a telephone box where he sat on a narrow seat. He searched in his coat pocket and produced some coins, put a couple into the machine and called the operator while his other hand was delving into another pocket. Deftly he produced a slip of paper as he spoke into the mouthpiece.

"Operator, I want a London number. Pitsea … Pitsea eight, eight, nought, one, one, yes, that's right. Yes, I'll wait."

He sat there studying a picture of the local pub and was just licking his lips in anticipation when the line crackled and a voice spoke into his ear.

"Hello Bill," he said in answer to the hello, "it's John. I got here about ten this morning. I saw Denny and I got the full story from him … What? No, he hasn't seen George Ward either, not since he vanished. Looks like it is a full dose of the usual … No, I'd say we want the full works on this one. Bring Trevor with you. See you when you get here…That's right, see you tomorrow morning then. I'll be staying at a local hotel about two miles from here, Rayburn Hotel, Stuart Street, in Darcy. You'll find it. It's near the river. All right, see you tomorrow."

He hung the receiver on its hook, studying it and the way the phone wire curled up into a spiral.

"Well, well," he muttered to himself, "let's see what tomorrow will bring."

He shouldered out of the box and headed for the place where he had parked his car earlier.

The morning came into being, accompanied by a gentle rain that wet the streets and the rooftops with a slick that shone like silver in a watery sunshine. The weak bars of sunlight penetrated the inner gloom of the hotel dining room where Meary, an early riser, was finishing off a plate of toast and marmalade. He looked up to see the lean figure of Bill Drew, his young colleague, peeping through long flowing curtains that divided the room from the hotel lounge. He at once saw Meary and slipped into a spare chair at the table, placing a bulging briefcase on the snow white tablecloth before him.

"Morning, Bill," Meary said, watching as Drew, without preamble, was undoing the two straps that held the case closed.

"I've arranged for a lorry to bring ladders and scaling equipment," he breezed, opening the case up and extracting a sheaf of typewritten papers. "I've also got written permission from the local council to search the cemetery."

He had a fresh face that was shiny with eagerness. He

tapped a sheet of paper with shortened fingernails.

"This here is a detailed description of the local topography, which includes a map of the area with the cemetery and the outlying district for several miles around." He beamed at Meary with a note of triumph in his voice as he said, "So you can see, I've not been idle, John."

"Good man, Bill," Meary said, swallowing the crust of the toast and wiping the marmalade traces from his mouth. "And now I hope we can get on with discovering exactly what happened to Mr Ward, gravedigger."

He laid down the napkin on the table before him and was about to rise up from the table when a waiter came to inform him he was wanted on the telephone. Leaving Bill to gather up the papers and return them to the briefcase, he followed in the wake of the waiter to the telephone. Waiting for him to return, Bill finished strapping the briefcase together and was just returning a pencil to his inside pocket when Meary swept back into the room.

"Come on, Bill, there's no time to lose!" he exclaimed, holding the curtain back for the young man.

"Has something gone wrong?" Bill enquired, grabbing the case.

"The council," Meary spluttered, "they're at the graveyard now, filling in the hole!"

CHAPTER THREE

The graveside was a hive of activity when the two men finally arrived. Council workmen were grouped around the grave and a big man with a cloth cap was waving a lorry laden with rubbish to approach the hole, with quick gestures of his hands.

Meary swung the cemetery gates aside with a strong flick of his fingers and quickly made his way through the leaning gravestones, where he stepped between the approaching lorry and the hole. He lifted his hands above his head, trying to make himself heard above the roar of the engine exhaust.

"Stop this!" he bellowed at the big man, who raised a hand in a signal to the driver to halt the progress of the lorry.

"Now, what on earth are you doing?" the big man demanded, confronting Meary.

"You *must* stop filling in the hole at once!" Meary shouted as the engine dropped to a lower tone.

"I have my orders, whoever you are," the council worker said. "Now, please step aside so that I can carry them out."

Meary shook his head.

"Are you in charge here?" he asked, pointing to the hole.

"That *must* stay open. A man's life may depend on it being left as it is."

"I'm the foreman in charge," the big man said. "What's this you say about a man's life depending on it being kept open? We've had explicit instructions saying the well must be filled in, and this we are doing."

Meary waved an official looking piece of paper in the man's face.

"This is my authentic permission to examine the site of the grave with a view to entering it."

He handed the sheet of paper to the foreman, who was now surrounded by half a dozen council employees, and waited while he read it. The foreman took off his cap and scratched his head.

"Well, it looks all right as far as I can see," he said, handing it back, "but I must have it in writing that the work is stopped because of a prior requirement of an inspection of the well."

Meary nodded in quick succession and assured the man that his need to examine the site was official, adding:

"My friend Bill here," he indicated the presence of the waiting Bill Drew, "has the necessary paperwork that I am sure will satisfy you and your superiors."

The foreman nodded and waved the waiting lorry away again. Meary breathed a sigh of relief as the lorry backed away from the hole, then settled down to wait for their own transport.

Two hours later the rainfall had eased to a dull grey day and Meary and Drew watched the arrival of their own van load of equipment, with rising excitement. Meary personally supervised the offloading of the covered vehicle, working until the sweat rolled off his brow, placing the different requisite pieces where they were most accessible. Swiftly the metal tripod that was to support their weight was bolted together and raised over the entrance to the grave. A heavy block and tackle, still dripping with grease and oil, was slung from the three-inch thick steel legs of the tripod and hung down over the yawning hole, spinning in the breeze of the autumn day.

Coils of new Manila rope, fresh from the mill, were broken open and threaded through the blocks and led over to a capstan that was being erected by Travis, the van driver. The ropes were wound around the roller that tightened and held them, stopping them unwinding. Over the hole a bo'sun's chair was fixed to the end of the ropes, circling slowly. A metal handle was attached to the capstan where it was held by a metal tongue slipped in between the greased cogs. Several thick wooden planks were laid across the hole with just a three feet by three feet opening left for the eventual entry into the grave.

It was at this juncture that Meary decided to call a halt to the work and produced a Thermos flask full of hot coffee and three tin mugs.

"Right now," he said, sitting on a fallen gravestone, "I suggest we have a brief rest before proceeding."

Travis pulled a wood splinter from his thumb and eyed the other two.

"Do we have to draw lots for whoever is going down first? If not, I'd like to volunteer."

Meary smiled at the apparent eagerness of his colleague.

"Now, now, Dave," he said, laughing through the coffee steam, "you'll get your chance to find out what's down there in due course. I was thinking of asking young Bill to do the honours, eh Bill?"

Bill's face lit up at the possibility of crossing the threshold of an unopened grave, even though he knew that George Ward was the first and may be down there now.

"I-I'd like to, John," he stammered, "but surely as it is your project you've got a right to the first sighting?"

Meary shook his head.

"I've had my discoveries," he said, sipping the coffee and holding the mug between his legs. "No, it's for you two to decide who's first."

Travis produced a coin, tossed it and won. With the help of the others he was strapped into the chair and waited as they took his weight on the turn of the roller. As the rope tightened he was suspended over the black hole for a little while before the rope turned through the block and he was slowly lowered into the gloom of the tomb opening. The glow of his hand torch lit up the start of the entrance and the bright rays of light winked through the plank gaps and slowly dissolved as he sank lower into the hole, finally leaving the opening with just the movement of the descending rope.

At the capstan the taut rope holding the weight of Travis slowly unrolled from the roller amid the metallic clanking of the iron tongue slipping from cog spline to cog spline. The two men took it in turns to swing the heavy metal handle around, holding the rough Manila rope in a taut line as it gradually payed out through the straining blocks. The line went slack as the chair reached the cave floor and they paused to regain their breaths.

After a few minutes the muffled voice of Travis floated up from the hole and the chair was hoisted until it reappeared, ready for the next rider, who was Meary of course. Before he entered the tomb he uncoiled a long length of electric cable and lowered a robust metal protected lamp through the plank gaps and, hand over hand, dropped it into the gloomy void below.

"Can you see anything?" he yelled into the hole, and back came the muffled voice of the man. "Nothing yet, John, it's huge and dark down here! It'll be better with the big light."

Meary grunted with the effort, and picked up the heavy cable. As he walked he released it bit by bit until he had only the connecting plug in his hands, and this he put into the socket of a waiting portable generator. Bill was on hand to work the controls as Meary grasped the cranking handle and turned it in a circle. Immediately the petrol engine coughed into life and, at Bill's insistence, caught and gathered speed. As it settled to an even rhythm, Meary flicked a switch on the side of the generator to the accompaniment of a muted cry from below.

The sides of the pit were bathed in harsh light that struck up from below. After leaving Bill to oversee the running of the equipment Meary made ready to descend into the hole. He nodded to Bill when he was strapped into place in the canvas chair and waited as the other man took up the slack rope over his head. He was then lifted bodily from the wooden boards before dangling over the waiting cavern, looking straight down into the shafts of electric light coming up. Reversing the rollers, Bill got ready to release the rope then gently the rough Manila line began to crawl through the block and Meary's suspended body sunk into the hole, swaying slightly with the movement, disappearing from sight with every passing second.

Through well-oiled wheels the taut rope slowly lowered Meary into the big rock chamber that on first sight seemed vast and weird. In the half-light the jagged rock walls passed by his eyes and the damp musty odour of countless ages rose up, pervading and stinging the linings of his nose. Then he was through and into a big subterranean cave, which appeared to gain in stifling intensity the farther he was lowered. The rope twanged and the chair creaked in unison as the expectant clutch of the waiting Travis grabbed at them and guided them onto the rock shelf on which he was standing. Meary released himself from the chair and, stooping down, grasped the metal grill of the electric lamp protector and held it high above his head. The bulb was powerful and emitted strong rays, but it failed to penetrate into the gloom of the cavern corners.

Meary set the light on the rocky floor and, unclipping a long-handled torch from his leather belt, turned it on for a cursory look about his person. The probing beam of the torch darted around from rock wall facings to corners until it finally alighted on the ground where it lit up the pile of yellow dust.

"Curious," he muttered in a low undertone as he bent down and grabbed a handful of the dust and let it trickle through his fingers. "This must be the yellow dust that Denny saw, but what caused it to boil up in such a .way to frighten him?"

He was interrupted by the distant voice of Bill yelling through the hole above, enquiring whether everything was all right. Meary assured him it was, and the yells faded away as, satisfied, he returned to his job up above.

In the meantime, Travis had hauled the thick electric cable across the rough rock floor to the farthest reaches of the mysterious chamber and promptly discovered a skeleton lying in a prostrate position in one of the corners. His excited cries brought Meary to his side and together they gazed down at the sight, thinking the same thoughts.

"It's got to be that of the gravedigger," Meary said after awhile, "but that's impossible because he's only been missing a few days and this thing hasn't got an ounce of meat left on the bones."

"It could be rats, but even if that was the case there would be something left," Travis interposed. "These bones are dry and ready to crumble."

Meary's torch circled and exposed a few articles of clothing lying several feet away from the skeleton. The light danced on a pair of hobnailed boots.

"They certainly look like they come from the skeleton and those are the sort of boots a gravedigger would wear."

Travis shook his head vehemently.

"I hate to disagree, John, but if I was to date the skeleton I'd say it was at least ten years old, possibly more."

"On the face of it, it does look that way," Meary argued, "and ordinarily I'd agree with you, but we are faced with other factors, such as the testimony of the poacher, Denny, and Ward's sudden disappearance. Now, why would Ward take off all his clothes and lay there naked for the rats to gnaw at him?"

Travis remained silent at this obvious conclusion and could only shake his head in confusion. The next discovery came in the shape of the sarcophagus. Travis, holding the lamp aloft, saw the dark hump of the funeral pile and pointed in its direction saying:

"John, there's something on the other side of the room."

Together they strode through the pile of knee deep dust and beheld the huge wood and iron coffin atop its supporting bed of roughly hewn stones, and stood there amazed at the sight.

"It's a sarcophagus of sorts," Meary announced, hardly able to contain his excitement at finding the coffin. He examined it by the light of the torch. "There's some sort of indentation chiselled on the side of the thing. It looks like writing, but it is almost illegible."

He turned to Travis, who was touching the stone slabs of the coffin.

"What a find. Do you know what this amounts to?" His face was working with excitement. "It's possibly the find of the decade, Travis." His voice rose in tone as the true import of the find registered on his mind then he sobered suddenly as a thought occurred. "We've got to get it to some place where we can examine it at our leisure," he continued. "I never expected such a find as this, Travis. It must be very valuable."

"Invaluable," Travis agreed, and walked around the huge pile of stones. His voice echoed off the stone walls as he spoke. "There's no way of opening the thing as far as I can see. There are more indentations on this side of the coffin – indecipherable though."

"Now, this is where a colleague of mine by the name of Lund may be able to help," Meary said, placing a thick pair of wide-rimmed glasses on the end of his nose. "I've been glad of his help in the past. He is a past master in the art of hieroglyphics, so I'm sure he'll make something out of this little affair."

"What about the skeleton, John? We've never really sorted that out. It looks like we are no more nearer to solving the gravedigger's disappearance than we were a couple of hours ago."

Meary picked at his lip, eyeing the rock pile. He felt sure the answer to Ward's disappearance was somehow linked with the coffin, but he could not fathom out how. It looked so solid and impregnable sitting on the rock table, so it was difficult to imagine such thoughts. Still the feeling remained. His train of thought was interrupted by a yell from the grave hole. Bill wanted to know where the fuel container was as the petrol tank on the generator was running low.

Meary was pulled to the top in the chair and stepped out of the half-light into the twilight of an autumn evening. They searched for a solid hour for the fuel, but found none. Meary finally conceded defeat with a sigh and decided that, although there was ample petrol in the van, they still needed a further supply if they were to continue. This he conveyed to Travis by shouting down to him.

"The petrol should last another two hours at least. I'll use the opportunity to get a lift into the village and contact Lund. Be back in about an hour or so."

With this parting promise he left, never dreaming that it was the last he was to hear from the man down below, for fate was to step into their different lives in a way so unexpected it was a wonder they retained full control of their sanity. Even though a grim fate was in store for one of them, they were happy with the knowledge the discovery had made for the trio. With this in mind, Meary and Bill got into the van and set out for the village, driven by Meary, the leader of the project.

They passed the cemetery gates and as Meary swung the steering wheel to turn towards the distant village a saloon car suddenly appeared from nowhere and smashed into the side of the van with devastating force, pushing the vehicle and its occupants down into a narrow ditch at the side of the road. The other driver, who was unhurt, left the wreck of his car and, leaping onto the overturned van, wrenched the door open. He pulled the moaning figure of the young man, Bill, out of the van and immediately re-entered, looking for the driver.

At the impact of the two vehicles Meary had shot forwards in the seat and collided with the dashboard, which knocked him unconscious. He was lying on the wide seat, on his side, oozing blood from a cut high on his forehead. He was breathing slowly from his mouth, which was half open. Although groggy after the crash, Bill's help was enlisted and together they dragged the inert Meary from the van and set him on a stretch of grass several feet away from the vehicle. Leaving Bill to cradle Meary's head in his lap, the driver of the other car left to report the accident to the authorities. Within a quarter of an hour an ambulance squealed to a halt and two burly ambulance men took over from Bill. The two were transferred to a local hospital where Meary was looked after by a doctor whilst Bill was discharged after receiving a sticking plaster to a small cut on his face.

It was several hours before Meary regained consciousness. After awhile he was able to make out the anxious face of Bill looking down at him, and a further hour elapsed before he was able to collect his thoughts together and talk to him.

"What happened?" he questioned, still fuzzy in the head.

"We landed in a ditch," Bill replied, smiling weakly.

"It all happened so fast," Meary said, pain slicing through his head. "I remember coming out of the cemetery gates and then nothing more until I found myself here."

"The fool in the other car caused the accident by driving on the wrong side of the road, but he dragged us both from the wreckage. The van is on its side in the ditch and has probably been inspected by the police by now. You've been out for four hours or so, old chum. I was worried about you, so I stayed here waiting for you to recover."

When Bill left it was about half an hour before Meary remembered about Travis. On recollection, he shot up in bed and called for the nurse.

"I've *got* to get out of here!" he said forcibly to the doctor. "A friend of mine could be in mortal danger if I can't get to him in time. Please help me get dressed. I've got to go to him!"

The doctor and nurse tried to restrain him.

"He'll be all right," the doctor said, trying to placate him. "You've got to get some rest. You have had a bad knock."

Meary struggled hard to get out of bed, but eventually collapsed exhausted, breathing hard. The doctor administered an anaesthetic and watched as his patient closed his eyes and subsided into a comfortable sleep.

Bill tried to arrange for alternative transport, but was unable to hire a car until the early hours of the morning. At 6 a.m. a sleepy taxi driver, constantly yawning, took him to the petrol station where he managed to buy five gallons of petrol. That caused another problem because he had no money to pay for it and had to borrow from the driver. With the promise of an extra large tip, he managed to persuade the taxi driver to drive him back to the cemetery where he had the necessary funds..

He finally arrived at the gates of the graveyard at seven in the morning and, with the curious driver treating him and the graveyard to several queer looks, began to lug the heavy petrol can through the gates. It was then in the distance he saw a light. His astonishment was total. By rights the generator should have run dry hours ago, he thought, unless Travis has found the fuel, but that is impossible. Travis is still in the pit with no one to pull him up. What then, another person pulled him up? Who would that be at this hour in the morning? Bill gripped the metal handle of the can and hoisted it high. Well, I'll soon find out, he mused, and strode towards the light. It was then he realised the generator was silent.

His footsteps faltered as the light became brighter. His staring eyes reflected the greenish glow. A cloud began to boil up, rising in a tortuous writhing mass that twisted and turned into a swelling ascending vortex. Circling to a madly spinning spiral, it gyrated and danced to fantastic contortions, hovering like a gigantic octopus that rose from the grave like some hideous green bloom. The nearer gravestones and piles of excavated soil around the hole reflected the green light rays with shadows of eerie fire, and Bill shuffled to a stop, recalling what the poacher was supposed to have seen. Through his own awe at the sight, he had no doubt it was a vivid re-enactment of the incident, but witnessing the phenomenon as he was, it was so frightening he could go no closer. His feet refused to go on and he stood there trembling with fear. Instead he opened his dried mouth, dredged up a tiny morsel of warm spittle and croaked out the name:

"Travis! Travis, where are you?"

The grave still maintained the stillness and silence associated with the graveyard. Lack of response from Travis only made the matter worse. His pounding heart hammered against his ribs and he fought rising panic that blanched his face to a sickly pallor, desperately imploring him to turn tail and run until the sickening sight was no more. He resolved to try once more. He dropped the can on the muddy earth of a trampled grave, cupped his hands together and shouted as loud as he could. The hoarse sound ripped the quiet from the little graveyard and echoed off the surrounding confines of the containing walls—no answer.

The cloud seemed to slow its movements and hang over the grave like some huge bubble. Again Bill yelled out:

"Travis, where are you?"

His voice rang loud and clear in the crispness of the early morning air, only this time in a noise that had the effect of freezing the very marrow of Bill's bones, came the hideous sound of demented laughter. As far as he could tell, the flesh creeping sounds were coming from the opening underneath the swinging bo'sun's chair.

CHAPTER FOUR

"But I tell you I saw the green glow," Bill insisted. "It was like a strange cloud that rose up from the hole, like nothing I've ever seen before."

His voice had a slight inclination to hysteria and his lips trembled with the memory. Meary listened with interest and looked at the young man with a good deal of sympathy. He reminded him of himself when the aura of excitement of a new job had worn off and been replaced with a degree of reality.

"And this sound of laughter, could it have been Travis laughing?"

"*No way,*" Bill said with feeling, "not that kind of laughter. It was a hideous sound that seemed to rise up from the grave like the laughter of a demented lunatic. In my association with Travis I have never heard him utter such a sound."

Meary could see he was disturbed by the sighting at the grave and was plainly shocked by his first encounter with the paranormal. The man was young though, and if he was to continue in the footsteps set out by Meary then he was destined to see and hear other strange sights and sounds.

Meary prompted him a little further.

"When you heard this laughter, did you hear anything else?"

"Like what?"

"Well, sounds of anything being shifted, or being opened or closed. Any squeaks or strange noises you couldn't account for?"

Bill shut his eyes for a minute as he tried to conjure up a recall of the incident. He opened his eyes slowly with the new light of recollection in them.

"Now that you mention it, John, there was this small noise, sort of an under sound that would not be noticed with everything else going on all around."

"Well," Meary said with quickening interest, "anything you can throw some light on will be of use to us, no matter how small it may be."

"Yes, it was as I was approaching the grave for the first time. The green cloud was in place over the hole and the glow was just getting near its zenith. There was this grinding sliding noise, so small it was barely audible. My attention was taken up by the cloud, so this other thing completely slipped my mind."

Meary was sitting up in the bed and looked decidedly better after his refreshing sleep. He was sporting a blue bruise on his forehead and a gauze bandage on his right wrist, but appeared unaffected by either. He tapped the thick rim of his eyeglasses on the swell of his thick lips and thoughtfully stared into space.

"First Ward, and now Travis is missing," he said almost to himself. "I wonder how many more will disappear before this affair is over?"

Beside him, a still slightly shocked Bill was rerunning the day's horrific events through his mind, still describing them with not a little awe and dread in his voice.

"There was this bubbling gurgling sound; unearthly and unnatural it was, just like I imagine the Devil's laughter to be."

"Perhaps it was," Meary said in a musing voice. "Strangely enough, the Devil is attributed to have strong laughter, so it could be the work of our old adversary, Mr Lucifer himself."

Bill's face blanched.

"My God, Satan!" he said, horrified. "Surely with him involved we are getting out of our depth, John. To take on the Devil is an almighty task even you with your experience would be wise to ignore."

Meary chuckled at the apparent innocence of the young man and decided to put him at his ease.

"I said perhaps it *might* be, not *is*, Bill. However, it doesn't seem likely because of the associated events. They're not the same."

Puzzled, Bill looked at him with worry lines corrugating his forehead.

"I don't understand what you are getting at, John," he returned. "Just what are these incidents you speak of?"

"Well, the coffin for starters. By the looks of it, it has all the hallmarks of a strange burial that took place ages ago, and nothing else. On the face of it and until we know to the contrary there is nothing sinister in it. However, it coincided with the disappearance of the gravedigger, Ward, and that is where all coincidence vanishes, especially now that Travis is also missing."

Bill went to interrupt, and Meary held up a thin hand.

"I know you didn't see Travis," he went on, "but that isn't to say he has gone like the other man." Meary paused for breath, looking at Bill before adding, "If Travis has gone though, I'll do everything in my power to find out why."

Bill smiled at this assertive undertaking, showing a set of even white teeth as he did so.

"That's exactly how I feel about it, John, but how do you account for Travis not answering when I called, and what is more worrying is whose laughter was it that came up out of the hole?"

"I can't say right now," Meary replied, making to get out of bed, talking to Bill at the same time, "but I mean to find out a few more answers before this day is out, Bill. From someone who does know a little bit more about the subject than we do."

After getting dressed and assuring a concerned doctor that he had made a remarkable recovery, he thanked him for his help and, with the ringing of the doctor's advice to take care of the wounds, echoing in his ears, he hurried from the hospital. Striding purposefully along, accompanied by his eager friend, Bill, he went straight to a taxi rank where they hastily clambered inside a waiting taxi. Meary muttered an address to the driver and soon they were speeding to their destination in a town ten miles distant.

The autumn countryside flashed by in a continual panorama of flaming colour. The golden fields, bursting with fat stalks of ripened corn, stretched out to the horizon in undulating waves that rippled and rolled in time to a gentle

September breeze.

In time, roads and tree-lined avenues took over from the countryside and the taxi presently drew up and halted beside a neat detached house with whitewashed walls that blazed out in the warm autumn sunshine. A dozen fruit tress, laden with fat apples and pears, shaded the house from the street, and the wide front garden was divided in two by a short gravel drive that started at a wooden five-bar gate and ended at a richly carved front door. The gate squealed for the want of a little grease, but yielded to the touch and swung open wide on strong, black iron hinges.

Together they crunched up the drive and arrived at a square brass plate that announced it was the residence of G E Lund, Chemist. There were other figures and letters to the name, but the passage of time, weather and countless rubbings of the plate had all but erased them. Meary pushed a button on the door frame and somewhere in the house a bell rang. After another push at the doorbell the door inched open to allow the features of a thin faced woman, who looked them up and down before enquiring what they wanted.

"I'm Meary, John Meary. Your husband must've mentioned my name. We attended college together some years ago."

When her face registered surprise at their appearance, Meary introduced himself again.

"Meary, George Lund and myself were at college together." He turned to Bill, saying, "This is my associate, Bill Drew. We are working on the case of the missing gravedigger over at Wyvern Valley. George knows all about the affair; he was the one who recently alerted us to it."

She opened the door wider and, with them following,

led them to a side room where she gently tapped on the door panel.

"Come," said a muffled voice in answer to her rap, and she opened the door and ushered them inside, closing the door behind them with hardly a sound.

The room was in semi-darkness due to the curtains being tightly drawn together. In the centre, crouched over an illuminated microscope, was the portly figure of the biochemist, Lund. They stood there looking about the room and trying to see in the gloom. Suddenly the man straightened up and, striding to the window, flung the curtains opened wide. Immediately he espied Meary standing there and crossed the room with a big smile on his face.

"John Meary. How nice to see you again. It's been ages since we last met. How's that little business over at Wyvern Valley? I've heard nothing about it since the gravedigger went missing. You come in connection with that, John?"

He was wearing a pair of thick horn-rimmed glasses and he was studying them through the polished lenses. He turned them on Bill and listened as Meary introduced him as, 'My colleague, Bill Drew, who is learning the trade'.

"You were right," Meary went on, "we have come in connection with the missing man, but only in an associated way. The real reason is because of the find we discovered in an underground chamber under the graveyard."

Lund digested this morsel of information for a few seconds before answering.

"I've heard about this underground burial crypt and of Ward's strange disappearance because of it. This other discovery of which you mention, I must confess intrigues me."

Meary smiled in a knowing way.

"I thought that would be your reaction to the news, George. I am fully aware of your enquiring mind and of the way you will ferret out any possible answers to every question."

"Well, some of them anyway, John, but do excuse my interruption and go on with your account. I can't wait to hear about what it is you have discovered. I've heard rumours that witchcraft and the like have been practised lately at the village."

"Just rumours with no foundation in them, George, nothing more."

As Meary plunged into what had taken place at the cemetery, Bill was gazing at a huge array of bottles, glass phials, rubber tubing and other paraphernalia of the chemist, and seemed fascinated by the sight. Meary was continuing his story of what had happened at the cemetery and was launching into the gist of the tale.

"After Ward vanished we entered the tomb and found this massive coffin sitting on a pile of stones." Meary's face lit up and a little shade of excited sweat was showing above the full lips. "To say we were excited is an understatement."

He looked around at Bill to confirm what he was saying. Bill swung around from the bottles.

"Quite right," he said.

"But this is a magnificent find, John," Lund agreed. "I'd like to see it as soon as possible. When can we do so?"

"I was coming to that. On the wooden casket was, I think, a description of the occupant. I must add it was a poor light, but we think it is the name or otherwise of the person or thing lying in the coffin."

"I see," Lund said, and that is where I suppose I step in?"

"Precisely that, George, to coin a phrase, the words are all Greek to me, but with your understanding of Egyptian mannerisms and so forth I thought perhaps you might be tempted to take part in the actual opening of the sarcophagus."

"Thank you, and I accept the offer, my friend." Lund fell silent for a moment before saying, "So you have no idea what the words say? Perhaps it is indeed the name of the occupant and no more?"

"There is another matter of which you should know, George. The other member of my team is missing. Travis, our driver and very fine friend, was inadvertently left to hold the fort while we were away and during this time was also posted missing."

"Missing, you say?" Lund said in surprise. "Did he say anything before he went?"

"We were in a slight accident, Bill and myself. We ended up in hospital and that is where I spent the night. It was during this time that Travis vanished."

"But he can't just disappear," Lund protested. "The man must have left a message, a note to say where he has gone, anything?"

"That's impossible, George. We had this system of lowering each other down into the tomb. With a man on top winding a canvas chair down into the hole, we kept one on top all the time to pull it back up again."

Meary looked at Bill, who took up the story.

"After the accident I left John at the hospital and got a taxi back to the site to pull Travis back up to the surface. I walked through the gates and that is when I noticed a light over the grave." Bill licked a pair of dry lips as the memory came flooding back. "As I got nearer it seemed to bubble up into a balloon-like shape, getting bigger and greener by the minute." Bill's voice became hoarse and he coughed into his hand. "I was scared, so I yelled out for Travis. I got nearer the hole and hollered out again – nothing. I was about fifty feet away when I called again. This time – and I'll hear the sound to my dying day – there came this weird laughter, coming up from the hole."

Now it was Bill's turn to sweat, and a gentle shine glistened on his brow.

"You have my sympathy, Bill," Lund said, turning the events over in his mind. "I can imagine your fright." He turned to regard the young man. "Where do you think your friend has gone?"

"I wish I knew." Bill sighed. "There is no other way out except for the chair and that was there exactly as we left it."

Lund looked at Meary and saw the light of agreement in his glance.

"This gets more interesting by the minute," Lund said. "Did you report it to the police?"

Bill shook his head.

"Not yet, Mr Lund, I wanted to make sure that Travis is really missing before involving them."

"Good man. We don't want any panic, we don't want sightseers trampling over the graves, and that includes the police. What's your plan of campaign now, Meary?"

"First of all the raising of the coffin to somewhere where it can be examined," Meary explained.

"This will present a problem because without Travis the

task will be that much harder."

"I'd like to volunteer," Lund enthused. "I've done quite a lot of excavating in my time, so it will come as nothing new."

"You're hired, George," Meary said, laughing and then becoming serious. "There is something else," he added, fixing Lund with a look that foretold something urgent. "We found something, Travis and I, we found a skeleton and he is pretty much sure it is the remains of the gravedigger, Ward."

"A skeleton in such a short time, John, this I've got to see."

"And so you shall, in a short while from now, just as soon as I can arrange for lifting equipment to bring the coffin to the surface." Meary stood up and held out his hand. "Nice to have seen you again after all this time."

He watched as Bill also took the proffered hand and stood up.

"I'll keep in touch, George," he promised, "just as soon as I can."

Back in the taxi Meary gave instructions to the driver to head for the cemetery, and settled back against the cushions to await the outcome of the coming return to the grave site.

Everything was as before, with the exception of Travis. Meary stood on the piled up earth, pondering the question, eyeing the chair and the seemingly yawning chasm staring back at him. In his mind's eye he imagined the man waiting for their return from the petrol station, of his hours spent in the hole wondering when they would eventually return and then realising something must have happened to the pair. Meary chewed a thick lip and kicked soil down the hole.

Down on the tomb floor the dislodged earth rattled against

something solid. This had the effect of making up his mind and he spoke to Bill, who was standing several feet away.

"I'm going down, Bill," he decided, speaking in a low voice.

"I'm coming too," Bill returned in a determined voice.

"You forget we need someone to pull me back up again. There's only you and me, so I'm afraid I'll have to go alone."

"What about the things that happened here, the two missing men and everything?"

"You mean the evil laughter and the green dust cloud?" Meary asked in a determined voice. "I don't intend to let things like that put me off. I've made up my mind. Please make ready."

Bill reluctantly started the generator and gripped the iron winding handle of the windlass, fitting the square bar onto the roller axle and dropping the metal tongue into place between the iron cogs.

"Ready," he said in a husky voice, feeling the tension of the rope as it drew up the slack, then waiting as Meary eased his bulk into the embracing straps of the chair.

John waited for the other to begin lowering the chair into the gloom of the yawning hole several feet below him. The block squealed as the rope slid through the wheels. The chair trembled and started to descend into the hole. As before, the rock face of the surrounding tomb wall passed by his eyes and quickly moved away when he entered the tomb proper. The quietness of the still air covered his ears and the thick closeness of the surrounding atmosphere entered his lungs, so much so that he wanted to sneeze it out. He resisted the feeling though, pinching his nose with thumb and finger, well aware that his highly pitched senses were searching the gloom with all the force he could muster. Within himself he fought the desire to panic, repeating over and over again that the tomb was empty of anything meant to harm him and instead, if it was so, the owner of the laugh was trying to contact him.

The chair gently spun on its axis and his legs touched down on the accumulated dust pile. The electric light bulb burned brightly on the cave floor and the hand torch, still emitting a dull ray of spent radiation, was lying nearby on the dusty floor presumably where Travis had dropped it. Meary bent down and retrieved it, shaking it to revitalise the beam, but failing, so he stuffed it into the pocket of his jacket.

Above him the echoing voice of the young man floated down to him.

"You all right, John? Is there any sign of Travis?"

"None yet, Bill," he answered, extricating himself from the chair straps. "I'm just about to have a look around though. If there is I'll jerk on the rope.

"Perhaps he was taken ill. If it is so you can put him into the chair for me to pull up. Can you manage that, John?"

"Should be able to, he is only a small man and light as well. If not, perhaps we can get a doctor to come down here."

"Good idea, John. If you find him, perhaps you can stay with him until I can get the doctor?"

"Right, starting to search the tomb now, Bill. I've found the hand torch, so he must have left it." Meary dragged the light cable across the floor until it lit up the bulk of the coffin. After noting the sarcophagus was as before, he trained the light beam about him, looking for the missing man. The rays of the lamp fell on and lit up the skeleton, only this time there was an addition — a second skeleton lying side by side with the first. Travis?

CHAPTER FIVE

Meary was not really one to panic at the sight of two skeletons lying side by side on the cave floor, but the fact that two men were missing and two skeletons were there before him somehow seemed to unnerve him a little. He stepped back from the sight, dropped the torch in his haste and, staggering to the rope, tugged it for all he was worth.

"Quick, pull me up, Bill!" he shouted breathlessly, and climbed into the seat as fast as he was able, feverishly fastening the straps about himself with excited fingers.

The journey upwards seemed interminable. Slowly the fetid air gave way to fresh and he gasped it in with huge breaths that made his head spin. The rocky face of the tomb passed by his gaze and he broke surface, pale in the face and serious eyed. Bill anchored the windlass and, at Meary's side, undid the straps and pulled him out of the chair.

"Did you find Travis?" he questioned, helping Meary aside then staring at him as his friend gazed back down the hole.

"John, what did you find down there?"

Meary held him in a fixed look as the young man asked

the question. He had hardly been able to train his thoughts on what he was being asked through rushing pulsing questions of his own that kept on leaping and dancing in his brain.

"I think I've found Travis," he said at last. "He's dead. He's lying in the corner."

"What do you mean, you *think*, John? Surely there's enough light to see if it *is* Travis. If you think it is—"

"I'm almost sure," Meary interrupted. "That is to say there are two skeletons now, not one. Travis is missing, so I've put one and one together, simply making two–two skeletons. Can you come up with any other solution, Bill?"

"I-I-I don't understand," Bill stammered, going pale. "Travis a skeleton? W-w-why that's imp—"

"Impossible?" Meary interrupted again. "But that is how it is looking, Bill," Meary said huskily. "Both of them lying side by side, it beats me, but that is how it looks to me."

By this time Bill's complexion had changed from pale to white and it had the effect of stifling speech. He just looked helplessly at Meary, shaking his head and groaning. Suddenly Meary shook himself and seemed to find reality. He put a hand in the arm of the other and led him away from the graveside, heading for the cemetery exit.

"This has got to be reported to the authorities then I'm going to hurry up the arrival of the crane." He was puffing with the exertion of pulling Bill along, and paused at the gate to gain his breath. "We've no time to lose," he wheezed. "Even n-now it might be too late. The two things lying in the tomb might be a warning of sorts. I-I only hope we've enough time left before anything else starts to happen."

He found a telephone box and got through to the hire

company without any untoward delay.

"Hello, is that the person who is bringing the crane? It is? Can you make the delivery tomorrow instead of the next day? You can't? Why not? It's not available until then? I see, well, the next day as arranged, but be advised I'll never use your facilities again. What? Well, I'm sorry too, but it is a matter of extreme urgency, if not life or death to an unwilling participant in the near future. That is how important it is—goodbye!"

Meary slammed the receiver down and made a face at Bill, who was eyeing him through the window. He screwed his brows together, trying to remember another number, stroking the chin bristles of an emergent beard.

"Hello, George," he said to the chemist as the line crackled. "Another important development; Travis has turned up we think, but not in the way you think. We have another skeleton to match the other. No it's not a joke, George, I wish it was. There are two skeletons down in the hole and I can't for the life of me understand why. Pardon me? Yes, you can come over to see for yourself—tomorrow? Yes, that will be fine. Goodbye."

Outside Meary relayed to Bill what had been said and, returning to the grave, stopped the generator, watching the light in the hole fade to nothing. For a moment or two he stared at the gloom rising up from below, trying to picture what had taken place. His eyes steeled to slits and a silent oath slipped out from between firmed lips.

"Tomorrow I'll find your secret or die trying!"

With that he turned on his heel out of the cemetery and eventually to his room where he slept a dreamless sleep.

Meary awoke on the stroke of 6 a.m. ready and determined for anything. Bill arrived just as he was drinking his second cup of coffee, and accepted a cup with a hand that was steady, not spilling a drop. He smiled in return to Meary's greeting and waved to a window beaming with sunshine.

"Nice day for whatever turns up today, John," he breezed, trying to look cheerful.

Meary gave him a look and swallowed his toast.

"Let's hope the job goes as well as the weather," he said dryly. "I'm also hoping Lund will be able to shed some light on the subject."

Lund's smart black saloon car was waiting as they arrived and soon they were all grouped at the graveside, looking down into the gloom and the quiet of the underground tomb.

"Yes," Lund was saying, "I understand what you mean about getting it to the surface, John, but if I can just give it some cursory examination before you do, perhaps I can help."

Meary nodded in acquiescence.

"I'm sure your help will be invaluable, George," he said, smiling broadly. "I only hope you will be able to use our primitive methods of lowering each other into the hole." He indicated the chair hanging loosely over the yawning hole, adding, "Rough, but effective until we can use the crane in order to hurry things up a bit."

The rope creaked as it lowered the chair into the hole, taking with it the portly frame of the chemist. Meary, now dressed in overalls and a cap, waited for his turn to descend into the grave. Bill turned the windlass, watching the greasy cogs interplay as they clacked noisily together and the engine of the generator, purring smoothly in the autumn air, echoed off the assembled gravestones with a gentle popping noise.

Pretty soon Meary joined Lund on the tomb floor and, with the addition of a further couple of high powered electric bulbs, the hole was lit well enough for them to see all there was to see. There was also a sack of tools for them to use, and Meary was in the act of untying a length of restraining twine. He pulled the sack open and tipped the tools out onto the ground, watched by the chemist.

The first full sighting of the sarcophagus was breathtaking. The huge wooden coffin was resting on a bed of flattened stones arranged in a rectangle fully twenty feet in length and six feet in width, and this pile, four feet high and table shaped, supported it. The coffin was made of oak boards with iron corner brackets to the top and bottom. Wrought iron bands of black metal crossed the oak boards at intervals of every two feet, giving the sarcophagus an enormous size and giving the impression of extreme weight. The coffin, some twelve feet in length, was roughly constructed of undressed wood and covered with the dust of the time it had lain there. By the presence of a few rough indentations on the side of the box, there appeared to be a name inscribed on the boards, and Lund donned his spectacles to get a better view.

"It's in old script," he announced. "Almost illegible through time, but as far as I can make out it says, *Brighold*, nothing more."

"Could that be the name of the occupant?"

"Possibly, but not knowing anything about it, that's all we have to go on. Usually they put the name on to indicate who is inside, so we will never know who until we see what is inside."

Their voices echoed around the chamber and reverberated from the corners, giving a weird effect to their speech. The coldness of the rocky room seemed to settle in the strange light coming from the bulbs, producing an edge to the timbre of their voices and a very slight feathery vapour to their breath. Neither man noticed any difference though, being entirely immersed in the excitement over the coffin. Meary looked long and hard at the tools held in his hand. The metal of the hammer and chisel gleamed in the brightness coming from the bulbs. Without any effort he found the crack between box and lid, and inserted the tip of the chisel into the hairline split. The heavy hammer blow smashed into the quiet of the cavern, driving the chisel deep into the crevice between the warped boards.

The coffin shuddered under the blow, but resisted it. The second stroke drove a fracture between the boards, causing a dark line to run the entire length between top and bottom. The third smash opened a gap an inch wide and the light started to enter the breach produced. Meary paused, examined the fissure with a finger and disturbed a quantity of dust in the slit. It trickled from the warped wood and blossomed on the floor, spreading out on the rough rocks projecting upwards. Dropping the hammer on the floor with a crash he inserted the chisel into the crack and with a grunt levered on it with all his might, opening up the coffin to his eager gaze as the lid teetered on an imaginary axis and with a deafening crash fell to the floor.

For a minute as the dust rose up and covered the scene, the contents of the coffin were momentarily obscured. The seconds ticked by and gradually all was revealed to them. Two pairs of eyes, eager for the first sighting of the occupant, initially expressed surprise and then shock as the full import of the sight that met their eyes. Lund, holding his glasses closer to his eyes edged nearer, leaning over to get a better view, while Meary, still clutching the chisel, also gazed with fascination at the thing in the box.

"It's some kind of figure," Lund said at last, "a statue of some sort." He shook his head in bewilderment. "But why in a coffin and buried here in this place?"

"It's some sort of figure of a man, I think," Meary whispered close to Lund's ear.

He bent down and brought the light closer. It was indeed the figure of a man. Complete with all the attributes associated with the male species, it lay there naked and blatant, ready for the whole world to see.

Lund reached into the coffin and touched the thing.

"It feels like stone," he said, spreading out his fingers and running them across an expanse of the material, "and yet it doesn't; sort of a hard leathery feeling to it."

Meary ran his eyes from top to toe of the thing.

"He must be all of eight feet in height," he announced, "big and muscular too by the look of him."

The Brighold was indeed a sight to behold. As Meary had surmised, it was a huge size and awesome too. The features were of a man in his late fifties, with muscular body and somewhere close to eight feet tall. The skull, although almost hidden by a wooden block supporting it, was complete and without blemish, although the surface material seemed to have run together and fused into something approaching a hard skin. The lines of the nose and the thin lips' surface had this effect as did the eye sockets and ears. Overall, the figure seemed to exhibit this rather curious effect with the stony flesh of the occupant lying there like some giant slab of stone.

"Well," Lund said after awhile, "rather confusing to view it at first sight, but very exciting, John. We must get it up into the daylight where we can see it better."

Meary had by this time picked up the coffin lid and was studying it.

"George," he said excitedly, "there's some sort of inscription on the lid—drawings and writings." He lifted the lid into view, adding, "Perhaps this will shed a little light on the subject of whom or what the thing is."

Lund was still studying the Brighold, and pulled a piece of decomposed cloth from between its legs. Immediately a smell of such rank and utter decay rose up from the figure that he was forced to turn his face away to breathe fresher air. He completed the move with nose turned away from the smell, holding the scrap of material up to the light to study it closer.

Meary scanned the indentations on the lid with eager gaze. Although badly affected by the passage of time, erosion had been mainly arrested by its constant time spent in the dark. Characters depicting various scenes were etched on the wood and, underneath each group of pictures, words were cut, possibly explaining the meaning of the pictures themselves. Meary counted twenty or so of the scenes and said as much to Lund.

"Looks like you've got quite a job on, George, probably the life history of the man in the coffin in so many pictures and words."

Lund turned aside from his ardent perusal of the cloth and eyed the lid.

"This is indeed a great find, John," he enthused. "The wealth of information in one coffin is staggering. It looks like we will have an almost complete assessment of the Brighold and whom he was, which is remarkable." He took the lid from Meary's grasp and gazed at it. "I shouldn't wonder the scenes will explain why the coffin is here and what circumstances put him in this place."

They replaced the lid on the coffin and stood looking at it until Meary broke the silence.

"That being so, perhaps it will also give us some sort of insight into what the skeletons are and if they are the two missing men."

By this time they had wandered over to the skeletons and were looking down at them. Lund was the first to speak by pointing out a notable thing that had been overlooked in the excitement caused by the disappearance of the men. He rummaged around the fingers of the skeletons then straightened up, holding out a signet ring and asking:

"Do you recognise this, John?"

Meary took the ring between thumb and finger, turning it over in the palm of his other hand.

"The last time I saw this ring it was on the finger of my friend and colleague, Travis."

Lund compressed his lips to a firm line.

"I can think of no reasonable explanation to fit this puzzle," he said after awhile. "The answer may lay in the coffin, it may not. Even so, I'm positively aching for the chance to examine the find in the confines of my own laboratory, so the sooner we can get it up out of the hole, the sooner we will find out a few things, but even now, looking at it logically, how do you account for these?" He tipped the toe bones of the nearest skeleton with his shoe. "And what about the dust cloud wavering above the grave like some gruesome sentinel waiting, it seems, to attack any intruder?"

Meary searched Lund's face with an earnest look.

"And of course there is Bill's testimony. He swears he heard laughter coming from down here. Now, I have got complete confidence in Bill. He's not one to imagine—"

Lund was shaking his head as Meary was talking, and it was at this juncture he interrupted him.

"Perhaps he did," he expounded, spreading his fingers. "All these things I can't explain and neither can you, John. It's a complete mystery to me at the moment and that is why I have high hopes of the coffin revealing a few of its secrets, but right now, my friend, I have to return to my house to get everything ready."

Meary nodded his head and led the way to the waiting chair. Up above, Bill was wiping his hands on a piece of rag and greeted the two men with a smile.

"I hope you two men found out what you were looking for," he said, killing the generator motor by tripping a lever and waiting until the sound died.

"More than we thought possible," Meary answered.

He told him of the opening of the coffin and the peculiar resident lying in the sarcophagus. He also mentioned the drawings cut into the lid of the coffin and of the strange language employed.

To the tune of a gentle hiss of rain, the mobile crane arrived at the cemetery and pounded a painful path to the grave, knocking over several stones on its way there. The driver, an overweight man in a greasy cloth cap and dungarees to match, swung down from the driving seat and proceeded to drape a pair of rusty chain links onto the massive iron hook swinging from the crane arm. He climbed back up again and, to the ear-splitting roar of the engine echoing through the cemetery joined by a jet of blue-grey exhaust smoke that shot into the air spattering the onlookers with oily water spots, he manoeuvred it into position.

"I'll need one of you to oversee what is happening down below," he said to the waiting men.

In answer Meary detached himself from the group and, dodging the chain lift dangling over the open hole, sat himself in the chair and signalled to the waiting Bill. Taking it in turns, Lund and the young man lowered Meary into the tomb and waited as the rope slackened, denoting his arrival on the rock floor.

Raindrops dripped down into the tomb and splashed onto John's upturned face as he waited for the chains to arrive. Attached to the lifting hook was a pair of leather encircling straps, heavy duty raising jacks and several metal runners for the coffin to slide over. The leather straps were lined with wool inserts, meant to limit the damage to the coffin on its way upwards.

Soon Meary was joined by the driver, who expertly lifted the warped box with the aid of the jacks and positioned it so that it began its slide from the rock pile to the floor, supported by the metal runners. It then travelled across more runners as the crane, now operated by the driver, pulled the huge mass across the dust over to the spot from where it was to be lifted. At Meary's direction the coffin began its journey upwards. Dripping dust-ingrained rainwater spots, it arose into the air amid a clanking of metal chain-links and creaking leather straps.

Down on the rock floor Meary followed its progress with anxious eyes, noting with some satisfaction that the coffin just squeezed through the hole with hardly six inches leeway on either side of the warped wooden boards of the base.

By the time Meary's head broke through into daylight the coffin was in place on the back of a lorry procured for the purpose, and covered with a tarpaulin. Bill was just tying a rope to it to anchor the coffin to the lorry floor and the crane was backing away, still emitting clouds of sooty exhaust smoke and making a racket enough to wake the surrounding dead.

Within an hour the crane departed, churning up a few old graves in the process and leaving deep tyre tracks in the muddy soil. Lund fussed around, obviously delighted with the way they had progressed, congratulating the other two.

"I'm looking forward to examining it," he said, beaming at the others.

His face was gleaming with rainwater, but its effects did little to dampen the enthusiasm shining in his eyes. His laugh was infectious because in spite of the rain they both saw the funny side of the situation and roared with laughter together, rainwater coursing down their separate cheeks.

That night the dust bubble returned, only this time an angry looking orange core could be seen in the middle of the mass. The cloud seemed to whirl slowly, with a miniature vortex that gained weight and substance with each passing minute, pulsing and heaving in turn to the waxing and waning of the bubble. Green flares arose into the atmosphere and vanished into the dark of the night. The whirlpool gained momentum with each spasm and lit up the surrounding graves with the evil fire. Orange tipped flames, inundated with hideous grainy yellow fingers and blood red spines, leaped into the night sky.

All about was the smell of Hell; a rank stinking odour of a thousand reeking graves, foul with the decay of death and fetid with the rank decomposition associated with rotted flesh. The sickening smell seemed to hang in the air, pervading the atmosphere and flowing on the tiny up-thrust of every emergent draught springing into being in the cemetery then, like some hideous crab, the boiling motion seemed to subside into a lesser fury and the claws of fire to withdraw into the green body of the monster. The eddying orange vortex lost its ferocious whirling and with a final burst of dispersed energy, sunk like a dying candle flame into the hole from which it had burst forth.

With other things to occupy their thoughts, the trio were gathered together in Lund's laboratory, gazing with rapt awe at the sight of the strange fellow occupying the wooden coffin. Meary and Bill were observing the body with curious glances while Lund was studying the long wooden lid with the aid of a powerful magnifying glass. He was so intent on his job that it produced a thin film of sweat on his brow, which he chose to ignore. Instead his searching eye found and read the intricate message written on the aged wood and, as the story unfolded, his attention was gripped by a fascinated mind. Only once did he utter a sound, which was when a particularly indistinct part of the story was almost unreadable and his, 'Ahh! I see!' of recognition rang out.

Several times the others glanced at him, ready for a great revelation, but the chemist just sat poring over the lid, not seemingly wishing to divulge any information at that moment. Of course the man in the box was interesting, but three hours of waiting for something to happen induced a gradual feeling of boredom of which only the intensely occupied Lund was unaware. Several times Meary sighed and exchanged glances with Bill, but they were lost on Lund, that is until with a sustained uttering of, 'At last the full story is emerging!' he put down his notebook and with eyes widened with the full story, proceeded to enlighten them.

"It's a queer tale," he began, consulting the book, "but reading from picture one, the story goes as thus:

This is the witnessed testimonial of I, Titus Nethanial Brighold, revered physician to His Most Supreme and Admirable Excellence, the Sovereign King and Emperor, Phillus of Upper Gonderia and Tredo. In the half year of Janus with the spring moon full and bright over the land, in the year barely past the onset of 1309, the great sickness came over the land. It cut down the population without favour, causing distress and suffering to many. In the beginning it started when a great starvation of water beset the natural wells of the domain and every soul who drank the liquid from the still ponds and lakes in the upper realms, died a mysterious and painful death.

On such a day when the masses of the dead reached from end to end of the country, I went to the area where the sickness was first sighted and that day witnessed the extraordinary power of the wind. It was something to behold as it searched with feverish fingers into every fissure and crevice, blowing the strange yellow-green dust abounding there into a myriad of hills and mounds, which magically seemed to transpose to a mantle of red that glowed in the dark as the sun set in the west. I was afraid of this metamorphosis, sure that it was of a fiendish purpose and convinced it was the work of the Devil. Then the mad rain came. It smote the earth without respite for twenty-two days, crushing all plant life and animals alike, opening up deep ravines and bottomless gorges from which hideous aromas of corruption arose. That this malignant rainfall was the cause of the sickness, I had no doubt. The passage of the plague from the core of the earth to the plains where our people dwell was lined with the corpses of the dead and dying, the land itself bearing testimony to the yellow and green poison coating the virgin soil. I travelled a long way, seeing overflowing sepulchres and churchyards, and the frightful and devastating smell of the yellow death flies on the breath of every wind and wallows in the deep tarns of the northern mountain country.

Reading my report, His Excellent Majesty summoned me before him and commanded me to wipe out this foul malady, for the fear of contracting the disease was in his face, with the fate of the royal family of great concern to him. He promised me vast riches for the salvation of his people and gave me title to one tenth of his kingdom for my promise of relief from the sickness. I protested I was powerless, but he would not listen to my pleas. He gave me a mandate to try anything to rid the country of the plague.

In the next three years the sickness waxed stronger and spread to the imperial palace where it claimed the lives of four of the king's favourite wives. Afflicted by this tragedy, in his misery the king had me cast into prison where I awaited the results of his displeasure. There were others who were jealous of my receipt of such vast favours and plotted my downfall. Seizing this opportunity, they had me tried on a false charge, found guilty by the very men who accused me and sentenced to death. Others who were loyal to me tried to get the sentence overturned, but only succeeded in obtaining the king's clemency in part.

In the land was an alchemist who specialised in potions and spells. He was known to possess the secret of turning human beings into stone, using some sort of powder and other ingredients to a secret formula. He was able to cause the subject to die for a specific period, thereby imprisoning them without incarceration, before awakening them when their sentence was over. The king thought this a fitting punishment for my supposed crimes and ordered my living death for a period of five years and no longer. Within days of the king's decision I am brought into the house of Tolmaar the alchemist to suffer the punishment to which he has condemned me.

It's here that the story is taken by another who witnessed the implementation of the sentence," Lund said, continuing to read.

"*He was secured to a table where he was forced to consume various powders and liquids, quickly lapsing into an unconscious state. A funnel was inserted into his mouth and other prepared solutions were administered. In his insensible state other things were inserted into his body and the transformation began. Within an hour his flesh was darker and had developed a hard looking shell, gaining a grey colour with patches of intermixed blue. This quickly changed when the second phase began. His breathing was suspended and heartbeats were absent. The third, the evolvement of the stone-figured flesh, was more pronounced. The facial features of the man seemed to fuse into the bare outlines and the sockets of the eyes, sinking deeper into an enlarged skull. Arms and legs gained weight and girth and, like the body, hardened into a shell-like skin covering. The fourth and final part of the operation was the ultimate granulation of the flesh into stone. The formulation was so pronounced that any recognition of the stone man and the former physician, Brighold, was cast in memory only.*

The figure on the table was huge in comparison with the ordinary man and we were hard put to carry him off to the charnel house. A special coffin was made for the giant, of iron bounds to hold his enormous bulk. From there he was transported to a cavern especially cut in the rock where the sarcophagus was laid on top of a table of rock, lying there to wait out the five years of the sentence."

Lund stopped his monotone and consulted the book.

"It's here that the tale has a twist," he said. "More words added a little time after the event, which had me stumped for awhile." He continued the story. "According to the later script:

Disaster came upon the scene. In the fourth year of his incarceration, catastrophe struck. The disease claimed another

71

victim in the shape of the alchemist, Tolmaar. He died without revealing the secret formula of the antidote for the re-transformation of the stone man. Now the sentence was forever and, unless a cure could be found, he was doomed. The Brighold, as he was then called, was buried here waiting for the day when a cure could be effected.

In the hope of a more advanced people finding the stone man and releasing him from his accursed prison inside the shell, we have collected all the known earths, liquids, powders, ashes and sands of the alchemist, Tolmaar, and sealed them into fifteen bags, laying them in the coffin with the Brighold. May the divine God in all His mercy help in his hour of need."

Lund scrutinised the notebook then, and holding it close to his eyes he continued.

"Then it goes on to say:

Grave despoilers beware of the dust, for it has properties only the alchemist has control over and is there to safeguard the slumber of the Brighold.

And that is us in a way," Lund continued. "Probably that is why the dust has risen up against us and considers us grave robbers."

"Are you seriously suggesting that that bubble of dust has somehow reasoned it all out?"

Meary's laugh must have been infectious because Bill, on hearing it, joined in the merriment with a subdued snigger of his own. Even Lund smiled weakly at the absurd suggestion, but quickly adopted a serious side after consulting the notebook.

"After a lifetime of expecting the mundane and getting something entirely different, I'll reserve my judgement.

Right now I suggest we examine the coffin for the fifteen bags buried with the Brighold."

"My thoughts too," Meary replied, scanning the figure of the stone man with a rippled brow. "He looks a hefty fellow and heavy too, I'll wager." He dipped a questing hand into the box and felt the rock-like skin. "It's hard and cold," he announced, "with the feel of granite. Sort of granulated and rock hard."

Bill tried to lift a massive arm, but only succeeded in going red-faced when he trapped two fingers underneath the huge limb.

"It'll have to be some sort of mechanical lift," Lund decided, and helped Bill remove his finger. He peered into the box. "I suppose the bags are hidden by the Brighold. If we want to see them it will mean lifting him up."

He produced a block and tackle, and fixed it to an overhead beam, letting the rope falls and hook dangle over the coffin. The three men, sweating profusely in the warmth of the laboratory, laboured to lift the left leg, but were only able to clear a big enough hole underneath for a rope to go around. Seeing this was inadequate, Lund circled the leg with another length of rope and tied the ends to the hook. He tightened the block rope with a quick pull of the rope and as the others stood back to watch, tightened the loops. With a sustained pull, he inched the leg upwards, pausing to examine the massive knee joint for any signs of bending. There was none, and the great stone leg rose slowly into the air, causing the coffin to emit loud creaks as the hoist took part of the weight.

Lund tied off the rope to an adjacent hook and stood

peering at the uplifted leg then looking closely and intently into the box.

"Aha!" he said, in a voice thick with triumph. "I think we have succeeded."

The others stepped forwards to watch as he groped into the box and produced a leather bag, holding it on high.

"Gentlemen," he said, smiling at them, "you are looking at a part of history hundreds of years old."

Meary, suitably impressed, could only stare at the bag and for a moment was speechless. He raised a hand and fingered it, noting the smooth texture of the animal hide and the rough leather draw cords holding the folds of the neck together.

"It's magnificent," he whispered, finding his voice through a dried throat, "just magnificent George."

Within the space of an hour all fifteen bags were discovered and were set on an adjoining table, where they sat, resting on the metal surface, waiting for the inevitable foray into their contents.

"First of all we must analyse the contents," Lund suggested, "and that must be my major concern at the moment."

"And what about the Brighold?" Meary queried.

"I'll examine him in due course, after I have prepared a report about the bags' contents." He shrugged a shoulder. "First things first, of course. I have a wealth of information to work on and very few hours to study the results of my tests."

Due to the lateness of the hour, Meary and Bill decided to call it a day and, taking their leave of the chemist, headed for their respective hotels.

After divesting himself of his overalls, Lund washed his hands in the wash basin and dried them on a nearby towel roll. In his mind was a burning desire to investigate the contents of the bags, to find out why they were so important to the Brighold that they were included in the burial. He lifted one of the bags and emptied it into a metal dish resting on the table. To him the little pile of dust looked no more than a handful of dried earth, with a few green lumps of unknown composition intermingled. He prodded it with a mixing spoon, spreading the mixture around the dish. An evil smell of decay and corruption arose, causing him to wrinkle his nose in disgust. He quickly returned the substance to the bag and closed it tightly. Finally he yawned and, after a cursory glance around the laboratory, turned out the light and exited through the house doorway.

Stirred up dust motes floating on the force of his passage from the room danced for an instant on the whirling tides of excited air before subsiding into a gentle fall to the floor. The wall clock, pointing to the hour of eight, perforated the blanket of sudden silence with its constant tick, and the faint sound of the departed chemist filtered through the walls of the laboratory.

Time seemed to stand still and wait with suspended breath. The silence deepened and gained depth with the going of the light. Only a single moonbeam, gaining access into the room through a crack in the shutters, searched through the gloom and alighted on the rows of leather bags resting on the table-top, and nobody human bore witness to the issue of green dust beginning to form into a small bubble over the tops of the bags.

The smell came soon afterwards; a searing corruption of decay and putrefaction that spread from the bubble to the atmosphere around it. Intensifying and gripping the very air, it pulsed and oscillated in dancing waves, spreading and circulating, scattering and stretching, making for the coffin and the stone man resting therein. Within a little time the bubble settled onto the wooden confines of the coffin, making small rivulets of green powder down the sides and dripping green with the force of the penetration. Bit by bit it seemed to infuse into the stone skin of the Brighold and sink beneath the granite-like grey surface.

Very soon the eyes of the Brighold blinked open.

CHAPTER SIX

Meary and Bill waited all next day for a phone call from the chemist, but it did not come. They were becoming impatient for some sort of summons from Lund, so finally succumbed to the temptation and called him. After a fruitless half an hour of continual dialling they gave up and decided to visit the chemist instead.

The building was shuttered up the way they had left it and not a sound was to be heard from the house or the laboratory.

"Strange!" Meary muttered, starting up the gravel drive. "He said he was going to be busy, but he usually answers the phone no matter how busy he is."

"I suppose he forgets what day it is when the work is *that* important," Bill said, striding beside him. "Strange as you say, John, perhaps we can get the lady to explain."

Bill rang the bell several times and Meary knocked on the door. The house remained as morose as before. Not a sound was heard in any part of the building and not a movement of any sort disturbed the dormant façade. Now an inner feeling of doubt began in the pit of Meary's stomach and branched outwards. He bit at his lip, thinking furiously. Small sensations of nagging uncertainty were eating at his nerve centre and no matter how he tried to dispel it the feeling persisted. He breathed in a deep lungful of cold fresh air, trying to shake off the morbid throes of impending doom.

"Let's try around the back," he suggested, shrugging the mood off.

They entered the side gate together and trudged to the rear of the building. Immediately they turned the corner they pulled up in horror. The damage to the French doors was total. Bits of splintered wood and glass fragments littered the back lawn and shrubbery. Torn and stained curtains hung from the remains of the doors and were draped over a wrecked chair. A solitary lady's shoe was lying in a pool of coagulated blood and a wrenched off hand with ligaments sticking up from the bloody flesh, lay on the confusion of wood and shattered windowpanes.

Bill's yelp of surprise and disgust was followed by another from Meary. They stood ogling the horrific scene with bulging eyes and faces drained of every vestige of colour, both unable to believe the evidence of their own eyes. The shock held them rooted to the ground, unable to go forwards to see more, but equally powerless to step backwards and retrace their steps.

"My God!" Meary croaked through disbelieving lips.

He then lapsed into numbed silence, unable to really comprehend what the grisly sight actually spelled out. He was spared further worrying thoughts however, for with a loud burp Bill threw up the contents of his stomach and hung over it, retching violently.

This gave Bill a little relief, but it had the added effect of jerking Meary out of his shocked state. He handed him a handkerchief and waited as he wiped his face clean. He patted the young man on the shoulder and stepped forwards without him. If he thought the first sight of the wrecked house and the carnage wrought there was all, he was sadly mistaken. The inside of the house represented a slaughterhouse and the smell and reek of blood fumes wafted on every indrawn draught blowing through the gaping hole that used to be called the French windows.

He crunched through shards of splintered glass and sidestepped articles of violently ripped clothing decorating upturned pieces of broken furniture. His shoes kicked aside other items of electrical gear and stopped short at the entrance to the laboratory. Skirting the buckled door hanging from its hinges, he fought his way over the piles of smashed bottles and rubber tubing, and eventually stopped before the metal table where they had stood the night before. As he had feared, the coffin was gone and the Brighold as well.

As fears raged like demons through his racing mind he had to ask himself if the stone man was responsible for the carnage and always arrived at the same answer, *yes*. He was surprised by the sureness of his innermost reply, but it was not unexpected. In his role as a believer of the occult and other mysteries he was always prepared to expect the dark side of man's nature, and this was no different, he decided. Man again, whatever the circumstances, was responsible for the happenings, good or evil, and that was the end of it. The Brighold responsible, he thought, don't be ridiculous! The thing is made of stone and hasn't the power of life any more.

Or has he? Strange how he is missing, and his coffin too!

Meary stooped to pick up a dog-eared notebook and stuffed it into his coat pocket without reading it. He was just examining a fallen wall clock, which strangely enough was still ticking, when hearing a movement behind him caused him to whirl around in alarm. He was relieved to see the ashen features of the young man framed in the doorway.

"It's just sickening," Bill muttered through incredulous lips. "There's blood up the stairs too, where someone mortally wounded dragged themselves upstairs. Also the family pet, a dog, has been torn to pieces." He leaned on the doorpost wilting with his forehead touching the wooden frame. "I asked myself who would do such a terrible thing," he went on, almost talking in a whisper, "and I always came up with the same answer—the Brighold!"

"I was just thinking along the same lines until I realised how ridiculous it seems blaming him," Meary said. "He is solid stone as you saw. I can't see him jumping up, committing all these atrocities and carting his coffin away as calm as you please."

They found the woman in the large front bedroom. Her wounds were pretty extensive with injuries to her neck and throat. She was lying on the blood-soaked bed with her spine exposed through a large cut in her delicate looking flesh, from which her life blood must have literally gushed. One leg crossed the other and the look in her eyes must have reflected the terror she felt because they were wide open and staring in horror.

Of Lund there was no sign, so they naturally assumed he was lying dead somewhere outside. The two men exited through the innocent seeming front door and, without any untoward delay, reported the murder to the local police.

Now the buzz of excitement passed to the village community, and voices were raised against the continuation of any more work in the graveyard and the filling in of the burial chamber to make sure this happened, even though Meary explained it was shutting the stable door after the horse had bolted. This was in reference to the flight of the Brighold, but he despaired when they seemed to ignore his warnings and demanded that the hole be filled in and all work stopped.

When the investigation of the murder was undertaken it was conducted by a police inspector called Harding, and he started the proceedings with a quick reference to the element of basic doubt contained in the opening paragraph in Meary's statement.

"It says here that you and others were present at the laboratory conducting an experiment on the corpse the night before the murder or murders took place. Is that right?"

Meary, sitting across from him in the station inquiry room, gazed at the angular policeman sitting at the polished desk and met the level look with a jolt of annoyance. He had been sitting in the hard wooden chair in the waiting room for over an hour and after the recent episode at Lund's house felt none too pleased with the outcome or the investigation into his private affairs.

"We were there, the three of us," he replied, returning look for look. "Bill, Lund, the chemist, and myself."

Harding dropped his eyes to the typed lines again.

"It also says here that you left the corpse in the charge of

Lund when you decided to end the day's work and go home, is that also correct?"

"It was not a corpse as you are intimating, Inspector."

"You mean it was still alive?"

"Well, no, in the proper sense of the word, sort of suspended animation."

"So you were experimenting on a live person?"

"Well, yes and no. He died hundreds of years ago and we were trying to establish how and why he died. We believe we've found the history of him, the Brighold."

"This … er … man, Brighold, where is he now?"

"That's just the point, we don't know where he is."

"I don't understand, Sir, you said he was dead and in the coffin. How can a dead man get up and walk away?"

Meary fought to control himself. This numbskull inspector is deliberately trying to make me say something incriminating, he fumed inwardly. Don't fall into his trap; the truth will come out no matter how many times it is asked. He took a couple of deep breaths before answering. He nodded to the statement with a dipped motion of his head.

"My statement says quite categorically that we were trying to discover the origin of the man in the coffin by inspection of the occupant and the surrounding box, and that is what we did. We have official permission to conduct these experiments, validated by governmental paperwork, which I have in my possession."

Harding acquiesced with a hurried nod and slipped down a few lines. Looking directly at Meary with a thin nose angling over the edge of the paper, he asked a direct question.

"Mr Meary, have you any idea who killed the womam found in the upstairs bedroom?"

"None that will make a lot of sense, but my colleague Bill and I think it might be the work of the stone man, although that will have to be ascertained with a lot of proof."

"And how are you going to produce this proof?"

"By finding the Brighold and conducting a lot more tests."

"Supposing this Brighold man doesn't want to be found?"

"Even so, they have to be made. It will be harder without Lund, but we must carry on the tests if we are to succeed in our work. If he is lying wounded out there somewhere —"

"Meary," Harding said, interrupting, "we found Lund lying in a wood a couple of hundred yards from the house. We identified the body by a wallet we found in a coat he was wearing. The head of the corpse was missing, but it was discovered in another part of the wood farther on."

He stared at Meary to see his reaction to the news, but the other had long ago fortified his mind to expect such an outcome and could only shake his head in silent sympathy.

"I'll have a description of the alleged assailant if I can, Sir?" he said as a matter of course.

"He is composed of stone," Meary said in a monotone, "weighs somewhere in the region of forty stones or more and is reputed to be seven feet eight inches tall. He is grey-black in colour with massive arms and legs of the same material. Oh, yes," Meary concluded, "he has no clothes, he is entirely naked."

"Naked, you say?" queried Harding.

"As the day he was born, so women police officers, be warned."

"Hmm, he's a lusty fellow," Harding said, "we'll need all the resources we have and more to catch this felon." He leaned forwards in the chair and levered himself upwards, coming around the corner of the desk with practised steps. "Keep in touch in case we want to see you again," he said, smiling.

He opened the glass panelled door and waited as Meary stepped through, almost bumping into Bill, who was waiting outside. Bill opened his mouth to say something to him, but thought better of it as Harding called:

"Mr Drew, please come in."

Instead he closed one eye in a wink and stepped into the room. As Meary left the police station he was undecided on what course to take and, after a few seconds of thought, headed for the village post office. He raked through his pockets, spent the last few coins on calling a London number and within minutes was speaking to an old friend and associate, Dave Hollis.

"Hello, Dave, guess who? That's right, John. Look, can you get down here right away? Pardon? Well, it *is* very important. The project is standing still for want of expertise... We need a very capable man and naturally I thought of you. Yes, some very exciting things have happened here, too many to talk about over the phone. I guarantee it won't be boring, Dave, far from it. Okay, I'll expect you tomorrow. Bye."

Meary stepped into the street just in time to meet Bill on his way from the police station. He pointed to his parked car at the side of the road and waited as the young man climbed into the passenger seat.

"Dave Hollis will be here tomorrow," he announced, slipping behind the wheel, and as Bill's eyes lit up with interest, "you'll have a lot to talk about since your last meeting at school. He's a good man to have around, Bill."

Under Meary's direction the car sped away from the village and soon ate up the miles separating it and the laboratory.

"I wonder where he is now?" Bill muttered from the corner of his mouth. "Where can it hide, the size it is?"

"The stone man?" Meary queried. "Probably thirty or forty miles away by this time, he'll travel fast I bet."

Actually he was a lot nearer than that. The Brighold had found a haven far underground in an abandoned section of a little known sewer system, into which he had blundered on his flight from the chemist's house. The offensive aroma did not bother him, for he had no sense of smell. His lungs, for so long unused inside his chest cavity, knew not the breath of fresh air and the suspended state of his organs, so vital to his other body, were supported by the presence of an unknown quantity of chemicals and other concoctions congealed in his dead veins.

The dim light filtering in from the outside held no terrors for him. He was barely able to see, even in the daylight, but relied on a voice in the recesses of his mind, warning him of any imminent danger. He did not require food, for Tolmaar's amazing compounds seeped through fine capillaries and cracks, running through the stone format. No longer lying dormant, it was the mainstay of the energy needed to push the enormous bulk of the Brighold forwards.

The rock formation of his physique was powerful. He

exuded strength and durability, which accounted for the easy way in which he had dispatched the chemist Lund and the woman. Although he had been asleep for hundreds of years he did not need it. His strength never wavered and was always the same. The only thing that bothered him was the continual squeal of noises in his head; some a rushing of wind and others a pounding reminiscent of the diggers excavating his grave. These he could remember, although the potions administered by the alchemist wiped out most of his faculties.

Lying beside him was the open box of the coffin with the lid close by. The fifteen bags of compound lay in the box, right where he had put them after his journey across open country. Somehow he knew the bags were important, not because he had knowledge of what they were, but because of their presence in the coffin. It seemed to him that they formed an intricate part of his body, like the colour of his slate-grey skin and the scrape of his tremendous limbs rubbing together as he stumbled forwards.

His upper body and arms were discoloured with peeling bloodstains, testifying to the severity of the attack at the house. Under his fingernails were little bits of flesh and bone, torn with tremendous force from the bodies of his victims. Sewer rats, big and vicious, scampered between his feet. Smelling the blood, they nipped at his flesh and appalled, recoiled with blunted teeth. He neither felt nor acknowledged their presence, but sat on a mound of rotting rubbish, waiting for the guiding voice to tell him what to do.

Water dripped in a steady stream from the roof. A discoloured waterfall of muddy water and other decaying matter poured onto the uneven ground in a constant river, which spread outwards to form a small lake and emptied through a hole in the side of the sewer pipe. Through the years, the water had worn a path through the concrete wall of the pipe and in time had undermined the supporting soil so that it had partially collapsed. The Brighold, in his search for a bolt-hole, had stumbled on the hideaway, not because he wanted security, but because the voice had ordered it so.

He sat upright, like some gigantic stone monolith, silent and motionless, arms hanging down and trailing in the litter around his lower limbs and feet. His body was unmoving in the still air, neither living or dying, but suspended in time, with life in the form of teeming rat hordes scampering about in their eternal search for food, and fat flies swarming around the putrescent pile of decomposing rubbish that had collected in the base of the pipe over many years. About twenty feet before his eyes rose an entry chamber, with the first three feet of a rusty iron ladder just in sight. Water dripped continually from the chamber to join the slow flow down the pipe to other water inlets and then on to the faster flow coming from the other source.

The Brighold sat there without moving for five days. The inhabitants of the sewer had grown used to the silent stone man. He was a part of the sewer now and they treated him with the same trust they afforded the other dead occupant of the pipe; the partially eaten decomposed body of a tabby cat.

It was on this particular day that the powers controlling the sewage system of the village decided to examine the whole complex because of complaints about the smell arising from it. A newer system had been built and ran its course above the old set of pipes, now derelict.

Overhead, an inspector of pipes in the shape of one, Tom Porter, was sloshing through six inches of muddy rainwater, looking for obstructions of any kind that could explain the cause of the obnoxious odour coming from the sewer system. He espied the rusted in, circular iron disc leading to the lower galleries and, after a strenuous wrestle with the encrusted lid, succeeded in dislodging it. Porter, clad in waterproofs and rubber boots, swung the heavy iron lid aside. The interior of the chamber was brick built. Most of the bricks were in a crumbly state and looked decidedly dangerous. An iron ladder, thick with rust, ran down to the lower level, fixed to the brickwork with driven in iron ties. Porter tested the first rung with a few stamps of his boot and, finding it supported his weight, swung the rest of his body into the hole, dodging the stream of dirty water entering the chamber as he did so.

Pieces of crumbling mortar and fragments of decaying brick rained down on the lower level, causing him to regret his decision to inspect the chamber. He started to climb back up, scrambling for the top rung and the gaping hole a couple of feet above his head. Luck was with him and the ladder held just long enough for him to launch himself through the opening and onto the upper level floor before it parted from its moorings and crashed down to the bottom level with a resounding smash. He wiped the water from his face with his sleeve and gazed into the hole, noted the buckled ladder lying at the foot of the chamber and thanked his lucky stars for the escape, although how much of an escape he had had was debatable because the terrific crash of falling iron had jolted the Brighold from his lethargy and forced his eyes open.

Fright never came to him and, to a certain degree, neither did pain. He experienced inner pain though, mostly in his head, but sometimes in his body. He very vaguely was aware of a spasm in his chest, slight, but not unduly painful. The sudden crash of the ladder revitalised a shudder of movement in his huge bulk and the tremor gathered force until it flooded into the millions of cells secreted in tiny capillaries scattered over his body. With this source of energy entering his system he was able to shift his enormous weight into movement, and this is what he did. He turned his head in the direction of the fallen ladder and through his dim sight made out the cause of the noise. Towering above everything else he slowly got to his feet, brushing the dome of the sewer pipe with his massive head.

Inside he yearned for somewhere to rest, to lie down and drive away the demons drumming in his head. His partial memory told him the only place he had been at rest was in the tomb. A confusion of primary thoughts tried to piece together the train of events leading from the burial chamber to his place in the sewer. He tried, but failed to understand it, and the thought just vanished from his head. He had no knowledge of his journey to the laboratory. He only heard the voice commanding him to awaken, to leave and take the bags with him, to escape from the attentions of the man who wanted to dissect his body and remove his brain.

The urge to return to the tomb was strong in him, but he lacked a driving force, a vital spark necessary to impel him forwards. The rats, scattering at his sudden movement, watched him from the safety of a dozen holes in the fractured pipe, ready to flee at the first sign of danger. He stooped and retrieved the coffin by holding it in one big fist and tucking it under his arm. He brushed the bags with the other hand to make sure they were there. He picked up the lid with a scooping movement. Still he hesitated, waiting to be led, unsure of himself and waiting for the command of the inner voice, but still no word came into his head and somewhere inside a feeling of panic materialised and enlarged into fear. He was desperate to return to the safety of the tomb, but not how to start for it.

He stumbled forwards, a tottering walk that swayed the huge bulk into a sort of feet-apart lumber, scattering small objects in the way of his enormous strides. He crashed through hanging obstacles, hardly slowing the gait, and brushed aside the ruins of the derelict sewer pipe with powerful thrusts of his granite-hard arms and hands.

Outside at the sewer outlet he squelched through thick mud and greasy water, his weight causing him to sink into it up to his knees. He fought the clinging mud and effluent water with flailing arms, while piston strides of his great legs carried him across the swampy ground. His feet touched firmer ground and he pulled the coffin onto a patch of weedy grass growing at the side of the boggy watercourse. Now he could feel the touch of the wind on his face and the warmth of an autumn sun on his back. He felt the twinge of remembrance within the realms of his memory, a sensation so remote it hardly raised a quiver, but even so it registered a sort of passing thought closely allied with another lifetime gone forever.

The clinging mud did a lot to cover his nakedness, the cloying skirt encrusting his lower limbs, hanging down like the folds of an overcoat, coating his waist to his feet in a brown evil smelling layer of drying mud. Through his dim sight he saw objects before him as shadows, and with the many encounters he had with trees and other obstacles, if he had been of a softer matter, he would have suffered immensely. However, he stopped at the obstruction and sidled around it with sideways motions of his body, feeling for the roughness of it until it faded from his grip or came to an end. Using this unconscious method of movement, the forest ended at the foot of a hill, and pasture with grazing cattle came into view.

The village, several miles distant, nestled in the valley of a gentle range of rolling hills and on the edge of the village, operating a lawnmower, was the park keeper.

The engine was acting up today and kept stopping and starting. He managed to start it for the sixth time, but it ran ragged for awhile until it packed up again. He never heard the sound of the Brighold's approach because of the din from the engine. He only felt a presence near him and, straightening up, turned to behold the horrific sight of the stone man standing thirty feet away. In turn, surprise, horror and fear, leaped to the keeper's face. He stepped back fast and just as quickly fell over the lawnmower. He stayed where he was, on the ground, staring in abject terror as the figure drew near and halted a few feet away.

Now the awe-inspiring horrific sight of the Brighold met his gaze and with it came the sickening smell of the grave and the mud-encrusted filth adhering to the stone spectacle. He screamed out in mortal terror, scrambling on the ground with feverish kicks of his heels and tearing at the tufts of grass with madly grabbing fingernails. His cries turned to sobs as the shadow of the stone man came between him and the sun's rays.

A policeman let them into the lab where Meary produced Lund's notebook and started to read the hurried scribbles of the chemist. After they had gone, he read that Lund had returned later to the lab to re-examine the compound bags. To his astonishment they were in place in the coffin with the occupant resting on them as if nothing had been disturbed. Lund, unable to believe the evidence of his own eyes, tried to retrieve them only to find the Brighold opening his eyes and looking at him.

'I was in total shock,' he had written. 'His eyes, devoid of any pupils and glistening like quicksilver, followed my every movement as I stepped back in fright. A huge hand tightening into a fist rose above the sides of the casket in a threatening movement and the head turned towards me. In blind panic I fled from the room and, after locking the lab door, told my wife to call the police. I searched for a weapon to defend myself, and my wife went upstairs and locked herself in her room. I can hear the monster barging about in the lab, smashing things, now he is tearing at the door and breaking through …'

The notes ended there and Meary pursed his lips in thought, convinced the Brighold had interrupted the writing and attacked the chemist. Obviously the monster had taken the coffin and the lid, so the likelihood of their getting any more information about the Brighold was practically nil. To confirm this view, Bill returned from an examination of the garden with a solemn face.

"No trace of the stone man," he reported. "The rain has completely washed out his footprints, so we've no idea where he was heading." He sighed. "We can scour the countryside, but he has a good head start on us. I don't rate our chances of finding him willy-nilly, John."

"And neither do I," Meary concurred, closing the book. "I think our best method of continuing the search is to go back to where it all started, at the tomb, so if you have finished here perhaps we can get started and return to the cemetery."

The metal gates of the graveyard loomed up before them as before, but with the addition of a rusty iron chain and a solid looking padlock holding the gates together. Meary looked at it with fury written on his features.

"That damned council!" he fumed, "they know I have a government backed mandate to do these operations. Just because of a few cowardly councillors who lack the courage to act against local busy-bodies poking their noses into what doesn't concern them. They make me sick!"

Leaving the car outside, they climbed the wall and made their way over to the gaping hole with the tomb below. The equipment was still in place where they had left it and, although wet through with the recent rain, the chair was swinging on the end of the rope, as if waiting for the order to descend into the depths. That looked more than likely because Meary was inspecting the generator preparatory to entering the chamber with that 'no nonsense' look on his face designed to brook no interference. However, Bill thought he had to make something crystal clear and voiced his opinion.

"There are only the two of us, John, and Hollis will be here shortly. Don't you think it's safer to wait for his help before you venture down there again?"

Meary turned a quizzical eye on him.

"There's no time like the present," he said, "but if you're not up to it we'll wait for him. That is, of course, if you want to lose several hours' work waiting for him, do you?"

"No," Bill replied in a numb voice then he seemed to brighten as a thought occurred to him. "I'd be willing to take your place. I've not been down there yet, so it's something I'd appreciate."

Meary smiled at his assistant. The young man was obviously concerned for his safety and was willing to face danger for him.

"Thank you, Bill, but it won't be necessary. You are most able working the equipment up here while I'm doing what I consider I'm best at." When he saw Bill's crestfallen look he continued, "You'll get your chance sooner or later, so don't look so down, lad."

Bill's gloom cracked into a smile as he took the petrol can that Meary was offering him.

"It's a bit late with the Brighold tearing across country the way he is. I shouldn't wonder the police will pick him up shortly." He turned a quizzical glance in Meary's direction, enquiring, "What do you want to go down into the hole for? There's nothing there now."

Of course Bill is right, Meary mused. The only occupants were the two skeletons and the dust, but the lingering feeling of something extra being present persisted. Deep in the well of Meary's subconscious mind an open sore of doubt remained and as much as he put the idea aside it came back to him with renewed vigour. There had to be something somewhere helping the Brighold, and like a chink of light entering through a barely perceptible cleft in the darkness, it revealed a quick glimpse before it was extinguished, which was so with the snapshots of evidence mounting up before his eyes.

The generator engine fired into life and the soot of long idleness shot into the air from the exhaust pipe. The carburettor coughed before settling down to a smooth and contented hum. Bill seized the windlass handle and fitted it on to the square end of the roller, waiting for Meary to climb into the seat.

Familiar patterns of rock formations passed by his eyes, moving upwards. The great opening of the cave, still maintaining an unearthly silence, settled around him like a smothering blanket and the rancid air, liberally laced with the floating motes of yellow dust, entered his lungs with a clammy dense feeling that almost made him throw up. When his feet touched bottom, he wriggled out of the chair with practised hands and gave the usual signal on the rope by pulling it. After a pause the outline of his assistant came into view.

"Everything okay?" he called, shaking the rope.

Meary assured him it was and gazed about him. Everything was the same as they had left it, he decided, from the pile of disturbed stones serving as a platform for the coffin to the skeletons lying side by side in the corner. At least it all appeared the same, and to the unpractised eye, would have been, but Meary had a sixth sense, gained in the years fighting the supernatural and creatures inhabiting the unnatural world.

He cast a wary eye about him and jumped as a lump of rock the size of a tennis ball hit the floor beside him and bounced away into the gloom of a cave corner. He stepped back, following the flight of the missile with narrowed eyes and looking up at the figure of his assistant still framed in the light.

"Was that you, Bill? Did you knock that rock into here? I'm right under your line of fire, so be careful," he shouted.

Bill's voice, mutely echoing in the chamber, came to him as through a void, which had the effect of blanketing it.

"It was not me, John, it must have come from down below."

His cry was fainter now as the stifling air of the tomb seemed to deepen and circle around. Meary felt the pressure beginning to build and said a little prayer to himself. He was accustomed to the powers of darkness asserting themselves, and mentally prepared himself for the assault to come. When it did come, it came in a form so bizarre it fairly took his breath away. He coughed, trying to dispel the taste of the fetid air, and the sound, muffled by the thickened air surrounding him, vibrated on his nerve cords, enclosing and confining him to the repeated stabs jangling at his very soul.

"Why don't you show yourself, you immortal coward?" he yelled. "Why don't you want to be seen by us mere mortals?"

On the myriad tide of floating particles of yellow dust welling up from the floor came the same demented laughter that Bill had witnessed.

CHAPTER SEVEN

The demonic laughter rang in the air and jumped from every corner like a rubber ball. Meary heard the strains die away before he deigned to speak.

"Show yourself!" he thundered. "Show yourself, whoever you are. If you have the desire or the will to make yourself known then do it, *now!*"

A lull followed, which seeped into the dense air of the chamber and seemed to add to the thickness of the cloying atmosphere. Even time seemed to hang still, as if the owner of the laugh was mulling the demand over – then it came. It was deep and resonant, with tones so powerful it caused Meary to inwardly wilt.

Who are you to desecrate my tomb? Be gone or I will visit a curse on you.

The sound of the spirit brought a panic to Meary and he fought to control it, but his inner soul soared and danced with the victory dance now that he was in communication with the laughter maker.

"I am here to find out about the Brighold. I am not a

desecrator of graves!" he protested

The sepulchral voice rang out again, louder and stronger.

If you are not a desecrator then why are you here? What do you want with the Brighold?

Inwardly tickled that he was making contact, Meary gathered his inner resources in one tremendous leap.

"I wish to know more about the Brighold because mankind wants to help. I am just a small part of a group of people who need to know about our ancestors and how they lived."

I have control over the stone man and no one else, the voice bellowed. *You are the one who stole his body so that you will profit from the discovery. That is why he was removed to a place where another was about to perform an examination.*

"We only meant to help. Lund read his history on the lid and was about to reveal it to the world."

Lund was preparing to remove his head! the voice replied, just as strongly. *I ordered the disposal of him with as much feeling as I'd have for any wild animal.*

"He was examining the Brighold so that, with the aid of the fifteen bags of compound, he would be able to —"

The bags are composed of rubbish, the voice interrupted. *Don't you think I would have used them before if I could?*

"But why were they included in the burial? The Brighold seems to think they are the answer to his problem. He carries them about with him as though they will help him regain his mortal soul."

Meary was pleading with the voice, although he was talking into the space around him. He found the experience more than trying and made it plain.

"Can't you appear to me so that I may argue on the same mutual grounds?"

That is impossible, came the reply. *I have only the power to project my voice to an outsider. My visual form died out in the final months of my life on earth.*

Meary filled his lungs with the fetid air and prepared for his last appeal to the tomb minder.

"Since the discovery of the Brighold two men have died as a result, one a very great friend and colleague. They died needlessly and in peculiar circumstances. I need to know why they died and who murdered them."

The direct cause was the yellow dust. It has the power to eat into solid flesh and lift off the skin. The internal organs are quick to follow, leaving the skeleton. It is simple, but effective. It renders the desecrator without life. He who seeks to despoil the resting place of the dead deserves nothing less!

"But he was nothing more than a scientist," Meary protested, "doing a job for the benefit of mankind. He didn't deserve it."

Do you know who I am? Do you know to whom you speak?

"Yes, Tolmaar, I am aware of your prowess as a sorcerer. I am also aware of the fact that it is you who is directly responsible for the fate of the Brighold. You administered the lethal mixtures to him and it is you who will be held to account."

For a breathtaking moment Meary was afraid he had gone too far, accusing Tolmaar. He waited for the reaction and wilted as the curses of the alchemist rained about him. It started with an almighty growl and grew into a howl of unsuppressed anger. Tolmaar's voice waves danced on the fetid air like steel nails driven into the quaking flesh of the trembling man.

You dare to threaten me, you insect under my foot. I'll grind you to the dust from whence you came. Tolmaar's voice thundered in the surrounding half-light and echoed throughout the cavern until the very portals rocked from the strength and power of the onslaught. The attack then wilted and began to subside, and the cavern ceased to reverberate with his cries, until only a whisper of its former vigour came to Meary.

Beware the Brighold, for he is death. Beware the yellow dust, for it is also death...

The timbre of the voice altered and began to fade. Meary began to panic after getting such a response from the sorcerer.

"Do not desert me," he pleaded. "I have so much I want to discuss with you, please stay."

I cannot, the voice said hoarsely. *Other powers greater than mine are intervening and I must do as they wish.*

"What about the stone man? He is causing havoc wherever he goes. You must control him, Tolmaar. You are responsible for the murders and mayhem he is perpetrating. You will stand before God to answer for all these crimes, Tolmaar."

A silence ensued that cut into the fetid atmosphere like a knife. The cave seemed to stand back and hold its breath at the interlude. Shadows deep and dark began to encroach on Meary and the air became sinister and evil. He felt the crawling demons, creeping, slithering, seeking out his flesh, pricking and stinging, needling with fingers of pointed fire.

It was then Meary looked all about him and, with rising alarm, saw the bright yellow dust beginning to form pools around his feet. He knew the reputation of the dust and thought it was time to make a speedy withdrawal. Not without some form of protest, he thought, retreating.

"So *this* is your answer, you devil!" he stormed. "But mark this! I will be back, on that you can count, and then we will have a reckoning you will not like or countenance."

He felt the first stinging fingers nibbling at his flesh as he strode over to the chair. Frantically he jerked on the rope and was instantly gratified to see the shadow of his assistant framing the entrance.

"Pull me up, Bill, *quick!*" he shouted, looking at the encroaching dust as he was climbing into the chair.

The rope tightened and his feet parted from the stone floor just as the dust reached the spot he had just vacated. He was blowing with the effort and grabbing great lungfuls of the stinking air. Bill was there to swing the chair aside and give him a hand to release the strap restraints.

"I couldn't hear you for awhile," he said in a nervous voice. "The air seems so thick down there it's almost my idea of the underworld, Hades."

Meary could see some sense in the comparison, but his mind was too full of his own experience to enlarge on the theory.

"I've just been talking to Tolmaar," he explained, giving the hole a quick look over his shoulder, "but right now I think we ought to be going because within a lttle —"

"*Tolmaar!*" Bill repeated incredulously. "But I thought he was ... "

"Dead." Meary finished the sentence for him. "He is, but his spirit is still very much alive, and so is the yellow dust cloud he set on me."

He was mopping his brow with a handkerchief, all the time casting anxious looks in the direction of the cavern opening.

"You mean Tolmaar deliberately told the cloud to attack you? Why I-I didn't know he had the power to control it from the grave. This is incredible. I don't know what to say."

Trying to listen to Bill and watch the beginnings of the yellow tentacles streaming like hideous fingers from the hole was too much for Meary to bear. He grabbed his assistant's arm in a fierce hold and dragged him away, both of them standing open mouthed and incredulous at the fearsome yellow issue vomiting and revolving as it spewed from down below.

"It's frightening, I know," Meary said. "It killed the two men down below with its fearful properties and it meant to do the same to me."

"But what is it for? What is its purpose?"

"To guard the Brighold, I'm thinking, possibly manufactured by Tolmaar to deter would-be grave robbers. He threatened me in the brief intercourse I had with him. He warned me to beware of the two deaths—the Brighold and the dust. I dared to argue with him and he set it on me. The man is as big a maniac in the grave as he was on earth."

Leaving the big dust bubble rising into the air they retreated to the car and made their way to the village.

For several miles the Brighold stumbled on. He crossed muddy ditch and ploughed field in his search for the tomb. He wandered with arms outstretched in the way of a blind man, which was as he was, with dim eyesight barely able to see more than four feet ahead. Once or twice he fell into a swampy patch and groped his way out of the soft mud with flailing arms and extended legs. On more than one occasion his great height, coupled with a surge of massive strength, saved him from another burial in the perilous muddy embrace of a bottomless bog. The coffin was still clutched in his enormous hand and the bags, now but a vague memory, at the bottom of a fast flowing stream several miles back, were soon erased from his short and conscious thoughts.

Back in his tracks the dismembered body of the park keeper lay. Already it had been discovered by a passing pedestrian, who was quick to raise the alarm, and a police van was already on its way to the scene. The incident went swiftly out of the Brighold's mind, for the bloody murder of the man meant only a passing obstacle in his search for the tomb. He had swept him aside as if he was a bush or a twig. His blows were hard and lethal to an ordinary man. One crushing punch from the granite man was enough to kill him stone dead, and that is how the park keeper had met his fate, plus the Brighold tore him in half because he thought the voice wanted it so. The unfortunate keeper was a victim of the Brighold's head noises and he had paid the terrible price. Unheeding, he plunged onwards, threading a diagonal line across the outskirts of the village, going away from the cemetery.

When the night came he fell into an open ditch and sat in six inches of muddy water, the coffin by his side. The night sky was clear of rain clouds and the stars were ablaze above him. He studied the glow for awhile and vague bits of memory stirred in the remnants of his mind. Memories so far back in time it was as though they barely registered. Snatches of thoughts and dreams intermingled in a kaleidoscope of colourful snapshots flashing inside him. He had a momentary vision of sick people dying for water, calling for help to fight the plague, before the dream broke into pieces in his mind and vanished. Since his awakening, he had blindly followed the commands of the voice in his mind and this is for what he was waiting, but lately the flickerings of a previous existence seemed to engage on his consciousness and awake in him a spark, just the tiniest of particles that had a peripheral life before dying.

The cold water bubbled and fizzed around his legs as air pockets shot to the surface in the little pool and popped open. A solitary frog, mistaking the flesh of the Brighold for a bit of rock, hopped onto his knee and crouched there, looking up at the stone mountain. The Brighold stirred not, ignoring all about him, waiting for the darkness to lift and the day to begin. He hardly felt the cold or the heat, so the extremes of temperature never really bothered him.

The raw wind that played about his person and whispered in the pool brought no reaction from him. The cold mist, tinged with the filmy frost of approaching winter, settled on the hard flesh of his beetling eyebrow sockets and the other outlines of his facial contours. Often his eyelids, like leather flaps, blinked to clear away small obstacles that entered his eyes, but they were hard to remove without the added lubrication that tears provided. His eyes, dark without irises, stared into the misty gloom unheeding as the quivering frog hopped onto the other leg and crouched there, staring up at him. The slow moving water, once muddy with the violent movement of his enormous bulk, started to run clear, eddying about his huge body with a gradual drift that lapped at him with gentle wave-like motions.

The dark hours began and started to run full course. The stars disappeared behind bubbling rain clouds that had accumulated overhead then, as the stone man stared into the night, the rain began. It ran down his face and coursed over his massive shoulders in a gentle stream. It cascaded down his glistening body and ran away to join the now swelling waters of the quickening watercourse, stirring it into a fast moving body. The strength of the raindrops increased, hitting the gentle surface of the stream and producing pimples of rain that danced up to meet the onslaught.

Upstream, the surge of rising water carrying various flotsam of leaves and twigs, turned the almost empty ditch into a deep well of flowing water. It rapidly emptied into the lower part of the watercourse and flowed down with this extra force, to where the stone man was lying. The muddy swirl of the rising tide, overflowing the gently sloping banks of the waterway, swiftly rose to chest height on the Brighold and, as he settled into the mud bottom of the stream, soon rose to the level of his armpits.

The icy water gushing about him provoked no response. He was neither bothered by the chill nor the force of the water, ignoring it as it flowed by. A few wisps of straggly hair, the remains of a healthy mat in some distant past, dripped streams of rainwater from his enormous head and trickled into his staring eyes, also without response. He was waiting for the light and nothing seemed to enter his field of purpose.

Later on the clouds strung out in the sky and a watery three-quarter moon ducked in and out of them at the insistence of a quickening wind.

Less than a mile away from the Brighold's resting place, the poacher, Denny, was readjusting a wire rabbit snare and by that same moon set it to a different rabbit run. The recent happenings at the graveyard were now a distant memory and any misgivings he still harboured about meeting anything supernatural were tempered by the fact that the graveyard lay in an entirely different direction to where he now stood.

As he covered ground in his search for other snares he little knew that his footsteps were heading in the general direction of the stone man and the horror to come. The woods and bushes were fast coming to an end to be replaced by grassland and the occasional tree. The fields were waist high in weeds and coarse rye grass making his passage through them difficult to negotiate. He ploughed through the tangled undergrowth guided by the periodic appearance of the moon gliding through stringy rain clouds.

Very soon, stumbling on thick knotted weed clusters and sharp bladed grass leaves, his breathing became laboured. He gasped out plumes of breath, which were misted in the moon's glow, and he felt the trickle of warm sweat running down his brow. Several times he stepped into soft boggy ground where his wellington boots were almost forced from his feet by the strength of the suction. His clothes were saturated with water from the raindrops hanging from the twisted growth and he could feel the coldness striking through the coarse material of his upper trousers. He was beginning to regret his decision to take a short cut through the grassland and was relieved to see, by a fleeting glimpse of moon glow, that the edge of the field was in sight.

He neared a stretch of circling hedgerow, made a dive for a hole in a dark patch of shrubbery, missed his footing on the water-filled ditch and was cast into the freezing waters of a rain-swollen stream, loudly cursing his luck and the ditch in which he was sitting. The chill of the water took his breath away and for a few seconds he sat there numb with cold. His teeth chattered and a violent fit of uncontrollable shivering seized his body. He fought to stand upright in the flowing water, but slipped on a bank of slimy mud. His clothes served to weigh him down as he floundered in the water. His heavy overcoat wrapped itself around his face, shutting out what light there was. He wrenched it from his eyes in an explosion of desperation and succeeded in tearing it off just as the full force of a naked moon lit up the surroundings.

Denny threw the coat away and in the same motion saw the figure of the stone man sitting in the same water, less than six feet away from him. Terror, quick and stupefying, numbed Denny's mind and he screamed and floundered in the water, kicking up a wall of foam and lather in his panic to escape. Beside him the screams of horror reverberated into the mind of the Brighold and jerked him out of his lethargic trance. He turned his head in the direction of the sound, and the madly thrashing body of the poacher darkened the area of his vision. The moon revealed the scrambling form of Denny slipping and sliding on the muddy bank, desperately trying to escape, but now well and truly anchored by the additional burden of two gallons of muddy ditch water overflowing from his wellington boots.

Rapidly becoming hoarse from his constant screaming,

Denny now turned terror stricken eyes at the movement of the monster and, as a result of his inability to escape, tried to cower away from the menace. He ceased to struggle as his mind numbed in horror at the sight, but rather squirmed away from the fearful apparition.

For his part, the Brighold felt vaguely disturbed by the noise of the man and, in an attempt to halt the screams, reached out to stem them in the only way he knew. His rock-like fingers took a hold on the right shoulder of the poacher and dislocated the joint with one tremendous pull. Now the pain-ridden cries of the man increased in volume. His body, trailing the fractured arm, writhed in agony, his terror creased face deathly white in the moonlight, twisted in pain and abject fear. He started to shake violently, cowering and cringing from the awesome fingers as they searched for a further hold on his quaking flesh.

The demented cries of the poacher echoed within the portals of the stone man's mind, creating images of past suffering that seemed to inflame still further a desire to stifle the source of the noise. Terrible stone fingers, dark with the red blood of the terrified poacher, with one concerted effort wrenched off the wounded arm and dropped it into the icy water. Trailing weeping blood vessels and writhing tendons, the member, issuing huge clots of coagulating blood, slowly washed away and was lost to sight beneath the surface of the gently moving stream.

Denny was fast feeling the effects of the attack. His attempt to escape was further prevented by the loss of the arm and he floundered in the swell of the deep water and his own blood stains. His strength seemed to be ebbing away and his cries were becoming weaker. The banks of the stream, slippery with mud and meshing weed stalks, was almost beyond him. It seemed to be farther and farther away, past his ability to climb now. Oozing blood saturating his shirt sleeve, coursed from the hole in his shoulder and dripped down to the black water below. As his life's blood drained away and the paralysing cold climbed swiftly through his muscles and sinews, a curious calm entered his mind. He somehow sensed that he was dying and he welcomed the painless extinction into which he was slipping. Very soon all movement in his legs and lower body ceased to exist and even his gentle attempt to straighten his legs beneath the water was stilled. His heart, starved of blood, hammered and protested in his breast, and what remained of its blood supply fuelled the dying brain. Within a little this also ceased to function and the crook of a smile he had managed to effect was frozen into a death mask. His lifeless corpse slumped into the water, looking up at the brilliant moon with eyes that saw nothing.

Beside the dead man the massive hulk of the Brighold settled back to await the dawn, oblivious now to the presence of the body, waiting for the daylight and the voice to call him to his resting place – the tomb.

A red dawn painted the edge of the clouds to a fiery colour and the edge of the rising sun clipped the horizon to match the splendour. Long fingers of pink and yellow tinged the sky and as the emergent sun ascended the coming shadows of the new day rose to greet it.

Meary took the extended hand of the smiling Hollis and

shook it up and down.

"Glad to see you again, Dave," he enthused, copying the man's broad grin.

He took the arm of the young man and led the way from the railway station to his waiting car. Hollis was a tall man. Meary judged he stood six feet three if he was an inch, and looked likely to be a handful if he was called upon to defend his corner. He was clean-shaven and sported a deep tan after his time in Northern India. He towered over Meary and inclined his head to hear what he was saying.

"I'll fill you in as we go along," Meary said, opening the passenger door to his car and waiting for the long legs to climb in. "The story is bizarre, as you will see when I tell you all that has taken place so far. It might surprise you, to say the least, Dave. As I mentioned in my letter," Meary intimated, "about the queer set of circumstances surrounding the deaths of Travis and the gravedigger, George Ward."

Meary slipped into the driving seat and within seconds the car was in motion. He drew a deep breath and related all that had happened since that fateful day when the world had opened up below the gravedigger.

"Lately," he went on, "the man from the tomb is causing havoc in the countryside by attacking everyone he meets. He is frightening in the extreme and with his enormous bulk and strength is more than a match for the ordinary man."

"What about the police or the army? Can't they help in rounding him up?" Hollis queried, turning his head sideways to see the driver.

Meary was shaking his head as Hollis was making the suggestion.

"I don't want to involve the services if I can possibly help it, Dave," he said, shooting a quick look at him. "Sightseers and all that, you know what I mean."

"I certainly do, but of course if the public must be protected we may have to ask them for assistance in the long run."

"Yeess," Meary said thoughtfully, almost to himself, "let's hope that it won't come to that if we can safely get him under lock and key."

"From what you just told me that will take some doing, especially with him being the size he is and possessing sub-human strength. It might take a few men to capture him and drug him into submission, possibly shoot him if he proves to be dangerous."

Meary cast a look at the face of Hollis and at the set of his jutting jaw.

"Let's hope it will not come to killing him," he said, face clouding visibly. "Probably many hundreds of years of history and legend lie in the make-up of that stone man, Dave. I'd hate to see it all lost to the world before we have a chance of discovery. That is why Lund died and the way he did. He was on the point of finding out something we all want to know—the secret of eternal life."

"Oh yes," Hollis scoffed. "Eternal life, cooped up in a skin of rock, with not a chance of shedding it—some life that."

Meary grew silent for awhile. He was digesting this morsel of staid knowledge from a member of the younger generation and it rankled. True, the man spoke with logic, but he missed the point; a wealth of valuable information walked the countryside on two legs and it was vital the stone man was examined before something untoward happened to him. Meary, in his chagrin, pressed down on the accelerator and the car jumped forwards. The rusted gates of the cemetery came into view and he clicked the hand brake on with a jerk.

"If you would like to see the grave it is there for your inspection," he invited, getting out of the car and approaching the gates.

Together they swung through the squealing entrance, skirted the leaning gravestones and were soon leaning forwards over the yawning hole, looking deep into the blackness of the grave.

"This *is* intriguing," Hollis said, with excitement in his voice. "I wonder if Tolmaar is listening to us, or is he just not bothered with our company?"

"No telling," Meary muttered through thinned lips. "My last encounter with him left me retreating post-haste with the dust cloud hot on my heels." Meary took out a handkerchief and mopped his brow. "If we want to further any discussion," he continued, "we must ensure it won't interfere."

Hollis turned a pair of brightly burning eyes on Meary and echoed his last statement.

"You are willing to further any discussion after your recent episode with the dust?"

"I'd be ready to risk it if the rewards are great enough," he replied, gripping the upturned edge of a nearby gravestone.

"And I would be willing to accompany you if you so do it," Hollis said, holding him in a determined stare. "The only thing is how do we nullify the dust into something powerless?"

"Perhaps there might be a way," Meary said, almost to himself.

"You mean there is a way of defeating the dust?" Hollis burst out excitedly, his eyes shining.

Meary mirrored his delight with a smile of his own.

"Now don't get your hopes up too high, young man," he said, surprised by Dave's enthusiasm. "It's a theory and nothing but. I got the idea from listening to the evidence about the two dead men below in the tomb. In it Travis once mentioned about the dust being affected by water. He said the dust acted differently when the rain dripped on it. More like a carpet of mud that lay on the cave floor when it was wet. He went on to say that even the air in the tomb was bereft of dust when it rained."

"That's it, of course, something simple, but effective," Hollis said. "The ideal solution to the problem; we flood the tomb with water, dissolving the dust's ability to kill."

"That's not to say it still hasn't the properties left to make it difficult for us," Meary protested. "If we go down there we must be prepared for it. It is, after all, a theory and we should treat it as such." Meary's voice dropped a semitone as he held up a hand to warn Hollis. "Make no mistake about it, Hollis, that invention of the alchemist Tolmaar is dangerous. It can melt human tissue as though it is wax. I'm only surprised it stops at the bones. Why does it not dissolve them as well?"

An element of doubt was crossing the mind of Hollis and it showed by causing his brow to furrow.

"I can see what you mean," he said in a subdued voice, "but what can we do? We've got to confront Tolmaar. He is entirely responsible for all our problems, and it will continue for as long as he wants it to. He must be stopped before we are all murdered by that monster roaming the countryside."

Meary straightened up and looked the other in the eye.

"Well, all right," he said after a brief pause. "I'm entirely in agreement with what you say. I want to face him, but not on his home ground, so to speak. Not after the other episode where I had to retreat so quickly due to the unwelcome attentions of the dust cloud."

"What about the cloud then?" the young man queried. "If we just give damping it down a try, perhaps it would work."

His face was working overtime with the concept of the idea. He tried to convince the older man with the enthusiasm of his argument. He waited, looking at him, searching for a sign that Meary was in agreement.

"I will be with you at all times. Sort of a back-up to give you support against Tolmaar should you so wish it."

Meary took out a pair of spectacles and polished them with his handkerchief. He was doing it whilst giving him brief glances with a pair of worried eyes. In his mind's eye he again went through his recent brush with the alchemist and he wondered if the man realised what he was getting into. Just the magnitude of the powerful voice itself was enough to make the strongest of men tremble. Even the thought of facing that again was off-putting, to say the least.

"I suppose we could try it," he said after awhile. "We could hook up a hosepipe and drown the dust into submission. It may not work, but it's worth trying. God only knows we need a little bit of luck." He put the glasses back into a side pocket and glanced at his wristwatch. "Bill should be here shortly," he announced. "We need him to lower us down into the hole if we decide to go down today."

Hollis glanced down at Meary and grinned.

"I certainly hope so," he said. "I can't wait to cross verbal swords with Tolmaar. From what you say it will be quite a contest of wills between him and us." His face fell as another thought crossed his mind. "Supposing he doesn't want to play our game, he might ignore us and not answer our challenge."

Meary was looking into the grave, and waited awhile until he answered.

"If I was to judge whether he would accept our challenge to verbal combat I would say, yes. That is only my opinion, mind you, and not a fact. In my estimation he will rise to the chance of challenging us mere mortals because he considers us inferior. He will welcome the chance of grinding us into the dust from whence he thinks we came." Meary held the young man in a brief stare. "And," he added, "speaking of the dust, all this supposition is dependent on whether we can beat it."

Within an hour Bill squealed through the gates and without any delay hurried to their side. After greeting Hollis with a warm handshake, he listened to the intention of wetting down the dust to escape its dangerous tendency to attack them.

"Might work," he said after hearing the proposal. "Rainwater did the trick before," he reminded them. "Why not wait for it to rain again? Ordinary rainwater might succeed where tap water will fail. I mean with regard to the chemicals added to it, whereas rain falls as pure water."

"Hm, could be something in it," murmured Meary. "Anyway, I suggest we wait for the next rainfall and see if it works. You will have to curb your enthusiasm, young man, until it rains, then you can have your wish in confronting Tolmaar," he said to Hollis.

"Am I to go below this time?" Bill asked. "I've never been down there, John, and you promised me that I could."

Meary peered hard at Bill and wondered why he had made that promise. Things had altered since that time; a sinister aspect had emerged and he did not want him placed in danger.

"And so you shall, Bill, just when the time is right." He saw Bill's face change in disappointment, so added quickly, "but it will be soon I promise you, real soon."

Bill had to be content with this assurance and, with it ringing in his ears, made his way to the generator to ensure that the machine was working to the best of his ability. Hollis watched him go and with a nod indicated the departing young man.

"It's easy to see he is disappointed." He turned to Meary, suggesting, "Perhaps he should take my place and go down with you, John, after all he has been here with you from the start and he needs a bit of experience if he is to follow in your footsteps."

Meary shook his head in blank refusal.

"Please let me decide when he takes over," he said, looking hard at Hollis. "I need your expertise as I have said, so please don't interfere."

Hollis dropped his eyes to the mound of earth surrounding the grave.

"Sorry I spoke out of turn, John," he muttered.

That evening as Meary was reading the daily paper in the hotel lounge, the night porter came up to him and told him he was wanted on the phone.

"There's a man called Bill wants to talk with you about an urgent matter," he said.

"What we were talking about today is happening right now," Bill rasped into his ear. "It's raining hard at the moment and it is set to continue."

CHAPTER EIGHT

They were gathered at the graveside as before, but with a difference. The rain had stopped, but a silvery mist hung over the hole and covered the rest of the surrounding gravestones in a weird coating. It wreathed in gentle whirls about them and gave their voices a muffled effect as they talked.

Everything was soaked with rainwater, and the generator proved hard to start as it resisted every effort that Bill could muster, swinging on the starting handle in an effort to save the battery. He wiped the combined sheen of sweat and mist from his face with a wet sleeve, straightened up and leaned on the iron framework of the generator. In turn they each tried their best, but it refused to even cough out a plume of smoke. They stood by, staring down at the machine in baffled silence each bereft of any idea until Bill pressed the self-starter and it hummed into life. They exchanged glances of relief, and watched as Bill brought the large lights down below into being by switching them on.

Immediately the black emanating from the hole was transformed into a misty pale grey, striking up like a small beacon into the dejection of a gloomy day. As the lights came on it not only illuminated the chamber down below, but also had the added effect of lifting the trio's spirits. Meary broke into a smile and wiped the descent chair of clinging misty water, whilst Bill untwisted the lowering lines and put them in order.

In the space of thirty minutes they were ready for the actual entry into the cavern and Meary stood by ready to take his seat. He waved to them both as he sat in the chair and, as before, was filled with apprehension as he entered the rock entrance, eyeing the passing rock face as it went upwards.

His questing boots touched bottom on a mud-encrusted floor. He jerked out of the harness, his eyes trying to penetrate the dim corners, waiting for the dust to attack him. No movement of the whirling dust motes about him. He was filled with the realisation that perhaps the dust was beaten at last and joy welled up inside him. Now, he resolved, let's fight on a level playing field, Tolmaar, let's start where everything begins even.

"Okay!" he yelled. "Pull the chair up and come down."

The legs of Hollis, like dangling doll's legs started to emerge from the entrance, then his body came into view, looking down and blinking in the gloom of the cavern. Slowly the chair descended, holding the bulk of Hollis, who was twisting and turning in the seat, trying to take it all in. Meary met the chair and unfastened the restraints as Hollis was still casting curious glances about him, trying to see it all.

Meary, reading his mind, shook his head.

"It seems the rain worked. The mud beneath your feet is the dust in solid form. It also seems its inventor, Tolmaar, forgot to take into account the effect nature has on it."

Hollis stood erect, circling the tomb with his eyes.

"So, here we are at last," he said, with not a little awe in his voice. "I expected a bit more, but assumed a lot. It's just an empty rock room with a pile of stones in the far corner, which I suspect is the table on which the coffin was recently resting. Apart from that it is empty."

"Not quite empty," Meary corrected, pulling the ropes and watching the chair slowly ascend. "The two skeletons are still lying in the other corner, just as they were when we discovered them." He turned to face Hollis. "There is nothing else except the presence of the alchemist, who I suspect is listening to us this very minute."

Hearing this, Hollis gazed all around the tomb in all the gloomy corners, but failed, as the lights were placed in central positions that they illuminated, whilst the extreme parts were bathed in shadow. He shaded his eyes against the glare and squinted.

"I can make out two white shapes in the corner. They are the two skeletons I suppose, John?"

"Exactly!" Meary concurred, watching the chair disappear out of sight. He turned to the other and held him in a stare. "Now, I propose we set about doing what we intended to do."

In the naked glare of the manufactured light Hollis's face took on a determined set and he squared the slant of his shoulders with a shrug.

"You lead, John, and I will follow," he said in a hoarse voice, swallowing and setting his lips.

He waited as Meary nodded in assent, and stood aside when John cupped his hands around his mouth and called:

"Tolmaar! Tolmaar! Are you listening to me? We want to talk with you, Tolmaar!"

Meary's invitation to talk struck against the rock face of the cavern walls and reverberating, echoed and died away. It left a silence that the two men felt more than the request to talk.

"Come on, Tolmaar!" Meary insisted. "You, the master of all you survey, and us as dirt beneath your feet, wish to discuss with you matters we consider important! Tolmaar! Tolmaar! I demand you answer!"

In the interval it took to allow the sound to sink into the walls, Meary wheeled on one foot and glanced at Hollis. The white face of the younger man glowed in the half-light, tight-lipped and staring at Meary with wide open eyes. As they waited with baited breath, a thunderous volley of sound assailed their ears. It circled the extent of the cavern, dislodging stones and small rocks in its wake.

What do you want, you fool? it demanded.

Meary addressed the nearest part of the tomb, with a voice that was threatening to quake.

"Tolmaar, you must listen to us. The monster you created is threatening the population. He is killing people by the score and we think it is by your leave. You have control over him, so we demand you stop him before it is too late!"

The brief interval that elapsed between the ultimatum and the answer was swift, but as the two men waited with pounding hearts and stifled breath it seemed like an eternity. A roar of naked anger rent the air and a swishing grinding column of sound rocked the very vitals of the tomb. The atmosphere became fetid with the overpowering stench of rotting flesh, as though a thousand graves had opened up and discharged the occupants, spewing forth the contents in a putrid, reeking putrefying cascade of slime and decay that made the very air sickening to breath.

Although his blood felt as though it was curdling in his veins, Meary forced himself to face the poisonous atmosphere and, gathering his courage in both hands, filled his lungs with the fetid air and yelled as hard as he was able. The rush of boiling air ceased and the stench vanished as if by magic. The dead still air returned and gathered about the two men, and the steady drip, drip, of the misty raindrops returned as before.

You have just seen a tiny fraction of my anger! the strident tones of the alchemist boomed. *Now be gone, or I will tell the dust to destroy you.*

Meary forced a laugh, something he couldn't have felt less like doing.

"Yes, the dust, Tolmaar. It lies like the inconsequential threat it is; mud under our feet, and will remain so until it is dry." Meary let slide a small laugh, which was copied by the nearby Hollis. "Just an example of one vital component you failed to mention—the fact that the dust is powerless when wet."

So you found its weakness, Tolmaar thundered, *but I have others more potent, more terrible than you can imagine. Now, leave this place of mourning to the man who you disturbed from his last resting place, the Brighold.*

"Not yet, Tolmaar," Meary insisted. "All that rubbish about concern for the stone man doesn't fool me. You are the one who brought him into being in the first place. He has nothing to thank you for. Indirectly you are responsible for the many deaths he has perpetrated and you alone will be punished."

At this juncture, Hollis, who had remained quiet until now, filled with the fascination of it all found his voice.

"I'll attest to that, Tolmaar. I'll swear in any court, earthly or heavenly, that you were the cause of the stone man running amok, killing innocent people, I'll—"

You think I care about your courts or your puny punishments! bellowed the alchemist. *The measure of my strength is boundless. I can cause winds to blow and mountains to rise. I can command rivers to flow and the earth to dry up. I can make fire that burns down forests and consumes whole cities. You think I will listen to the rambling of insects, who I consider to be lower than the earth on which they exist?* His tone took on a threatening note and dropped down the scale of loudness. *Now, I repeat, leave this house of death, for I will—*

Hollis returned the alchemist's bad manners and interrupted him in full flight.

"Will nothing!" he shouted, trying to make himself heard against the raving of the voice. "Look!

You say you have all this power, but according to the records inscribed on the coffin, the sickness went on unassailable well after your death. I'll just ask you to explain one thing. Why, if you were so powerful did you not defeat the sickness?"

The answer to the question came almost at once.

I had my reasons, too diverse for you to understand. Suffice it to say that our king displeased me by casting me aside when he made Brighold the palace courtier in place of me.

Meary nodded to himself, looking into space.

"So you punished everyone because of the choice of courtiers. You were in fact jealous of the Brighold's success, is that why you refused to help?"

I suppose I was in a way, but that is not why the punishment was meted out to Brighold. His refusal to do as his Serene Majesty ordered was nothing short of revolt. The punishment of five years in the stone mantel was for this offence and not because of his inability to cure the people of the sickness.

"Well, according to the records on the coffin, it shows that a big injustice *was* done," Meary persisted. "Lund, our friend who deciphered the message, read it as it was written. The man was sentenced to interment for five years. As it happened, you died and the sentence was forever. Is that part correct?"

Yes it is, the voice conceded. *A lowly malady struck me down just like a common peasant,* the voice complained bitterly. *I thought I was immune to its clutches.*

"Yes, many a man, king or peasant has had these thoughts," Meary said. "They think they are immortal until the good Lord decides otherwise. Even so, the blame of inventing the hideous torture of turning a human being into stone lies at your door, Tolmaar."

"And the crimes of murder should be borne by you," Hollis said, breaking his silence. "You have the beast under your control, so you must bear the blame."

You awakened him from his eternal sleep! the voice thundered.

"The gravedigger accidentally stumbled on him in the course of his duties," Hollis argued. "For that unfortunate mistake you killed him. The dust ate him away just as it did our colleague, Travis, and, while we are on the subject, why did you kill Travis?"

Because he is a despoiler of graves, the same as you all are.

Where is the Brighold now? He is trying to regain his place in the tomb where he rightly belongs, instead of just wandering around lost in the countryside trying to find his way here.

"Why do you have him murder everybody he meets?" Hollis argued. "And the God awful way in which he dispatches his victims is nothing short of horrific." Hollis was into something he saw as disastrous and when he did so, he did it with all the feeling he was able to muster. "Tolmaar, right from the onset you controlled the stone man and anything he did, he did so with *your* full knowledge, no, with *your direction*. He is under your spell as he has always been. You are the one who gives the orders; you are the one to blame."

Meary took over the argument when Hollis lost his breath.

"That is the crime of which you are accused, Tolmaar. Call him back here so we can do something for him before it is too late. He is not responsible for his actions. He is a monster who is out of control. While he roams the country unchecked, no one will be safe. Call him back *now*, Tolmaar, or face the consequences!"

A furious onslaught of violent sound met this ultimatum. The wind whistled around the two men as never before and whipped up the carpet of mud. A whirling mud storm of great gobs of congealed dust flew in all directions. Flying like crazed demons, it filled the air with its screaming whirlwind of demented sound, pecking at their eyes and bodies with teeth of rock-hard dust. All about them the thunderous roar of Tolmaar boomed out.

You fools, he stormed amidst the bombardment, *you think*

you can threaten me with your puny talk of retribution! The Brighold will walk the earth forever if I think fit. All those who stand in his way will meet the same fate as the others. Now go, while the dust is still dormant. Go if you want to live, go while you still have the chance!

The two men wilted under the onslaught, trying to protect their eyes with hands held before them, whilst moving backwards to the centre of the cave. Meary, holding his coat over his head, tugged at the trailing ropes dancing in the wind. They hugged each other, feeling the nips of the mud trying to bite through their clothes. The wind whistled about them, stinging viciously at exposed flesh, pecking and biting with all its might.

The chair, executing a wild series of dancing swings, glanced off their cringing bodies and one man peeled off as Meary pushed him towards the chair. The figure of Hollis, trying desperately to protect his face from the missiles, was hoisted into the air, soon lost to view in the vortex of the wind storm. On the floor of the cavern stood the lonely figure of Meary, coat held tightly about his face, encircled by countless numbers of flying mud missiles stabbing at his form with vicious jabs of jagged edged dust conglomerates.

Swinging wildly amid the storm, and buffeted on all sides by the fragments, the chair touched bottom and lay over on one side. The guide ropes were straining against the wind, tugging and pulling at the fierceness of it, whilst the chair cushion fought the restraints binding it closely to the chair. Meary edged closer to it, still trying to deny the dust its intrusion into his makeshift shield. He cracked a slit in the material held close to his face and with one exposed hand pulled the rope for the signal to haul away. The fast-drying dust attacked the hand and succeeded in drawing blood from his wrist. Now ignoring the pain from the wound, he leaped into the rising chair, blind from the coat protecting his eyesight, trusting the other men to wind him up to safety, assailed on all sides as the dust dived, attacked and nipped any soft flesh that was exposed for an instant to its vicious attack.

Slowly, laboriously, fighting the pull of the wind, the chair ascended, entering the rock tunnel of the outer crust and coming into the light of day, bringing with it the form of the man who was still bound up with the coat. Dribbling blood streams coated Meary's clothes and trickled down his legs. His coat was almost in tatters where it had been so heavily attacked and even his face, covered as it was by the coat, bore the marks of the battle, with little cuts and bites that showed pinpricks of rapidly congealing blood.

With the other two men supporting him, Meary clambered over the earth piles and sat down on a fallen gravestone. He was trembling from his recent encounter with the dust and his chest heaved with the exertion of the fight.

"Well, mates," he said, managing to smile, "that's one encounter I don't wish to repeat in a long while." He was wiping a blood trail from his cheek, and studied the streak decorating the back of his wrist. "For awhile I thought my number was up when the dust rose to attack us." He was peering at Hollis as he was saying this, and ran his eyes over his assistant, saying, "How did you fare against the dust? I was so tightly covered it was impossible to see anything."

Grinning ruefully, Hollis dabbed at the cuts on his face with a handkerchief. He was incredulous and his eyes were wide with it.

"What an experience, John. I was expecting something to happen and it did. I confess I was frightened by the happening in the first place. When Tolmaar came through it was awe-inspiring, to say the least, but frightening just the same."

Bill was horror stricken at the sight of their wounds and said so.

"They look painful and horrible. What on earth happened down there? I heard nothing up here. I waited for what seemed hours for you to call, but all I got was silence."

"A lot happened to us, I can assure you of that," Meary rasped, dabbing his cuts. "We were attacked by the dust, but in another form. Tolmaar called it up to attack us in its drying state. It replied by assuming another form. It turned into balls that were sharp and deadly, and tried to bite and tear us to bits.

We were lucky to get out alive."

"Well, what are we going to do now?" Bill queried, looking from one to the other. "We need to contact Tollmaar, but to do so would be placing ourselves in danger. Perhaps we should call it off for awhile and concentrate on finding the Brighold."

Meary tied the handkerchief around a cut on his wrist and finished by tying the two ends together with his teeth. His lips were slightly blood-stained and he licked them with a pink tongue.

"Hmm," said Meary, eyeing the bandage, "it might well be what we will have to do for awhile until the wounds heal. Perhaps we are going about it in the wrong way. Every time, in my own way especially, Tolmaar has beaten me, and now the two of us. Perhaps it is time we considered something different."

"The dust danger was temporarily wiped out for a time," Hollis said to no one in particular. "I think the rain is the answer to the dust, but we need to ensure that a lot more rain has fallen, so that we can go down again."

"So you are set to go down again, Hollis?" Meary asked, fixing him in a stare. "After what we have been through?"

"Aren't you? We've got to! That demon controls everything he touches and has to be stopped before he controls the world."

Hollis was breathing hard with the exertion of his resolution. He has the light of battle in his eyes and no one will stop him, Meary thought, watching the young man. He was satisfied with the fight he was showing and was standing up to it more than ever when the enemy had the upper hand, something of which he, Meary, was vitally aware in the light of what had happened in the tomb.

"Good for you, Hollis!" Meary said, breaking into a smile. "Need you and others of your like to make it quite clear that Tolmaar won't succeed, no matter how he tries."

At the village police station other things were happening, things that the trio at the grave were adamant in their collective agreement to abhor. The constables were being issued with guns and rifles, and waited outside in the station courtyard for the inspector in charge to assign them to the search for the stone monster.

"I want you to search thoroughly for him," the inspector was saying, "but mark you he is a dangerous man and must be approached with the utmost of caution. If in doubt, withdraw and make sure. The firearms are issued for your self-protection and must only be used as a last resort, I repeat, as a last resort. The public must be protected from this monster, and you if you go out of here thinking the rifles can be used willy-nilly. Finally, I must impress on you that this thing roaming the countryside at will is murdering people in the most hideous way imaginable and must be apprehended in the quickest way possible. We don't want any heroics. I've heard he can tear a man apart with one hand, so watch it. You will be transported to a spot close to where he was last seen, so good luck and get him before he hurts anyone else."

Three lorries especially loaned by the army, waited for the dozen or more policemen to climb aboard, and roared away into the early morning sunshine. A grey dust cloud followed their departure, hanging on the sun's rays and drifting slowly sideways at the insistence of a gentle wind current. A few early risers from the village watched them go, each filled with the knowledge that a homicidal killer was on the loose, and clutching a notice issued by the police to lock all doors and windows, and keep the children home from school until the present emergency was over.

This state of affairs met the curious stares of Meary and his friends as they headed into the village. The streets were deserted and shops shut, including the post office from where Meary phoned and collected his periodical batches of mail.

"Something's happened!" exclaimed Bill peering through the windscreen of Meary's car. "The place should be teeming with life, especially at the post office." He twisted around in his seat and craned his neck as the scenery drifted by. "Probably the work of the Brighold and the police, I shouldn't wonder."

Meary pursed his lips together thinking hard. I wonder if it is the work of the police, he considered. If it is then it has opened up the possibility that they are acting on their own behalf and mounting an offensive against the Brighold themselves. That means seeking him out and destroying him, in direct contravention of their unwritten agreement to find out what it all means, and us, my colleagues and me, getting so near the truth. It rankled a bit and Meary was angry. He twisted the steering wheel in his annoyance and caused the other two to shoot looks of surprise at him.

The police station loomed up before them and Meary got out just as a solitary police constable was leaving the building. Meary smiled in a way he was disinclined to feel, and entered the building shutting the door with a distinct thump. Once inside, he made his way to Harding's office where a plump middle-aged woman was in the act of hanging up her coat. She expressed surprise at his sudden entrance and laid the coat on a nearby chair whilst giving him a shake of her head.

"I'm afraid Inspector Harding is out at the moment," she announced, sitting at her desk, "but he will be back later after he — "

"I must see him right away," Meary interrupted. "I don't know what he is doing, I only know that it is vital the police don't do anything on their own initiative."

"I'm afraid it is a little late for that, Sir, the inspector left over an hour ago with his entire force," the secretary said, shaking up a pile of typewritten pages before placing them into a tray.

"For what purpose?" he asked, although he was dreading

the answer to the question.

The woman regarded him through thick glasses.

"You are Mr Meary aren't you?" she asked, sitting down at the desk. "I remember you from last time. No, I can't help you I'm afraid. All I know is he left with his entire force. They were riding in lorries loaned by the army and, Mr Meary..." She was regarding him as his eyes drilled into hers. "They were carrying rifles and ammunition."

She was smiling as if to say, there, that is something you need to know, and judging by the look on his face, she guessed right, for without another word Meary hurried from the room and banged out through the same front doorway, scowling dark thoughts of betrayal by the police, and Harding in particular. He thumped into the front seat of the car, looking at the other two.

"You were right, Bill," he fumed, pursing his lips and eyeing the younger man. "Harding has taken it upon himself to hunt out the Brighold. He has issued the police with guns and is out hunting him at this very moment."

"Guns!" retorted Hollis with a look of horror. "Don't they understand what they are doing? They are destroying this once-in-a-lifetime chance of studying a man from the grave. They must not be allowed to harm him!"

Meary's face was set into a grim line as he headed out of the village. Beside him his two friends were gazing white faced at the passing countryside, searching for the telltale lines of blue uniformed men seeking out the stone man, or, if necessary, shooting him if he proved to be the menace he was said to be.

Bills sharp eyes were first to see the minute dots of the

policeman ascending a grassy rise in the local terrain and he pointed them out with a cry of:

"There they are, on the hill!"

Very soon the transportation lorries came into view and Meary parked the car alongside the nearest vehicle, clicking open the door as it squealed to a stop. Together they crossed a narrow road with hedgerows on either side, and started to climb the beginning of a steep rise. Ahead of them the police slowly came into view and the thin angular figure of the police inspector, Harding, detached himself from the main bulk of the cordon and hurried towards them.

"I know it was untimely to call for action against the stone man," he said when at their side, "and I also know about a government directive giving you carte blanche, but the amount of murders has increased lately and my boss is climbing up the wall about them, so you can see how I'm placed."

Meary was about to reply, but was interrupted by a couple of loud bangs that echoed around the surrounding hills.

"Seems like you have found him," he said dryly, indicating with a nod of his head.

Harding turned his head at the sound of gunfire and gazed at the line of policemen just cresting the hill. He studied them for an instant, wondering which man had fired the shot, or two as the reports suggested. A worry line crossed his brow and he vowed to give the culprit a dressing down when the operation was over. He cuffed a trickle of sweat from his sharp nose and addressed the trio again.

"That monster has terrorised the community enough. I have given my men orders to shoot to kill if he doesn't give up." He was talking to Meary again. "The lives of the people around here are in my hands and, by George, I'll finish him if he so wishes it!"

The face of Meary was slowly going a dark red colour as the inspector spoke, and his lips trembled with suppressed rage. As a foil to deny his frustration with the man, he took out his eyeglasses and wiped them on his sleeve. He longed to give the man a verbal tongue lashing and it was on the tip of his tongue to hit out, but he denied himself the desire. Instead he polished furiously and bit back the retort. However, he was not getting away with it, and Meary told him so.

"I intend to report this matter to a higher authority," he grated. "That *monster*, as you call him, belongs to the past and as such is as much ours as he is the world's." Meary was sweating now, more with temper than with the atmosphere. He paused to gain control of his feelings. "You said you were responsible to the villagers," he said, feeling the eyes of the other two watching him, "you also said you would kill him if necessary, but if we can convince him to go back to from where he came, would you agree to call off the hunt?"

Harding returned Meary's urgent gaze and thought hard. He was thinking about the stone man, but he was also giving his reputation as a policeman an airing. He had waited for twenty years or more to gain his place in the local community and if he considered carefully he could come out of it with the laurels to which he was entitled. However, a little germ of indecision still plagued his mind.

"How can you guarantee he will do as you say? You said he was not responsible for his actions. How can you negotiate with him? The thing is a monster as I have said." Harding's mind was made up as he spoke to the trio. "No, I'm afraid of the consequences. It would be devastating for the people if that thing from the past really went amok." He shook his head, saying, "I'm sorry, gentlemen, I'm really convinced I'm right. The hunt for the killer will go on as before." He made to move to the side to watch his men disappear over the hill. "Now, if you will excuse me, I'll rejoin my men."

He nodded to indicate the meeting was over, and started up the hill again. The three men watched him go and turned towards each other as he drew away.

"The man is a menace," Meary muttered. "He'll stir the Brighold into a rage and there's no telling what he'll do. He does not know the power of the forces against him. If Tolmaar pleases, he could lay this place to waste within minutes and with the stone man to help him God knows what he will do."

"Perhaps we can reason with Tolmaar?" Hollis suggested, but by the quality of the looks directed at him by the other two men, felt qualified to continue. "No, on second thoughts that would be too much to hope for. We must treat him by the same methods he employs to defeat us. We must *compel* him to do it."

They exchanged looks, and Meary shook his head in bewilderment.

"Apart from appealing to Tolmaar there's not a lot we can do, and you must know what his answer will be."

Meary sighed, inwardly racking his brains. He had little faith in asking for assistance from the alchemist, and dashed the thought aside without considering it, then Bill came up with an idea.

"Those bags of compound found in the coffin, can't we

come up with something of our own?"

"You mean say we have a cure for the Brighold's condition?" Meary enquired, wondering what he meant.

"Yes," Bill went on, "show him some bags of our own and claim it will take it away. It might be enough to fool him for awhile until we can get the Brighold under lock and key."

"Worth a try I suppose," Hollis said, watching the inspector climbing the hill. "Better than waiting for the inevitable outcome here, anyway they are set on killing him as I can't see him giving himself up peaceably."

"Do you think it is possible to find an antidote to the work of the alchemist?" Meary questioned, continuing his train of thought.

"It would take the combined efforts of half a dozen well known scientists to effect some sort of cure, and then they might not succeed." Meary talked in a small voice, almost as though he was talking to himself. "What a terrible torture the man endured encased in stone skin. What kind of person was Tolmaar to invent this form of punishment? He was a devil and still has the tendency to act like the Devil in his present state."

As they made their way back to the car they cast looks in the direction of the departing police. Harding was fast catching up with the main force of his men and as they watched, vanished from sight over the crest of the hill.

"Let's hope they know what they are getting into," Meary said, behind the wheel again.

The car U-turned, skidded on a muddy patch at the roadside and, gaining momentum, sped away.

The little line of blue uniforms, spread out to include as much countryside as possible, slowly drifted down a tree-speckled fold in the hills, searching behind every bush and cranny in their efforts to find the stone man.

It was well into the afternoon before their search was rewarded. Harding, complete with binoculars and loaded pistol, was the first to see him. The Brighold was sitting on the naked soil, leaning against a fallen boulder, legs splayed out and arms dangling before him. He gazed ahead of him and appeared lifeless to the watching policemen. Slowly, with rifles pointing at the silent figure, they surrounded him, hiding behind bushes and trees, ready to open fire if the enormous creature showed any resistance.

It was a novelty for all the men to see the Brighold. Harding himself had no knowledge of the size of him and stepped back in surprise at the sight.

"My Christ, the bloody thing is *gigantic*! How are we to take him prisoner? We'll have to get more help if we're to get him back."

It was then the Brighold seemed to wake up to the fact that he was not alone. He moved his massive head sideways and saw the shadows of the policemen hiding some thirty yards or more from him. As always a complement of nerves and fibres in the make-up of the man came into play. He felt rather than saw the build up of shadows, and an alarm bell sounded in the brain of the stone man, causing him to shift position.

Immediately this sudden movement unnerved the watchers and a particularly nervous constable, a thin weedy individual with a moustache and staring eyes, squeezed the trigger of his gun. The bullet thudded against the rock-like body of the Brighold and whined off into space, to the total astonishment of the waiting band of men. The man who had been the first to shoot goggled at the sound of the singing missile and prepared to run. Harding saw and heard what had taken place and looked with some misgivings at the .38 calibre hand gun he was holding in the palm of his hand. He stuffed it back into the holster with a shake of his head.

"No one to fire without my orders!" he shouted, waving at the scattered men, then he tried another tack. He stood up and yelled to the sitting figure. "I advise you to give up. We have you surrounded, so you can't escape. Just wait there until we arrest you and we will not harm you!"

He waited for the words to sink in and, in reply, the Brighold uttered not a word, but just sat there, gazing in the direction of the voice sound, trying to determine whether it was the voice for which he had come to look.

Slowly the group of policemen closed about their quarry, still undecided if it was going to put up a fight. They were about twelve feet away when the Brighold decided to climb to his feet. He pulled himself upright to massive height and towered above the force. He stood there, swaying on his huge legs, still trying to make out what they were and if they were some kind of threat. He was still deciding when another shot rang out, this time glancing off his shoulder and ricocheting away into space. This was new to the Brighold. He had never been shot at before and although the bullets were harmless to him they stung his arm with their progress. In his agitated state they represented another obstacle to his search for the tomb and he replied in the only way he knew. He stooped and scooped up the nearest man who was now five feet away and hurled him with all his force at a number of fallen boulders lying ten feet away.

The man screamed with fear and hit the boulders with a sickening thump, where he lay like a broken rag doll, spread across the ragged edges of the biggest boulder. As they stared fearfully at him, he again bent down and picked up the stick that had spat at him, and threw it at them with great force. Standing astride with great legs spread out, he overlooked them, waiting with crooked hands to tear, rend and kill, waiting for his tormentors to come within range so that they could do their deadly work and rid him of them for good.

Harding was positioned about twenty feet away and stood there thinking furiously. This state of affairs represented a change in the ordinary round of duties, such as issuing summons, typing out the daily routine of his men and reporting to his superiors, as it was able to get, and Harding began to regret his desire to volunteer in the first place. He distinctly remembered he had promised them swift action to clear up the matter, something he now saw as being doomed to failure. The thing refused to give up as he demanded, and was going to make a fight of it. Harding foresaw a lengthening of the situation and it troubled him. He looked all about him and saw the hopelessness of trying to take him prisoner. Also he realised then was how ineffective the guns were proving to be. He yelled at the beaten men to fall back and retreated with them to a safe distance.

For the moment the stone man, still trying to make it all out and ready to fight if necessary, was still in the same position, giant hands with blood-stained fingers hanging down, standing like some enormous obelisk, framed in the blue and grey of a lowering sky that threatened more rainfall – and that is exactly what happened. As they crouched on a small hummock on the slope of the hill it began to rain and very soon they were huddled together with the raindrops dripping from their helmets and saturating their clothing.

Later on, after about an hour, as the rain made steady progress down to their underclothes, they gave it up and returned to their transport, glad of the chance to get under cover at last. Harding in the driving seat and sitting in an ice cold pool of rainwater that had somehow managed to enter the cab, ground his teeth together in suppressed rage and wondered what excuse he could think up to satisfy his boss, the chief constable. He was not looking forward to the meeting one bit.

Above them the Brighold felt the coldness of the rain and of the way it coursed down his body. It was a curious feeling and provoked the onset of another sensation, set in place a long time ago when he was happy and carefree. It also brought back a time of terror when the great sickness reigned, with death the only release for the suffering. As always the fleeting thoughts of a previous life began as ethereal snatches of broken dreams held together by a frail thread of intangible reality and, as always, it disintegrated into the black despair of his own existence. From his leathery lips issued a cry not unlike the scream of a trapped animal bearing the hurt and agonising despair that the beast, beset on all sides by the hunter, howled to the Creator for mercy. He wilted then, sinking on his great hands and knees, to the welcoming security of Mother Earth, cradling his great bulk and bearing him in the comfort of her vast soothing bosom.

Whilst the Brighold was basking in the euphoria provided by the gentle rainfall, the trio was busily engaged in the production of some form of chemical designed to fool the alchemist. They mixed a quantity of substances together and filled three bags with the chemicals, tying them off in the manner of which Tolmaar was familiar.

"Let's hope he falls for it," said Meary, laughing as he weighed each bag in his hand.

The laughter was infectious and jumped from one man to the other.

It was at this time that the commanding voice of Tolmaar rang like a strident bell in the dormant mind of the Brighold, awakening him with the authority of its demand and causing him to come to life. He moved in answer to the call, giant arms and legs pumping forwards, more or less in the tracks of the retreating policemen.

For an hour his huge strides propelled him onwards, skirting the many obstacles in his way with the warning voice of the alchemist acting as his eyes. The darkness clothed him with its embracing mantle, hiding his enormous body from prying eyes. He strode through deep puddles and floundered through mud that rose to his ankles, moving in a direct line that would lead him to Lund's old laboratory where the trio were working.

They finished the task and placed the bags in a briefcase. They filed out through the doorway, switching off the lights as they left, heading for the place where Meary had left the car. Their footfalls were subdued in the fall of the rain, making their movements hard to hear. A street lamp made their shadows grotesque and ghostly on a brick wall ahead of them, dancing in time to the movement of their pumping legs.

They rounded the wall and pulled up short to see the huge bulk of the Brighold striding towards them.

CHAPTER NINE

Hollis, who was in the van of the little group, stared at the sight of the massive man heading straight for them, and pulled up short. In between casting ogling looks at his companions and quizzical gazes at the advancing monster, he was loath to carry on, and suddenly stopped, turning to the others. Meary, at the rear of trio, barged into the other two and was just going to reprimand them when he also caught sight of him.

"My God, it's the Brighold!" he whispered in a horrified voice. Meary had no notion of the stone man's poor sight and clutched at the arms of the other two, saying as he did so, "It's heading for the graveyard I'll be bound. We had best get out of the way because I think it is under the control of the alchemist, Tolmaar."

Thinking as one, they dived for the cover of a nearby garden wall and crouched there, hearts thumping like mad, hearing the squishy squelch of the approaching Brighold as he ploughed through oozing mud and puddles alike. The street lamps, passing his enormous black shadow from post to post, cast a fearful impression of him on the ground, which served to heighten the fright shared by the three men hiding behind the front garden wall. They pressed hard against the brickwork as he swept by, praying he would keep on going. They need not have worried, for they were just dim, shadowy figures to the Brighold and not to be bothered with for too long.

In his mind's eye he held only his urgent desire to get back to the cavern and no other. It represented security to him and, deep within its soul, a resting place where he would be safe from the outside world. It mattered neither a jot nor did it even occur to him that he was being manipulated by evil powers with other interests in view.

His footfalls died away and his giant shadow grew less. The frequently disturbed rainfall puddles smoothed to a level even the gentle breeze ignored. A silence settled on the village like an enveloping cloak that muffled and gagged any wayward sound. It assumed an air of the grave, devoid of any sound except the noise of the three men crawling out of their hideout.

Hollis swept a big volume of incredulous air from his lungs and let it out with a gasp.

"That, I conjecture, was the Brighold!" he exclaimed, extracting a leaf from his ear. "I might have guessed as much even though you told me. Heading for the graveyard and his erstwhile mentor as you said, John."

Bill scooped up the case where it had fallen in their hurry to avoid the Brighold, brushing it clean. "If he *is* making for the cemetery wouldn't it be confrontation again?" he ventured.

He had a naturally pale face and the light coming from a nearby lamp post highlighted it so that his skin almost appeared luminous. He licked a pair of full red lips with a pink tongue and swallowed hard.

"He's walking and we have a car," he reminded them. "We should be there within an hour, it will take him the best part of three even with those giant steps of his." He hitched up the briefcase to a comfortable level and held it close to his body. "I'd say we were in a commanding position even if the Brighold did turn up," he pointed out. "We would be in the tomb and him on top."

The other two nodded in unison. The night was cold and the chill of the rain-soaked air had the effect of stifling any conversation content to a few utterances. In effect now though, they had a tacit agreement and they went along the same road from where the stone man had emerged, convinced they were on a safe course at last.

True to Bill's estimate of the time taken to reach the cemetery, they drew up before the rusted gates of the graveyard just as the first light of dawn was breaking on the distant horizon. The gates squealed their entrance and swung together with a crash behind them. The few straggly trees lining the boundary wall of the cemetery appeared as skeletal in the half-light, bringing shudders to them as they passed by. The other graves about them rose up forlorn and gaunt on each side of the cinder track, each one dark with rainwater soaked earth.

The hole appeared, wreathed in the curling mists of early morning, still dressed in the paraphernalia of entry. The chair, shiny with dew and mist, glinted in the first light and the trails of rope hanging from the tripod twisted and fell into the gloom emanating from the darkness of the cavern. Pools of rainwater dotted the cemetery landscape and a trickle of mud-encrusted water, after carving a path down the surrounding soil deposits, fell soundlessly into the void.

Within a little while the tinny roar of the generator punctured the muffling cloak of the morning mist and the spurting smoke shot into the foggy air, echoing into the early morning with a clamour that reverberated from the distant countryside and beyond. In unison the lights in the tomb came on at the flick of a switch, and the preparations for going once more into the cavern were underway.

Bill took his place at the lowering end of the lines and, as usual, Meary headed for the seat and another incursion into the gloomy world below.

"I hope our *friend* is in a receptive mood," Meary said in a sardonic way, emphasising the word friend with a slight twist to his lips. "I also hope the rain has dampened down the dust. If everything is okay, I'll give you the usual signal on the ropes." He was addressing Hollis from the seat of the chair and managed a small smile. "I hope we have good luck this time, I think we are due for it. See you down there."

He swung the chair into the hole and sunk into it, waving a thin hand at them. The ropes sawed at the pulley, and turned it with a small squeal, paying slowly downwards as they lowered the man to the tomb floor. The rain-saturated lines, taut with his weight, slackened as he reached floor level. Bill felt the sudden tug on them and gripping the turning handle started to lift the chair again. His youthful face was shiny with the morning mist surrounding them and he waved aside a dark lock of wayward hair that had somehow managed to come apart from a mist saturated scalp. He dashed a dewdrop of water from his nose and watched as the empty chair, minus its recent occupant, rose up through the hole.

Hollis wriggled into the chair restraints and, after checking the ropes for wear, signalled for Bill to proceed. The face of Hollis was edged with concern and not a little trepidation. He well remembered the recent episode and the incident of the dust attacking them, and he was hardly ever to forget the vicious bites it had sustained in its other form. He bit his lip and mentally gauged whether he would wilt under the pressure of which he knew Tolmaar was capable. He shook his head to clear out the negative thoughts and tried to concentrate on the task ahead of them. With a shrug of determination he nodded to Bill and felt the tremor as the overhead block gripped the ropes in its tight embrace and started to lower the chair and Hollis to join Meary in the tomb.

Bill waited for the jerk on the ropes and tried to visualise what it was like down below. Now and again he heard voices drifting up from below as they talked, and curious noises of which he had no knowledge. He even thought he heard the sound of Tolmaar and flying dust as it attacked his friends. He was cut off from where it all took place with just a tug of the rope to tell him what was happening. Small wonder he felt just a little frustrated with it all. Everything seemed to be after the event with him. He was aware of his youth and lack of experience in the field. He sighed, exasperated with the speed of his induction into the paranormal.

The morning advanced and he glanced nervously about him. He thought of the Brighold and of his presence recently. If he, the Brighold, was to arrive soon it would be wise to inform the others before making himself scarce. He shuddered as though a cold chill had touched his flesh. The horror that walked the streets was due there within an hour. He turned it over in his mind and dreaded the thing's arrival. The thought provoked another shiver and he rubbed his hands together to get warm. His mind returned to the other two. There was no noise and no signal to start hauling the chair up. Everything was as silent as the graveyard and he smiled ruefully at the simile, hoping it was not a portent for the near future. He need not have been so concerned though. If he had been witnessing what was happening down below in the tomb, the sight at that very moment would have been enough to drive everything away.

A transformation was taking shape before Meary's and Hollis's astonished eyes. An inverted cone of brilliant light flamed in front of them. It whirled soundlessly on its axis with dazzling puffs of eye-hurting light balls ascending from the base, to run quickly to the point of the cone where it fizzed and burst. Above the cone a vivid blue light, circular in shape, teetered on the point. It balanced there as the balls disintegrated, each with a succession of light splinters penetrating the blue light bubble as they faded away.

As they gazed open mouthed at the manifestation it appeared to grow larger until it towered over the two men, still emitting the light forms and whirling like a huge gyroscope seething and undulating, squirming and writhing until it appeared to almost turn itself inside out. The whirling shape, gaining momentum with every successive movement, emitted fingers of brilliant fire that burst out like some hideous rainbow, raining searing sparks that showered up into a circular bow so bright it brought a searing pain to the eyes and caused the onlookers to goggle with horror and amazement. As the rays of the hissing, seething sibilant cone reared up ever higher, from its innermost core, right where the intense flames were thickest, stepped a tall, thin upright figure that reared up before them, fully eight feet from the tip of his iron grey hair to the soles of his feet, which were poking out from under a silver and gold flowing gown.

Swallowing a hard knot of hard mucous that had managed to form in his throat, gazing with streaming eyes caused by the glare of the fiery phenomenon, Meary squinted at this new apparition and tried to fight the rising tide of panic that threatened to engulf him. He forced himself to look at it, trying to gauge whether it was indeed the alchemist himself who had deemed to put in an appearance. Through the stinging salt of the streaming tears he saw the wraith loom up before him and stand off ten feet away. There it stood, arm outstretched circled by the voluminous sleeve of the loose fitting gown, pointing with a long straggly finger at the two men. It held them in an unblinking stare from cold grey eyes that seemed to bore right through them. The angry glance held a malevolence that was almost felt as a blow. The sound that issued from its two, thin cruel lips had the effect of freezing the blood.

Why have you come here again? he raged. *Must I use the powers that are available to me to convince you that I mean what I say?*

He lifted the hand and crooked his fingers in a threatening attitude, starting to chant in a high strident voice while lifting the fingers and clutching them tightly together into a firm fist.

"Stop this!" Meary stormed, finding his voice with an effort. "We want to have a discussion with you and you keep threatening us every time we try. Aren't you man enough to talk about it instead of resorting to violence?"

Slowly the fingers unwound and the steely eyes lost the look of anger. The arm lowered and was held at the side of the man. Behind him the cone seemed to subside and lose its intensity. The force of the light source faded into a dull red glow and ceased to rotate. The sparks lost the degree of brightness and dulled to a scarlet and then cherry, finally to black. The eye searing light of a few moments before glimmered to a half-light and the walls of the tomb dimmed and regained the former gloom. The whirling swishing sound of the violently induced air storm ceased its ferocity and calmed to nothing. Even the dust, always a participant in everything that took place in the cave, subsided into a gentle movement and settled to the floor, where it shivered to a lifeless mass.

Meary heaved a sigh of relief and wiped the tears from his cheeks. He cast a backwards glance at his companion and received a weak smile of encouragement in return. He returned the smile and squaring his spare shoulders to a firmer line turned to face the alchemist. Now he was able to see him more clearly. Tolmaar had a long flowing beard and hair to match. He was at least six feet six in height and lean in stature. He was clothed in a long capacious gown that had the effect of adding to his height and appearance. Of some unknown material and design, it shimmered in the fading light and emitted weird moving sparkles of brilliance that gave the impression of moving glow-worms. As the alchemist's hand touched it, it radiated fingers of fire that jumped with a lightning flash before being absorbed by the flesh.

As Mearey gazed with fascination at the facial age of the alchemist the thin lips opened to speak and his thunderous tones echoed around the chamber.

I have allowed you to speak, as you can see! Now you have a chance to state your case! Speak as you want, but be warned, I will not be fooled by idle talk. If your grievance is a valid one it will be heeded, so speak now!

The silence that ensued in the tomb after the verbal onslaught was welcomed by the two companions and they exchanged glances to bolster up the courage they each knew they would need. After a nod of acquiescence from the other, Meary turned to face Tolmaar and gazed fearlessly into the face of the man.

"First of all," he said, looking deep into the grey eyes, "I would like to thank you for giving us a chance to speak our piece. You must realise it is hard to talk under these conditions, so if we make a few mistakes we ask you to make some allowance for them. We after all are just mortals and prone to all sorts of errors."

He paused to let this sink in and to wait for any reaction from the alchemist. A cold silence ensued from Tolmaar, so he continued.

"As we have tried to say in the past we represent a part of the government whose task is to deal with any emergencies that might arise from situations such as these we have here. The reasons we have been chosen for the position is because we have met other circumstances in a similar vein and finished the job."

Meary swung around to glance at the waiting Hollis.

"My colleague and I," he said, returning to the alchemist, "are here to plead with you to use your influence to compel the Brighold to cease his killing of the people. He is terrifying the villagers so that they are afraid to go about their daily lives." Meary dashed a bead of sweat from his brow as he talked. "He is fearsome and terrible, frightening and horrible. The people are afraid of him and dread to hear of the monster. They cower in their houses wondering who he has done away with in his latest atrocity. The police appear powerless to stop him. He seems to be impervious to their firearms. It only remains for us to call out the military, and this I want to avoid because the sight of soldiers in the streets might cause a panic. This I must do at all costs if we are to prevent such a thing happening in the village. We'll keep it low key as long as we can. If you can guide the stone man back to his place of rest —"

"After we have a chance to examine him first," Hollis interrupted, in a voice fraught with excitement. "We must have a study of the man before his re-interment. This needs to be one of the conditions we must impose."

Meary nodded his head in agreement then spoke to Tolmaar.

"Even you will join us in making this proviso. Our whole existence, our reason for being here in the first place is our interest in what happened here. It was unusual to the extreme, an event that to my knowledge has no equal. An eventuality, an occurrence that has no parity, a phenomenon so extraordinary it beggars belief. The Brighold himself, surely it must be in your interest to see that he returns to the grave he once occupied? It must be an atonement for the wrong you did to him all those years ago. In some small way it will make it up to him for the indescribable torture he has been subjected to and the suffering he has had to endure. This and more you can give him if you will compel him to return here. After all, he has nothing but death awaiting him if he goes on murdering the villagers, something I'm sure you won't want to happen."

Meary paused to allow the alchemist to reply, but there was no response, so he continued with what he hoped was an appeal to the vanity of the man.

"What will it mean to you, a great scientist such as yourself? Your discoveries are stupendous and the way you apply them were stunning, to say the least. Why, if you would reveal just one portion of them to us you would go down in history as a great benefactor of mankind, someone whom we would all revere and remember, someone whom all people will respect and admire for all time."

Meary felt a touch on his shoulder as Hollis wanted to join in the conversation. Meary nodded to the younger man to take over the discourse, and moved to one side to allow for this.

"Tolmaar..." he began, and then stopped. "I was also going to appeal to the generous side of your nature until I thought, no, that's not the way to speak to you, a man of your stature, your expertise, your knowledge. Better that I treat you as an equal in morality, but far superior in knowledge of other things we know little about; the ability to turn a man into stone, to hold him in perpetual suspension of life, but not living or dying, to hold him between both worlds for hundreds of years without some form of mortification. That is an achievement in itself. Therefore, if you have the power over life and death at your fingertips surely you can grant this little request? We've seen an example of these powers. A man who can command the dust beneath our feet to do his bidding must be powerful indeed. It will be as nothing for him to command the stone man to return to his grave. A mere flick of the wrist and everything will be righted. An extended finger will call him to his interrupted rest and he will resume it for all time. We implore you, Tolmaar, call to him before it is too late, before he has a chance to cause more havoc. The immortal soul of the Brighold depends on you for his salvation. Surely you can't deny him that, seeing that you are the cause of his being here in the first place?" Hollis swung a hand to include Meary, saying, "My friend and colleague, Meary, asks and implores you to help us. We both agree to return him to you as soon as we are able."

Still Tolmaar did not say anything, but stood there regarding everything that was happening before his intense gaze. His eyes beheld them and fixed them in its piercing stare. As the time went by Meary and in turn, Hollis, wilted a little before the relentless eyes. They fidgeted and exchanged looks of desperation, anything to escape the steely gaze being directed at them. Finally the tall man spoke and brought smiles of relief to their faces. As he talked his figure seemed to float before them and they found it difficult to concentrate as it shifted from position to position.

You may wonder why I waited to answer you, he boomed at the two men. *If I tell you that I was examining your inner soul and your motive for coming here, would you believe me?*

"Well, yes, I suppose so," Meary replied, hesitating, "but how could you possibly know if we were telling the truth. We assure you of our best intentions and what is more —"

I know you are speaking the truth, the alchemist answered. *Your innermost thoughts are known to me as they have been from the beginning. You cannot lie to me and that is why I am listening to you now. You have spoken your case and now I will reply. Do you understand?*

Meary had difficulty in answering because of a dry mouth, but Hollis had no such impediment.

"You knew from the outset that we were genuine," he fumed, "yet you put us through this inquisition. Why didn't you just tell us from the beginning that you were aware of our intentions? You stand there in judgement of our —"

I do not have to justify myself to anyone or anything on Earth, Tolmaar interrupted, thundering the words so that they echoed throughout the chamber. *If you choose to come down here and dare to demand my presence, then you deserve what you get.*

The words tore through the tomb and echoed against the stone walls. The deafening sound hammered at the close hung air and whirled about their ears, pounding into the senses like a beating gong. They each clapped muffling hands to their ears to shut out the noise and waited for the terrific sound to abate. Slowly, as they waited with fingers in their ears, the blast of sound faded. Meary managed a weak smile and gazed at the alchemist.

"Yes, you have proved you have the power to see into us, you also have the might to cause other things to fly around." Meary breathed a sigh that was heard in the now still air of the tomb. "You cause other things to happen and I am in no doubt you have the power to inflict such indescribable horrors at your choice, but that being so we still insist on restating our hope that you answer our request, and it still stands."

Meary uttered another sigh, hoping to finally specify and bring back the point of their argument with the sound.

It is plain to see, growled Tolmaar, *that you want to get some sort of undertaking from me that I will end the murderous wanderings of the Brighold, even though you and your like are responsible for the awakening from the beginning.*

"Accidentally, of course," Meary quickly returned. "The gravedigger fell into the pit as he was digging, and no blame can be attributed to him, and let us not forget you murdered him with the dust that you control."

Tolmaar uttered what they took for a laugh of derision.

And I suppose the second man, Travis, also fell into the hole?

Meary was silent for awhile before he answered.

"No, it was with my direction he came down here. I know that in some small part I was responsible for his death and for that I am and remain deeply sorry. I lost a good friend and colleague when he died." Meary's eyes then blazed with sudden anger as he accused the alchemist. "But you controlled the dust as you did with the gravedigger. *You* killed Travis and *you* murdered the other man. If anyone can be held responsible for their deaths it is you, Tolmaar. You have to face our Maker for your crimes."

Tolmaar answered, but in a quiet menacing tone. His voice had an edge to it and cut into the still air like a sharp knife. Meary, expecting an explosion of gushing sound was momentarily caught off balance and stared at the alchemist.

I have paid for my sins a thousand fold, Tolmaar said in a quiet voice. *I was imprisoned here with the Brighold, not as you imagine by divine intervention, but with the full knowledge that it was of my own choosing.* Yes, he insisted as Meary expressed surprise by the lifting of his eyebrows, *I volunteered to accompany the stone man in his hours of enforced burial. I was in fact a prisoner just as much as he, but with a difference. He was here because of my mistakes and I was also condemned because of a little virus. I succumbed to the sickness and was buried in the same tomb as the Brighold. Poetic justice some would say, but if the truth is known, wide of its actual meaning. You and many like you scoff and say it is no more than I deserve. Well, it may be so. The higher power that rights all wrongs has the last say.*

Tolmaar ceased to talk and let a wall of silence descend. Meary gave Hollis a meaningful look and gave a grave wink. He was just about to mouth the word 'courage' when the alchemist spoke again.

Have you any idea what it means to be walled up for centuries, years of perpetual darkness that seem to take aeons to pass? During the period I cursed my incarceration and the desire to accompany the man whom I had wronged. Over and over again I bitterly swore that if I was granted eternal life I would spend the time in the preservation of my fellow man, but my pleas fell on deaf ears. Year passed after year and slowly I began to realise my death was just as permanent as the Brighold's. Madness took me, and in the tortured portals of my mind I began to form images and other ghostly shapes. In due course they took control of my mind and gradually shaped it, altered it until it became something of which I had no possession, until the time came for them to expand it to the desired avenues they sought.

The chamber was filled with witches and hobgoblins. Without end the spellbinding and illusions were being enacted before my eyes. In the blinding darkness spirits and other shapeless masses wreathed and heaved before me. Snakes squirmed and devils danced, a writhing, wriggling twisting whirlpool of convoluted horror that had me screaming for pity. I had no control over my screams. Year after year the hideous parade went on and so did my nightmare. I fell into a deep void to which there was no depth — the deepest well of my utter despair. I could not kill myself because I was already dead. I was in limbo between Heaven and Hell, and friendless. I was alone. Another pause and the alchemist alighted on the dust of the floor and fixed the two men in a fixed scrutiny. *Shall I continue or do I bore you?* he asked, peering down at the two men from his lofty height.

"Do please continue," Meary said. "Your account is quite fascinating. Do please go on."

The figure of the alchemist seemed to glide over the floor. As his trailing robe touched the ground little darting sparks jumped to meet the rock surface and were lost to view in the layers of yellow dust that caked the floor beneath his feet. Tolmaar slowly turned to face the two men, his beard swaying with the motion. His eyes burning with the passion of his discourse, held a faint glint of fire in them. He looked at them, but beyond them. The glimmer of recollection was in them. Like a dream his magnetic voice washed over them and held them in its spell.

It was then I began to find out that I was possessed of magical powers. I talked to the darkness and wished for light. It was astounding. Immediately a grey tinged form of daylight filtered down from above and clothed the tomb in its light. I was overjoyed beyond comprehension and immediately ordered the powers to end my sojourn in the netherworld. My disappointment was abrupt and instantaneous. The light went out for good and I knew this wish was never to be granted. I planned my life then.

With my new found power I conjured up fantastic creatures and things. I commanded the dust of the ages to do my bidding and was rewarded when it responded by choking the creatures I had formed. I saw I had a valuable ally in the dust and used it to protect me whenever I thought fit. So much for my well-being, but I had other and greater things to occupy my mind. I always nursed a burning ambition to create gold. As an alchemist I spent years trying to discover the secret of turning base metals into gold. In Europe the search for the means turned alchemy into disrepute and the elixir or Philosophers Stone, as it came to be known, was shown to be false. My excitement knew no bounds. I had the power of producing unlimited amounts of gold. I had succeeded where untold others had failed. My reason for living was revealed at long last. The only trouble is how do I return from the grave to claim my rightful reward? I learned the bitter thanks of a life's work coming to fruition too late.

"There is something you can do," Hollis said, "you can give the formula to us." When Meary swung around to peer at him, he explained. "Well, the expertise could be invaluable in the medical field. Think of the help it would be in providing machines for hospitals and schools. Unlimited funds would be available for research into cancer and other diseases. Heart problems would be a thing of the past and so would dozens of other illnesses."

"Very commendable, Hollis," Meary said, nodding his head. "I'm sure you are right. We do need a lot more things to help the sick and the infirm; however, I can see only grief and misery in this discovery. It would be the ruination of manufacturing such as the motor industries and steel, to name just two. Gold would become worthless and also money. Financial institutions would cease to exist and the stock market would fail. There would be wholesale unemployment as a result, and untold millions would starve, and all because the price of gold plunged."

Hollis blanched and stuttered in embarrassment.

"I-I didn't realise the effect it would have. I can see it has serious consequences for the world, even if it would do a lot of good."

Meary patted him on the shoulder and smiled into the eager face. The young man was learning fast and would make a welcome addition to the team. He swung around to face the alchemist again and was just in time to witness the man standing tall with hands held high aloft. Tolmaar was chanting some unintelligible words, his booming voice echoing through the chamber and rebounding off the walls like tearing thunder. The timbre of the pounding voice gained in depth and strength until the very walls seemed to rock with the power of the sound.

After a few minutes of this mind-blowing cacophony of strident prayer the alchemist stopped appealing to an unseen person, lowered his hands to his side and bowed his head. He raised his head after awhile and, seeing Meary scrutinising his movements, spoke in a tired voice.

I was just ensuring we would not be interrupted. Your other man at the tomb entrance tried to get in touch with you, but failed, as we were talking. I also failed because I did not heed the warnings.

Meary, baffled by his actions, shook his head in bewilderment.

"I don't understand," he confessed.

Your man is in trouble and I sought to help him, Tolmaar said. *The Brighold is at the gates of the cemetery...*

CHAPTER TEN

After the two men had finally vanished from sight into the tomb, Bill was at a loss to find something to do to pass the time. He greased the lowering tackle and the big pulley in the block, and spent awhile in cleaning the generator cover from a thick coating of grimy lubricating oil. He visited the tomb top several times and each time listened for any sign of the two men. As before, there was nothing and he turned away disappointed with each call, more frustrated than ever.

The morning was advancing and the rays of a watery sunshine bathed the lopsided irregularity of the gravestones in a weak glow, slowly dispersing the coils of watery mist that had gathered during the night, and holding the black earth of the surrounding soil deposits in an unearthly greyish light.

With a pensive look on his face Bill coiled a spare length of Manila rope and hung it on a nearby gravestone. His mind was working overtime, imagining what was happening down below. Once when he thought he caught the sound of fizzing fireworks from below, he cocked an ear to concentrate on it. The silence that came then was almost total. It was not repeated, so he returned to his task. He was young and imbued with a good sense of hearing, so he knew he had heard the sounds. His natural curiosity was aroused and he half-waited for any other sound that might arise. He found himself waiting for any eventuality, which did nothing but keep him on edge all the time.

He espied the bank of clouds climbing into the sky, just over the line of stunted trees encircling the cemetery walls. He sniffed rain in the air and followed his line of sight to descend to the stone wall that ringed the graveyard. His eyes followed the wavering line of the top-most flagstone and held it until the rusted lattice work of the cemetery gate came into view. He studied it for awhile, eyeing the scrollwork of the council credited crest mounted on the top of the ironwork. With his eye he followed a section of the gate downwards and was about to take his gaze away when a sudden movement beyond the gate caught and held his attention. For awhile it was hardly visible, just a faint hint of motion that hardly registered on his consciousness. Bill shut his eyes together and rubbed out the tiredness and the morning mist with a grubby finger. When next he looked, the movement was more pronounced. Oh, my God, he thought wildly, the Brighold, he's *here*!

His first thoughts went to what he thought was taking place forty or fifty feet underground, and for a moment he panicked. That was until he took a grip on his quaking flesh and forced himself to look at it calmly. He must warn the others, that was clear. With this in mind he started for the tomb top. He filled his lungs to bursting point and yelled at the top of his voice. He rattled the rope lines violently and tried to lift the chair. It was then that the faint sound of the alchemist's incantation wafted up to him. It was almost inaudible, a weak sigh that drifted on the dust particles and was almost lost, but he heard it and wondered at the host of foreign words that were uttered and expelled into the air. He arose and whirled in alarm when the thought of the Brighold's imminent presence returned. He hid behind the soil deposits and peered out with his heart thumping like mad, sweat shining on his brow.

As the time slid slowly by, he began to realise he was panicking for nothing. It must have been a trick of the light, he mused, and nothing to be worried about. He picked himself off the heap of damp cold earth and forced himself to walk the distance to the cemetery gates. Until he reached the gate, his vision was obstructed by the graveyard wall and in no small part by the screen of skeletal trees that surrounded the cemetery. He laboriously picked his way through soft earth and fallen gravestones, and crunched on the cinder path to the gate. He peered through the rusted, water wet ironwork and was met by the horrific sight of the Brighold, standing like some huge stone effigy barely some fifty feet or more from the cemetery entrance.

Repelled, Bill stepped back in surprise, cringing away from the apparition. His heart leaped in fear and he waited for the creature to burst in with murder, *his* murder in mind. He waited, praying with eyes wide open in dread. The sweat increased to beads on his face and ran down the sharp angle of his nose. He could not move because his feet were rooted to the ground. In trepidation he waited for the gates to collapse and the sky to fall in on him in the same instant.

After an interval of a long-lasting minute and second extending passages of time, he shook himself out of the lethargy. Now he rose to his full height, determination plainly written on his face. He gritted his teeth, returned to the gate and looked out. To his heartfelt relief the Brighold was in the same position. He was unaware of it then, but the spell cast by the alchemist was working. The stone man stood motionless with his hands at his sides, looking for all the world like some monstrous, hideous stone giant that had stepped out of a terrifying nightmare. Bill licked a bead of sweat with a pink tongue. Somehow the murderous figure had failed to reach the gates at the last moment, but the young man was not one to rest on his laurels for too long. With a final glance at the giant, Bill retraced his steps to the open grave and looked down into the hole.

To his surprise the ropes were jiggling about in the opening, denoting that someone wished to come up. Bill wound the chair to the tomb head and was pleased to see the head of Hollis come into view. He helped him to free himself from the restraints and calmly related all that had happened. Hollis listened to him for awhile before speaking.

"It's your turn to go down into the tomb, Bill. I know about him outside."

"Yes?" queried Bill. "But how could you know? He has only just arrived. He is outside the gates at this very moment. He is just standing there motionless and—"

"It will all be revealed to you when you get down there," Hollis said, smiling at his insistence. He looked into the young man's eager gaze and said kindly, "Bill, when you get to see what is down there, it will come as a shock."

"Shock! Shock! What do you mean *shock*, Hollis? I know about the two skeletons. Is there something else down there?"

Hollis pursed his lips and nodded his head.

"Nothing to be alarmed about, but it will be something to tell your children about, if you have any." He breathed in a deep sigh as he said, "Tolmaar is alive and talking to us, Meary and me. He stopped the stone monster with a spell he called out. He wants to see you and demands you go to him now."

"Why doesn't he come up here to see me?"

"You'll have to ask *him* why." Hollis hedged for a moment, trying to find the right words. "I'd try to avoid awkward questions for awhile, if I were you. He has been down the hole for some considerable time, so go easy. Meary has some expertise in the matter, so listen to him and take it to heart."

Hollis took him by the arm and led him to the tomb top. He fastened him into the chair and looked earnestly into his face.

"Take it easy, young 'un," he said, giving him an encouraging wink.

He strode over to the waiting equipment and slowly turned the handle. The white face of the young man descended and went out of view. The ropes rattled on their way to the cavern floor and the newly greased pulley, spinning silently in the block, eased out the tightened line. Hollis wiped his oily hands on a greasy cloth and, striding over to the hole, listened for any sound wafting up from below. The rope line was slack now and drooped after the weight was removed. He heard nothing of what was going on down below and he felt frustration just like Bill had done.

After awhile he went to the gates and, opening them, eyed the stone monster. It was so big and grotesque he was taken back for an instant. It was staring into space through hooded leathery eyes, motionless and silent, dwarfing a row of skeletal trees that lined the edge of the road. Keeping a careful eye on the monster, Hollis squeezed through the protesting gate and slowly approached him. The tremendous bulk of it reared up before him. The enormous hands, still stained with blood, hung down by his sides. The naked stone figure, marked with the scratches and chips of countless bullets that had glanced off him, looked like a massive lump of grey granite, and formidable to the extreme. Hollis did something then that no man had done since Lund had examined him at the laboratory. He extended a hand and touched him.

The skin, if it could be defined as such, was rock hard and cold. Powdery dust flakes overlaid the grey surface and stuck to Hollis's fingertips. He slid the hand over the outlines of a vein and felt something akin to hard string. The formation of the blood line had no life, no substance, for all the world like the stone it professed to imitate. Hollis wrinkled his brow in amazement. There was no doubt about it, it was undoubtedly dead. There was no bloodstream, and by the feel of it, no pulse. By rights it had no life and was most certainly dead. He, Hollis, had no explanation for the phenomenon. How can the dead walk? The monstrosity that stood before him belied belief, but yet, the thing walked and moved. Was that possible?

He walked around the giant, getting a good look at him, noting the damage to the legs from his arduous journey through the twisted and tortuous undergrowth he had negotiated on his way to the cemetery. Hollis took note of the wide back and the way its thick neck was joined to the enormous head. The whole presented a picture of massive power that was standing without motion, without movement, a huge figure, dormant now, but possessed of a strength that spoke of unnatural energy should the sleeping giant be awakened. Hollis shuddered at the prospect and tried to keep his mind on the examination of the creature. As far as he was able, he studied it closely. The upper parts were beyond his reach, but he got a good look at the man from ten or more feet away and in so doing made a startling discovery. He judged the stone figure to be some nine feet tall, an increase of two feet or more. The monster was growing bigger; something not accounted for in the furore surrounding the monster. If he was right this vital piece of information was important to the extreme. He circled the silent figure and retraced his steps to the gates.

He could not resist a backwards glance at the naked figure. He earnestly desired a camera to record the episode and cursed his forgetfulness in leaving it at his hotel. He thought of the wonderful pictures he could have taken. It was a golden opportunity lost and he ground his teeth together in rage, promising himself there would be other times. He squealed through the gate and, dodging the leaning gravestones, trudged back to the open grave.

With his heart in his mouth Bill watched the rocky walls of the tomb top pass by and the taut line of the holding rope pay out. Smoothly the chair descended to come to rest in the welcoming arms of the waiting Meary.

Bill gazed all about him and was too preoccupied in discovery of the interior of the tomb to notice other things. He let Meary release him from the chair and stood on the dust strewn floor where he waited, drinking it all in. For a moment, as his eyes adjusted to the gloom, he blinked and gradually saw. He grinned at his boss and squinted at the blanket of brilliant light that was the alchemist. He wilted a little at the sight, but swallowing a large lump of frozen mucous that had somehow managed to wedge itself in his throat he managed to force a shallow smile.

"It's Tolmaar," Meary explained in a whisper. "Don't be scared of him. He requested your presence here."

Meary looked into the clear blue eyes of the boy. True, he had youth on his side and that was a plus, but he had little experience of what he was about to witness. This would alter in time and as he aged. It was about to change in some small degree at this very moment. Meary led him over to the flaming light coil and stood him before it. The tall figure of the alchemist towered over his slight body and the young man wilted before him. Tolmaar's dark shadow loomed over him, probing his very soul and the recesses of his body. The gimlet eye steely gaze searched into him, feeling for any impurity to mar an innocent life.

You, boy! the alchemist said in a tremendous burst of sound. *What do you do here with these other men?*

Bill inwardly quaked at the mental onslaught and physically stepped back. He paled at the sudden attack and gazed at the alchemist with wide eyes.

"Please, Sir—" he whispered.

Speak up, boy! was the thunderous reply.

Bill cleared the offending spittle from his throat with a cough, and tried again—this time louder. "Please, Sir, you wanted to see me. Hollis told me. What do you want with me?"

I'll ask the questions, boy! the alchemist boomed. *All you have to do is answer them. If I see fit to let you question me I'll indicate so. Do you understand?*

Bill mumbled in the affirmative and tried to look at the man. Everything about him was designed to instil fear into the recipient. The tremendous voice and the overbearing attitude, coupled with the strange atmosphere and the pyrotechnics to back him, made a formidable show to support the man. Strangely though, Bill had the gift of second sight and saw something that the others failed to see.

Tolmaar had sensed that there was a medium close by and realised it was the young man, hence he drilled his gaze into the interior of the boy and tried to unlock his secrets. He had no doubt the young man was unaware of his own powers, but Tolmaar was, and he resolved to nullify them without delay. He did not welcome battling with another of similar power, even though the boy was probably not aware of his gift.

When the others depart you will remain with me in the tomb, Tolmaar rasped.

The tone and the matter-of-fact manner in his voice caused Bill to return the look with dismay.

"That is impossible," he said, shaking his head. "I have others who want to see me and be with me. I have my mother to think of—"

Earthly things that you can do without! Tolmaar

interrupted. *Do you realise that I am offering you eternal life? You will want for nothing because you will have everything. You will have powers no earthly being has enjoyed since the dawn of man's creation. You will live to the end of time. You will even have the power to create life. All this I offer you, if you will join me in the underworld.*

Fleeting thoughts of his life in the world above darted through Bill's mind. The kindly face of his mother came into view and with it the joy and pleasure she imparted to him with her presence. He had several firm friends he met almost daily whom he would miss, and a girlfriend who was more than a friend.

"My life is full of people I love," he said. "Even if I was to envisage such an existence it would be impossible. As it is, such an offer would be hopeless as well as unwelcome. I do not have any desire to bury myself in this crypt, and neither do any of my colleagues. My only desire is to help the people who have been hurt by you and to see that the Brighold is returned to his grave. I know that is what my colleagues have in mind and I will support them in this wish."

Bill spoke with all the resolution he could muster. He talked fearlessly and effortlessly, his voice a flash of light that cut across the dust-laden depressive gloom of the cavern. As his voice smote at the shadows about them a change in the manner of the alchemist took place. His eyes, most of all, seemed to brighten and flame with a phosphorescence so startling it seemed to fill the orbs. A slow glow of white colour radiated from his cheeks to his forehead and climbed rapidly into the rest of his face. His thin lips clenched to a firm cruel line, holding them in a vice-like grip that had the muscles standing out like ripcord.

Meary saw the change in his appearance before Bill, and gripped the shoulder of the young man. He shook his head in a silent motion to warn him. A red glow was issuing from the figure of the alchemist and gaining substance with each passing second. His voice screeched out then, and assailed the close air of the tomb with its vigour.

You dare to argue with me, boy! His cries seemed to tear at the walls with fingers of fire. *I give you the chance to be great and you refuse! I have never heard such impertinence, such arrogance!*

He paused to regain his breath, though on recollection Meary thought he didn't have to breathe. Bill stepped back a couple of paces under the verbal onslaught, gaping at Tolmaar. Meary stepped between the boy and the alchemist, his eyes blazing with the light of battle.

"You can't expect him to condemn himself to an end such as you brought upon yourself!" His words, laden with fire, exploded like crackling fireworks at the tall man. "He has a life on earth to pursue! He has a mother, and a girlfriend whom he hopes to marry some day. To ask him to join you in your misery is a blasphemy. The lad was right in refusing your request—"

Request! raged the alchemist. *Request indeed! It was an order. I do not ask any earth-dweller to do my bidding. If I think it is fitting I will tell him so. The boy will remain here after you depart. That is my ruling and I advise you to accept it.*

Unflinching against the blast, Meary struck back.

"He enjoys life to the full in the upper world," he said, with passion. "He is a free citizen of a free country and has the right of free determination. He has made his choice to stay on the earth not under it. When his time comes to join the earth in death he will, I assume, acquiesce. Until that time he has the gift of life to fulfil, and with that I aim to help him."

Tolmaar's rage increased. Sparks shot off into the oppressed air and showered down on the two people huddled together. The fetid stink of rotten carcasses laden with the odour of stench-ridden decay, drifted down on the pair, causing them to retch with violent sickness. The wafting smell, reeking and heavy with breathtaking fumes, encircled and held them, inhibiting their every inhaled breath until they gasped for oxygen. Still it persisted, entering their mouths and noses until it was nearly impossible to breathe. Every gasp for air was a battle for survival, each cough and desperate snatch for precious lifesaving oxygen was accompanied by a grinding and gut-striving desire to cough the fumes from their lungs. They were driven to their knees by the stinking onslaught. The air was so thick it was poison. They were succumbing to the attack of the foul air and they knew it.

Bill collapsed into Meary's arms and hung there, his breath sawing deep within his heaving chest. Meary, also striving for air, fought the tormenting atmosphere in vain. The searing pain in his chest could not be avoided much longer. He knew they had to have air before long or perish. With his arms around the shoulders of the wilting boy, before unconsciousness claimed the two friends, he looked up and through the din created by the alchemist's curse, heard him chanting another incantation. The two people, man and boy, slipped into insensibility...

Above, in the graveyard proper, Hollis received a bit of a shock when the chair started to lift of its own accord. With protruding eyes that followed the flowing rope line, he watched it pass through the pulley and wind itself onto the rotating take-up drum of the capstan. Before he had a chance to examine how it was able to effect the transition with no help from him, the unconscious body of Meary rose into view. He was slumped over the arms of the chair, with his head lying on the back rest. As Hollis ran to help him, he seemed to recover. He sucked in great gasps of air, his breast heaving with the effort of the task. With the help of the concerned Hollis he straggled from the embrace of the chair and collapsed onto the pile of dark earth that encompassed the grave.

With a multitude of questions buzzing in his head, Hollis helped John into a sitting position, waiting for him to recover.

"What on earth—?" Hollis began, and then saw his white face.

"He's got Bill," Meary panted, fighting to get up. "We've got to rescue him before he inducts him into the underworld. If he does, Bill will lose his mortal soul. The man is a fiend and he wants to use the lad to fulfil his dreams of immortality. I was powerless to stop him. He will use everything to get his way. We must get Bill out of there before it is too late—" he gasped as he was seized by another fit of violent coughing that had him doubled over.

It was then that the crash of the cemetery gates meant the Brighold was awake. The alchemist had made sure of any eventuality. He had awakened his huge stone servant with murder in mind. Blundering through the wrecked gates he still retained pieces of ironwork wrapped around his enormous body and was vainly trying to free himself of the offending loops. Fortunately for Meary and Hollis, it proved to be something of a tough job for the Brighold, and time consuming. He wrestled with it for some considerable time before finally ridding himself of the meshing encumbrance and dashing it forcibly to the ground. He straightened up slowly and pointed his face towards the two men huddled together.

His lumbering footsteps began again, making for the open grave—*his* grave where he had rested in peace for so many years. Within the Brighold it spelled safety and comfort for him. A vestige of reason dwelt in the stone brain of the giant, mainly composed of habit and an urgent desire to be where he felt safest. The tomb represented both to the Brighold, even though it meant sharing it with Tolmaar. As far as the coffin was concerned, he neither thought about it nor chose to associate it with the tomb. It was embedded in his subconscious, far beyond his powers to remember.

He dashed aside rather than skirted the gravestones. His huge feet, naked and exuding dust with each violent contact with the gravestones, pounded the soil into mud and stringy water. His weight was so vast he left tracks in the earth four inches in depth. As he advanced, his imposing shadow blotted out the daylight from the two men. He stumbled forwards then and appeared to miss his footing. He sank to one knee and stopped with his eyes not on the two men, but on the opening that was visible beside them.

Hollis, seizing hold of the opportunity, prodded the still half-conscious Meary into urgent life. He crawled on his hands and knees, dragging and, in turn, propelling the other to action. Slowly they made progress across the soil heaps and while the monster struggled to free himself from the soft earth managed to put the distance of several yards between them.

With a tremendous hoist of his weighty body, the stone man lifted himself from the sucking embrace of the mud and staggered the last few steps to the hole. He waited, swaying slightly, gaze fixed on the blackness. He seemed to be ready for something to happen, and it did. The yellow dust fizzed up then and bloomed out into view. It bubbled and heaved, circling and coiling like some hideous yellow serpent. The tentacles reached out and touched the huge body, encircling and enclosing it with the wreathing cloud.

As the two men watched spellbound, the Brighold was engulfed in a succession of blue and yellow sparks that rotated about him like a miniature whirlpool, and he appeared to assume the haze of powdery smoke. His huge body bulk trembled and seemed to lose its form. The body disintegrated into a thousand different pieces, each fragment exploding piecemeal before fading into nothing. Where he had stood there was nothing to indicate he had existed. The yellow dust retreated after the Brighold's disappearance. It writhed like some monstrous hideous snake, before settling and sinking down into the blackness of the open hole.

Across from the opening, the two men could hardly credit their senses. First, as if by magic, Meary had been wafted up to the surface on apparatus that was being worked by an unseen hand, and now the Brighold had vanished from sight, obviously the work of the same hand—Tolmaar.

Meary shook his head in bewilderment. The power of the alchemist was increasing with every minute. He wondered if it was possible to beat the degree of black magic being enacted before his eyes. Tolmaar was displaying such sorcery, such wizardry it was difficult to see how he was to be beaten. The signs foretelling a victory for him were pretty evident at this stage and Meary would be the first to admit it; however, right is might, Meary mused, although with an ironic twist in the tail of the tiger of virtuous justice. Meary sniffed to indicate his obvious displeasure. He rose to his feet and watched as Hollis copied his example.

"The thing just disappeared!" Hollis said, with amazement in his tone. "If I hadn't witnessed it myself I wouldn't have believed it." His eyes were wide with wonder when he nodded at Meary. "And you, you were pulled to the surface by an unseen power. How do you account for that?"

"I can't," muttered Meary. "We must attribute it all to the fiend that controls everything happening below and for that matter, our friend, Bill."

"Yes," said Hollis, slowly, "I was forgetting him." He sighed and looked at the other man. "How on earth are we going to rescue him from the clutches of that fiend now?"

"At the moment I haven't a clue," Meary confessed. "It's obvious where the Brighold has gone and it is evident the alchemist is in control over them."

He wrinkled his brow in deep thought and rubbed the beginnings of an emergent beard with the palm of his hand. They were still standing on the earthen hill, and they slid down the packed earth. The day was well advanced when they held a discussion about what to do.

"Any suggestions?" asked Meary of the other. "For myself I am bereft of any idea. It looks like Tolmaar has the upper hand, especially with all the might he has at his fingertips. I've never seen such power before. He has the Devil's own control over everything he sees. It seems to me he is able to command the thing to do his bidding at will. His influence is staggering to say the least. The man is gifted with evil to such an extent it stuns you with disbelief."

He paused to reflect on his own observation, and stared into space, his brow set into deep worry corrugations and his eyes troubled. Hollis was worried too. His tanned face lost its healthy glow and lapsed into sadness. In the face of overwhelming odds, he felt as helpless as Meary. The alchemist had triumphed over them and was continuing to do so. He held the boy and was in command of the monster. Hollis shook his head in dismay and also confessed to himself that he had no suggestions.

"There's not much we *can* do," Meary confessed. "He is too strong for us. He can conjure up magic at will, and all the time he is able to do it he will call the tune."

"But is there nothing we can do to beat him at anything?" Hollis asked with a shrug of his shoulders.

"It looks like it," John said. "He is too strong for us, superior in the extreme. He is too much for us and we may as well admit it. The man has beaten us I'm afraid."

In conjunction with the admission of the two men, Tolmaar did indeed hold sway. At that moment, with the help of his magnetic gaze, he held the helpless boy in his grasp and was preparing to fully induct him into his ways. The tomb was alive with wriggling writhing monstrosities, slithering and sliding on wall and floor. The fetid air was thick with stench and decay, and dripped blood spots that drizzled down onto the hideous assemblage below. Lightning flashed overhead to illuminate the revolting scene taking place below and to light up the solitary form of the boy, Bill.

Through glazed eyes that had no recognition in them, he stared at the mesmerising fingers of the alchemist and followed each movement. Tolmaar muttered incessantly. The strange language of the spells echoed around the cavern and reverberated on the rock walls. The intonations being uttered reached such proportions it almost deafened the boy, but he felt no ill effects. The waves of sound penetrated into his mind and blotted out his will to resist. He heard nothing but the voice of Tolmaar and was completely within his power.

He was dressed in a gown similar to that of the alchemist, but smaller. The boy's skin had taken on a pallor alien to his own healthy colour, and mirrored exactly the deathly pale darkness-induced complexion the wizard always wore. About his erect body, disgusting things with shiny scales entwined. Tentacles waved in his face and hairy creatures with hideous features danced on the end of swaying webs. Bill neither saw nor heeded them, his only interest laying in the shining pools of twin compulsion that were the eyes of Tolmaar. There was another feeling though, and even through all the power being directed at him, he felt it. It was as though a bar of silvery sunshine managed to fight off the depression and shine through momentarily, before the incantations took over again, and always calling, beseeching him to come away before it was too late. Bill struggled to recognise the voice, but it was difficult, *so* difficult, almost beyond his power to recollect to whom it belonged. It was fading into a background of the continual clamour and deliberate din.

Tolmaar's voice struck like a bolt into the mind and reason of the boy, drowning out all memory of his life in the upper world. The alchemist was a past master of the art of hypnosis and Bill represented a challenge to him. To his credit, Bill fought to keep control of his mind and triumphed for awhile. He yelled out, seeking to dispel the power being wielded by the alchemist, hoping for help from his colleagues.

When he saw the fate of Meary, who seemed to be spirited upwards with no help from Hollis, his courage flagged and appeared to be at rock bottom. He now knew terror in terms of things of which he was, until now, unaware. As the initiation into the underworld began and unimaginable creatures started to form, he screamed in mortal fear at the manifestations. He cowered from them as they squirmed ever nearer, coiling and wriggling, screeching and hissing, until he covered his eyes and ears to escape the terrible sight. He retched in agony as the horrible stench that accompanied them came, and no matter how he tried to prevent it, entered his nose and mouth, reaching inside him until it was installed within his very vitals, but the alchemist wanted more.

His voice climbed and reached a pitch so that even the surrounding din of the chattering creatures was eclipsed. Such strange unnatural sounds frothed from his thin lips, his face twisting out of proportion with the effort and taking on a transformation that terrified the boy. Before the eyes of the young man, he changed into something so loathsome and disgusting it literally caused him to faint with the sight.

Tolmaar was growing serpentine, but in a much more pronounced way than the things that writhed around the boy. He coiled and twined, wreathed and twisted, wriggled and squirmed until the tortuous rolls seemed to be endless. His gyrations continued to whirl then, but with a difference. The pace slowed and the sickening scene became more acute – he was affecting other changes. He assumed a long neck, from which issued a continual green stream. The teeth were of the some colour, and glistened with the rank slime that seeped out between the rotten stumps. A hideous pink tongue poked incessantly between the gaping jaws, drawing in, but mostly losing the dripping, yellow-tinged green streams. Tolmaar, or the creature he had assumed, reared up over the boy, peering at him through cruel eye slits. He had feelers attached to his upper body and used them to stroke the boy, all the time slobbering over his fallen body.

Bill awoke to the fondling and slowly regained his feet. He had no feeling inside and no will of his own. Within him he felt no enmity towards the alchemist, no hostility whatsoever, rather he was filled with the desire to embrace the creature that hovered over him in its menacing way. The eyes held him transfixed. They seemed to fill his head with strange dreams, draining him of the will to resist. The black irises of the slits appeared to grow and whirl until they entered his head. Bright lights danced around his mind and captured his spinning brain.

The induction of the soul was almost complete. Everything was now ready for the final phase and, as if to highlight how important it was, the noise reduced to a murmur and then a total hush. The monotones of the alchemist were heard then, repeating over and over such blasphemies that the air about them blanched with horror. The cavern darkened and the air grew denser. The temperature rose and brought sweat to the boy's brow, but he neither felt nor heeded it. He was transfixed by the hypnotic tone of the other's voice and followed it with urgency. He was unable to understand what was being said and it was difficult to follow, but he cared not. The mesmerising power exercised by the weird monotones of the voice had the effect of dulling the senses of the boy.

Several times, as he gazed into the eyes, he seemed to try to fight it. He breathed in the fetid air and with a shake of his head, emitted a cry of agony. His body twitched and shook with every convulsion. His slender frame was fighting a furious battle with the forces of evil and to his utter dismay he appeared to be losing. He was drawn to the hideous creature waving before him. His blood stilled, grew cold as his heart slowed. The malignant forces of evil, sensing victory, pressed onwards and entered the unsullied tracts of the boy's subconscious. He suspected nothing as the malevolent streams gained access. They engaged the boy's natural army of resistance and a fierce conflict ensued. The battle for the boy's mind had begun.

As if in conjunction with the alchemist, the thick layer of glistening toads that jumped and cavorted on the muddy floor, set up such a chorus of foul grunts it was difficult to hear any other sounds, difficult, but possible, for above the tumult and the turmoil, the frenzy and the uproar, there arose the demented ugly howls of Tolmaar, the arch demon himself.

CHAPTER ELEVEN

There was a sensation of movement, of rising, and of the brush of still air passing by him. Bill was ascending, but gently, with hardly a tremor. He wondered at the lack of feeling, but he put it out of his mind as the motion of his moving body continued. The light drew stronger as the grave floor neared.

Very soon a gentle draught of pure air wafted down to him bathing him with a cold fan, which was both invigorating and cheering. His lungs gratefully seized on the oxygen and drank deeply of its life-giving force. It coursed through his veins and surged into his vitals with energetic vigour. The light beckoned and called him. His breast yearned for its welcoming softness, tempting him, urging him onwards and upwards. He broke into the light of day and was dazzled by its brilliance. He blinked several times and twisted his head to take it all in. Familiar things stared back at him and the swaying chair hung from the block, standing out starkly against the grey sky. He smiled a thin smile, knowing he had no use for it now—he was a disciple of the underworld.

Bill was different in many ways. He had a clearer vision of what was happening; his thoughts were many and well formed, he had the ability to gauge well what he was about to do and the determination to carry it out regardless. First he had to do what the master wanted. He must prepare the way for him to re-enter the world, to vacate the confines of the cavern and re-emerge to his rightful place in the universe. The metamorphosis of the new disciple was complete, and the boy readily fitted into the role. He was indoctrinated into the ways of the alchemist and was an ideal pupil. The void created by the absence of good was gratefully filled by its opposite – evil. To the boy, who neither knew nor cared about the transition, it was just a continuation of the norm. The only thing now was the pleasure of the master.

The boy had vague thoughts about his role in the course of things and within his imagination felt his desire for reward. There it trailed off because his mind was set to another purpose. He was in fact satisfied to worship the master. His whole meaning in life now was to do as he was told and to make sure of the coming out of the master. This was vital to the cause and brooked no delay. His new life surged within him. Its added spice excited him and brought a certain charisma that blossomed within him. He was in perfect command of it all and, what is more, was fully aware of it.

Meary and Hollis noticed his presence just after he surfaced. Hollis saw the boy first and nudged his companion.

"Why, it's Bill!" he exclaimed excitedly. "How on earth did you manage to escape from ... "

His voice trailed off when he saw the gown. Meary

straightened up from examining the generator and, through his glasses, fixed the boy with a quizzical stare. His eyes came together in a deep frown and he whispered to Hollis.

"Looks like we are a little too late, the robe means that Tolmaar has him in his power." He sighed and jutted his chin forwards, saying, "Now it will be extra hard to undo the harm done by the alchemist."

Hollis was about to add more when the boy spoke. There was a slight tremor in his voice when he addressed them, and to emphasise his meaning he pointed with a raised finger.

"You both must be gone from here," he said in a quiet way. "It is dangerous for you to remain here. The master—"

"The *master*! Who in hell's name is that?" demanded an indignant Hollis.

Unflustered by the sudden interruption the youth persisted.

"The master has ordered me to tell you to go!"

He emphasised the order with a wave of his hand. There was no explanation of what had taken place down below and no indication of what he was feeling either. The boy dropped his hand and waited, seemingly expecting them to comply without any delay.

Meary could not help noticing he was floating over the hole. The gown the boy wore swayed slightly with any movement. It covered the legs to the feet and the many folds of material flared out from the boy's slender waist and flowed downwards. Many signs decorated its expanse. Weird and devilish, they presented an uncanny sight that did much to add to the effect of demonic happenings. Meary decided to reason with him. He smiled to put him at his ease.

"Bill, lad," he implored, "come, take off the cloak, stop this nonsense. Your friends are waiting for you at home. We need you to —"

"*Go!*" ordered the boy. "Go, or the master will cause you to regret it!" His lungs bellowed it out and he raised the hand, making a fist as if to add depth to the order. "Go and you will be spared the wrath of my master."

"I'll be damned if I will!" Hollis said, reddening with the effort. "Now you stop this tomfoolery and ... "

His voice trailed away as the boy lifted two arms and began to chant a torrent of strange and hideous utterings. He seemed to fall into a hypnotic trance and as the stream of shrill invective rose above him he added to the menace of the words by flexing and unflexing of his fingers.

As the two men stared with fascination at the sight, an unearthly glow started to come from the grave beneath his feet and bathe him in its hideous light. The creeping phosphorescence, tinged with an unearthly radiance of yellow and green, slowly climbed up the expanse of the robe until the entire fabric was coloured by the strange luminosity. The shrill incantations rang out across the deserted graveyard, hideous, animal like, darting from the boy's clenched lips — now raging, now hissing — unknown words that spewed from his throat and smote the still air with the force of their stunning blasphemy, resounding and echoing until the very stones set in the brown earth seemed to wilt under the barrage of shocking abuse.

As the two men gazed with trepidation at the apparition, they had the added horror of watching the start of another spectacle. The boy was soon surrounded by a gyrating, seething, creeping fog of yellow dust that welled up from the hole and curled about him like a monstrous snake. The venomous looking coils twisted and danced to a hideous slithering creep on its way up the slender body of the motionless boy. As the terrible cries grew less and the boy started to lower his arms, beneath his feet the hole began to disgorge a bestial array of peculiar creatures. Before their horrified stares appeared jumping toads with hair flowing from slimy bodies, screaming black bats stuck together in a struggling mass of congealed slime. and other shapes, too horrible for them to comprehend, slithered into the open, wriggling into spiralling corkscrews and squirming as they fought for space.

Now the boy was silent, but the repulsive expulsion of weird creatures continued. With a yellow bubble of oozing slime and popping gas fumes a disgusting apparition met their tortured gaze. Meary stepped back in horror as it emerged from the hole and broke the bubble, like the birth of a baby. The fiendish creature shouldered past other fearful creations and, slithering through this leaping heap of wriggling slime and secretion, pushed into the daylight. Wading through them like something sloshing through oozing mud, it cast its bulk upwards and rested on the lip of the grave where it lay eyeing the two men with a stare that was both baleful and direct.

With rising gorge that threatened to eject the contents of his stomach, Meary swallowed to dispel the urge even though the stench of the outpouring was overpowering. He fixed the latest thing to emerge from the hole with slitted eyes. As far as he was able, he could only describe it as a cross between a snake and a dragon. It possessed a flattened head and a rounded skull that flared out like the head of an enormous daisy. The petals dripped yellow mucous and seemed to emit steam that drifted above its head in hazy clouds. A single horn rose above meshing brown teeth and a solitary eye glittered in the crown of the daisy.

Meary shuddered in horror. The thing was a nightmare to watch, but he stared at it, fascinated by the unwavering eye and the drip of yellow tinged mucus that ran from its meshing jaws. He knew in his heart it was the ultimate of his knowledge of strange beings. Throughout the years he had had call to fight other weird creatures and, through this knowledge, eventually win the battle, but this account seemed to have no ending, nothing to foster a tiny shred of encouragement to which he could cling. He had a limit to his endurance and he wondered vaguely if he had reached it.

Meary also thought about whether his companion was suffering the same sort of reaction to the fearful sight displayed before them. He held his breath when he saw the whitened face of his friend. His eyes were staring and protruding with the effort and his lips were a bloodless thin line. Hollis's jaws were clenched together and jutted out into a rock-like line of frozen flesh. Meary caught sight of firmly curled fists that were held slightly outwards as though to ward off the evil. His slender frame, bending slightly at the waist, was tense and still, bathed in the uncanny light flowing from the horrific sight before them.

Meary turned his gaze back to the grave just as the creature reared up into the air to reveal the possession of a pair of leathery looking wings. The creature flapped them frenziedly, emitting an accompanying roar that echoed around the graveyard and bounced off the stone walls. The creature's howl of rage brought the two men to life. Hollis straightened up with a jerk, and Meary bent down to grasp the metal handle of the hoist. The handle was slippery with mud, and slid easily into the palm of his hand. The coldness of it struck and chilled the flesh of his fingers. He raised the implement high above his head and whirled it in a couple of tight circles before launching the missile at the creature. When it struck home on the head of the beast, the thing gave a tremendous howl of agony, falling down among the slime from whence it had come. As if from a signal, the skin of the creature burst open. The slimy belly, oozing and dripping disgusting mucous, split and disgorged a dozen black, scuttling hairy spiders.

Meary stepped back from this latest twist in events. He felt no alarm at the manifestation, rather at the speed of which it was being enacted. The spiders represented another phase in the onslaught being directed at them.

Hollis found his voice at last.

"Ah, I thought there would be spiders."

His voice was hoarse to the ear, which he immediately rectified by swallowing. He followed the passage of the nearest of the arachnids with interest and watched as they began to spill over the sides of the grave. He watched their progress as they filed over the heaps of chalky earth then he gave a hollow laugh and turned to Meary.

"Is this the best you can do, Tolmaar?" Hollis asked. "Why, with all *your* power I expected something spectacular!"

Meary had to return his smile. Now he thought about it, he had been expecting spiders too. The sorcerer's stock-in-trade included spiders and snakes, and it looked like Tolmaar was no exception. Meary watched the nearest spider and, striding forwards, lifted his boot and crushed the life out of it, saying:

"I wish it was as easy to crush its creator."

Hollis was looking at the boy, so missed this observation. Gradually the youth drifted to the side and hovered over a heap of earth where he stopped as though waiting for something. Unaware of the fact that the boy had changed position, Meary was in the act of pouring petrol on the remaining spiders. After dropping a lighted match on them he watched as they caught fire and shrivelled to a cinder. It was then he looked up and noticed the boy had moved. He rapidly changed position to be at the side of his colleague. He eyed the floating youth and the flowing robe, noticing his slack hands dangling down at his sides. The boy was obviously under the influence of the alchemist, evidently listening to the commands of the arch demon and doing his every bidding. He had his eyes tightly closed, and his pallid skin was drawn and sickly. He had no motion about his person and Meary wondered if he was breathing,

"We've got to get him out of Tolmaar's clutches," Hollis said, "but how? It looks like he's well under the influence."

He turned to Meary and they looked each other in the eye. Meary bit his lip in silent thought. At the back of his mind he could not help agreeing with Hollis. On the face of it, it seemed that the boy was indeed lost in the power of Tolmaar. Meary dropped the thought as Hollis's hand dug into his ribs.

"Aha!" he grated. "Something's happening I'm thinking."

Something was indeed happening. With a sudden burp the sickly conglomerate of writhing creatures disappeared into the hole. The yellow dust contracted and spiralled into the depths, and the boy moved to follow. Concern written on his face, Meary stepped forwards to prevent the boy from returning to the cavern. He stood in his path and raised his hand, pleading with him.

"Bill, lad," he began, "think what you are doing. If you return to Tolmaar you'll never get away again. The man's a devil and he'll use you until he has no need of you any more. He'll cast you aside and goodness knows what fate will overcome you."

The boy drew nearer until he was just a yard away. That was when Meary made a move that was to decide the actual destiny of the boy. He extended a hand to touch him and met nothing. Realisation flooded through him when the shock took effect, bewilderment, followed instantly by overwhelming dread. The boy was nothing but a shadow, a nonentity of light and shade conjured up by the alchemist; something like the dust that could be managed, but not touched, a thing ethereal, but not real.

CHAPTER TWELVE

With one accord the two men turned to each other, Hollis with a question written on his face and Meary with plain astonishment showing through a pair of wondering eyes. Hollis was the first to speak and did so after a gap of ten seconds had passed.

"What was that all about?"

Meary shook his head in disbelief. To him the shock of finding no substance in the boy amounted to a realisation that from the start the figure had not appeared at all and was just a resemblance, a copy conjured up by the alchemist, who no doubt held Bill's real body. Meary fixed the young man with a puzzled stare. He also had no doubt that Tolmaar did not want Bill to emerge into the upper world, simply because the boy had not been fully inducted into the underlife – not yet.

The arch villain of the piece was not sure of the boy's help. Bill was not under his spell, as the alchemist suspected, but yet maintained a certain degree of awareness, even though Tolmaar had almost passed a high amount of power at the lad. Right from the start he had shown resistance to the might of the power, and Tolmaar felt rather than knew the strength of his hidden gift.

Meary suspected the alchemist had noticed the difference in Bill's make-up, and that was uppermost in his determination to ensure the lad's survival. Now the first stage in Bill's induction to the life in the netherworld had begun, and Meary felt powerless to stop it. His thoughts leaped from one avenue to another, searching for the answer.

"That was not Bill," Meary croaked in a husky voice.

"But we *saw* him," Hollis argued. "He talked to us, he warned us, he even brought those hideous things to life. You saw it the same as I did."

"We saw what the alchemist wanted us to see, you should know that," Meary muttered darkly. "The forces he controls are no different from the creatures he produces, the more horrible the better for his purpose. He is waiting to frighten you with his creations and it looks like he has succeeded with you."

Hollis kept a hold on his temper and tried to ignore the barb. It was true the train of events had come thick and fast in the past hours and he was not sure as some of them were too completely fantastic to be relied upon; the alchemist for a start. Was he real or just a picture created by the power of the dust?

That opened up the possibility of the dust itself. Was the power in it producing the alchemist or vice versa? There was no contact with Tolmaar. All that ever emerged were thunder and lightning as he raged at them, just visual evidence with a background of noise and whizzing sparks to set the piece off. The setting was an offence to the nose. To Hollis it was fishy, as all attempts to circumscribe the paranormal appeared to him.

"There must be some sort of explanation for it all," he

said. "I'm sure we will rescue the boy—"

"I'm not so sure, Hollis," interrupted Meary. "You saw me try to touch him—"

"Yes, I saw you pass your hand through his outline—"

"Then all I ask is, is or was that Bill?"

"I would say no, if you really did reach out to touch him."

Meary let out a loud burst of frustrated sound.

"Are you in doubt about the evidence of your own eyes?" He flung out an arm and invited Hollis to try by saying, "Here, you try. Maybe it will be different for you."

Hollis hesitated. He had a burning desire to test it for himself, but stopped short in trying to prove Meary wrong.

"Let's not argue, John," he protested. "I'll take your word for it and let it go at that."

"Try it," Meary insisted with a growl. "I won't be satisfied until you see for yourself."

Hollis eyed the shimmering figure hovering over the hole and stepped forwards. With arm extended before him he approached the apparition. As with Meary, his hand passed through the boy's form and encountered nothing. He dropped his hand to his side.

"Now we've both felt nothing," he muttered.

"Exactly," concurred Meary, "but that is not helping the boy. He is still a prisoner of the alchemist and we are no nearer to rescuing him."

To confound the magnitude of their feeble efforts the shadowy outlines of the boy began to fade. The sharp outlines of the graveside formation appeared through his shape and he slowly vanished from sight. Meary gazed at Hollis with a mixture of fear and consternation. To say he felt helpless was an understatement. He stumbled over the muddy earth and stood gazing at the hole, trying to picture what he thought was happening deep down below.

"We've got to go back down below," he muttered, so low he was nearly inaudible to the other.

"Go below *again*!" Hollis said, aghast. "You heard what Tolmaar said. You heard him when he threatened you. The fiend is determined to finish you, as he is with all of us. He means to rule the earth and he'll see that no one stands in his way." Hollis blew a gush of air to emphasise his feelings. "He'll tread you into the dust he created. Mark my words, John, we need divine providence to intervene, and we have no way of providing such a deliverance."

Meary was adamant as he argued.

"Don't you see, Hollis, to rule the world he needs a divine pathway from the netherworld, something that will protect and guide him to the substance and light of this upper plane. He needs a spirit to shine forth its lustre so that the way is clear and unfettered. He wants a guardian angel who will protect and show him the way."

"I suspected as much," Hollis said. "To prevent such a thing from happening we must go below and rescue Bill."

"Exactly, as I was about to say," Meary said in a hoarse whisper.

Hollis mentally conjured up all that his words meant, and could not prevent a shudder from going through himself. His mind pictured the meaning and he shuddered again. Meary saw what was going through his mind and tried to make it easy for him.

"It will be better if I go alone," he said quietly, "anyway, we need someone to operate the chair." Hollis pursed his lips in a grim line and shook his head.

"We'll toss a coin, as always," he insisted. "Perhaps I can persuade Tolmaar to change his mind."

"I doubt that," Meary said, with a wry smile, "but if you insist we'll toss for it."

Hollis produced a coin and with a little groan called:

"Wrong!"

He stood to one side as Meary prepared to make another foray into the hole.

"Good luck," he said as Meary stepped into the chair. "I'll say a short prayer for you."

Meary gave a shallow grin and waited as Hollis began the process of lowering the chair. As the chair disappeared into the hole, Hollis stood contemplating it for awhile. He knew the danger into which Meary was entering and he was with him mentally as he descended. His thoughts raced ahead of the chair as the rope played out. He wondered if the giant man was still in a placid state and if the boy was normal. Tolmaar was not to be trusted and could be relied on to produce more of his nasty surprises. The recent revelations regarding Bill were something new to Hollis. Meary, bless him, was shouldering the blame of introducing the lad into the tomb and, typically, was determined to rescue him from the clutches of the evil alchemist. A tall order it would seem, but something had to done if Bill was to be saved.

Hollis felt the ropes go slack and knew Meary had arrived. He called into the black void of the hole, but there was no response. The dark stared up at him and the silence was virtually that of the grave. Not a sound disturbed the hush, not a drip of water—nothing.

The local council chamber was a hive of activity. Councillor Holt had received explicit instructions that a murderer was terrorising the neighbourhood and had to be apprehended without any delay. A special force of twenty men of the North Downshire Fusiliers, complete with armoured cars and bristling machine guns, had arrived in the village under the command of one, Captain Lewis. They formed two ranks in the market square and there heard of the bizarre and bestial doings of a stone man who was impervious to rifle bullets and possessed of enormous physical strength with which he literally tore his victims to pieces.

In addition to rifles they were equipped with hand grenades and anti tank weapons, so, as Cllr Holt was often heard to remark to the assembly:

"They are well armed with a veritable arsenal of modern weapons. Enough to start a small war if need be, but enough to take care of the malefactor."

Captain Lewis was only too happy to oblige by saying:

"We've heard of his murderous activities and of the people he has so far slaughtered. Make no mistake about it we'll put an end to his butchery."

The soldiers were deployed in searching the countryside for the killer. In addition, Inspector Harding was once more using his police force to guard the local school, the church and the Women's Institute. With this assurance in mind, the local gents repopulated the local Red Cow Inn, the buses resumed their visits to the village and the women walked their prams to the local park. The cemetery was still taboo though, and very little local life passed through the metal gates. A blessing it would seem because sightseers would be too much to bear in the present circumstances. So thought Hollis as he passed his lonely vigil waiting for Meary and what was taking place deep within the bowels of the earth.

He strode back and forth to keep his blood pumping in his veins. He tried coiling the ropes and cleaning the equipment, but still the time dragged. He earnestly wished he was in a position to witness what he thought was happening, to give some sort of moral support to Meary in his hour of need.

It was getting towards late afternoon when the first of the soldiers made an appearance. After a cursory push and inspection of the gates, a solitary khaki-clothed figure skirted the gravestones and stood watching Hollis. He was a corporal and was equipped with a semi-automatic rifle that he wore slung over one muscular shoulder. The soldier eyed the open grave and the chair swinging in the breeze. He nodded at the hole.

"Would you mind telling me what you are doing?" he questioned.

Hollis, fearful that the soldier was about to spoil things, answered with a nonchalant shrug of his shoulders:

"I'm trying to rescue my dog that has fallen into the hole."

The corporal scrambled over mounds of earth and stood there peering into the aperture.

"Who's with you?" he asked swinging the chair so that it did not impair his view.

Hollis compounded the lie.

"My mate's looking for the dog. I'm lowering the chair

down to him. If he finds him I'll pull him and the dog up."

The soldier scrutinised the hole.

"He's not making much noise down there. It's as black as 'Newgate's Knocker'. You sure he's all right?"

Hollis regarded the corporal with dismay. The soldier was an interloper and had the unconscious intention of interfering with events that were far beyond his understanding. This he would not put up with, so he made himself plain by remarking:

"It's no good examining the apparatus it is just a means of lowering people to the cave's interior. I have the situation well in hand I can assure you, so I don't need any help at the moment thank you, Sir."

The khaki-clad figure straightened up from his appraisal of the situation and smiled at Hollis.

"I wouldn't leave him too long in that place, the air in that cave seems to be a bit foul as far as I can make out."

He made to go and slid on the pile of excess earth that lined the gravesides, waving at Hollis as he made for the gates. Hollis watched him go and winced as the metal gates crashed shut behind him. He grimaced at the retreating figure and returned to the task in hand.

The petrol tank needed filling and he fell to the job with gusto, trying to shut out the sight of the swinging chair. He had only his vivid imagination to fall back on and it was doing overtime in the stretch of grey matter that constituted his brain. All sorts of schools of imaginative thought shot through his mind. Was Bill in any danger? Was his compatriot, Meary, suffering at the hands of the arch demon himself? Was the alchemist practising his black art at this very moment and, last, but not in any way least, did the ensuing silence portend another foray by the stone man, heralding the vicious murder of other innocent villagers? With these things in mind Hollis welcomed other thoughts, but try as he might they were denied him. He sought to refresh his mind, but still they seemed to drift into meaning. Once there they seemed to hold sway no matter how hard he tried to dash the doom-laden ruminations into nothingness.

Hollis bit his lip and earnestly wished their roles were exchanged, and if so the boot would be on the other foot, he resolved in a soundless hiss. Tolmaar would feel the thunder of his reply should he try to answer to the accusations he directed at the ageing Meary. Just let him try his Devil's black magic on me, he sniffed and thought. He'll come a cropper, I can tell you. He thought about the situation again and decided Meary was about right in his estimation of events. In the meantime it was situation normal up top.

It was then that Hollis cast a wary eye on the silent chair and thought he saw a tremor of the ropes. It is the wind of course, he thought. He sensed a slight stirring of wayward wind puff, and this time he was certain the ropes were moving. The movement was slight, but definite. Hollis waited, transfixed, preparing himself for any eventuality, then the smell came. The aroma of rotting bodies was joined by the emergence of the yellow dust stream as it squeezed out of the blackness of the tomb hole. As the whirling cloud twisted and swayed in the slight wind another horror made itself apparent as the dust parted. The tortured familiar features of Meary gazed at him with a blank stare and expressionless face.

CHAPTER THIRTEEN

Meary ascended into view, followed closely by the figure of the boy. The scientist stepped from the chair and waited there, swaying slightly, eyeing the awesome Hollis with unseeing eyes. The boy, turning away from Meary, beckoned to Hollis with a thin hand and waited as he trod the distance to the chair. The boy waited again as Hollis sat in the chair, signalling for Meary to start the engine, but Meary just stood there, hollow cheeked, the same vacant stare dulling his eyes.

For awhile Bill seemed to regard Meary through equally distant eyes, before opening his bloodless lips and intoning some unintelligible mutterings. The dust ceased to revolve and started to retreat into the realms from where it had issued. The chair trembled and the ropes tightened. The boy uttered further intonations and the chair began its descent into the abyss of the funeral hole, taking the intrepid Hollis with it.

Hollis, wide-eyed with anticipation and dreading the eventual encounter with the alchemist, twisted in the chair, watching the rock formation begin its gradual journey upwards, as the chair descended. The air shifted in the entrance and with it came a rush of papery objects that peppered his facial features with stinging suddenness, causing him to cover his face with his hands. They ceased, however, but the wind increased as the chair got lower, shrilling with intensity and ferreting out the natural openings of his face. In turn the wind lessened and stopped, to be followed by a tiny sound that heralded the arrival of the chair.

His legs were lost as they dug deep into the dust pile, cushioning his arrival, which he quickly exited when he thought of the evil of which it was capable. He waited for any reaction, ready for instant flight if the dust still had the same qualities. The dust remained dormant and in the dim light looked harmless, evincing a shadowy outline in the darkness that spoke nothing of anything but innocence. The silence is indeed the silence of the grave, Hollis thought. The semi-darkness seemed to add to the gloom. He skirted the dust and made his way to the rock pile that was the grave of the Brighold. He felt the inside of the coffin and ran his fingers around the lining that rested beneath the giant figure. It was, as he suspected, empty. The stone man must be here. He had seen him before Tolmaar had caused him to vanish, but what of Tolmaar himself? Where had the alchemist gone?

Meary had evinced some sort of response by demanding the presence of the wizard. He had shouted, lacing the demands with a few invectives of his own. Perhaps that is what is needed to call the alchemist to wakefulness. Hollis filled his lungs to maximum and hollered out to the rock walls, inwardly flinching as the sound echoed through the chamber and reverberated from the rock face. The wind died away and retained the sound, echoing in a breath of captured energy. The resultant effect was just as he expected–nothing.

The tomb seemed to hold its breath as the minutes ticked by, silence capturing silence and emitting not a tremor or vestige of a tremor. Hollis tried again and thundered:

"Tolmaar, are you heeding me? I come to challenge you, to ask why you are holding the boy, Bill. To demand you return him to his kin." The silence continued. "In the name of all that you hold dear, I implore you to release Bill and Meary."

A fizzing firework bounced off the rock walls and exploded in a shower of blue sparks and green particles, the sudden ignition bringing blue and yellow lights to the gloomy reaches of the burial chamber.

The demonic laughter reverberated around the chamber, chilling the very bones of the waiting Hollis. It dwindled to a snarl that had the effect of freezing what was left of Hollis's resolve.

You fool, the snarl growled, developing into a roar. *You think you can come in here and demand the boy. I have a great future for him. I will use him to do my bidding no matter if the world will end. I will have my way and enter the world in my own light. The boy will ensure it is so.*

As the voice paused, Hollis broke into a tirade.

"Tolmaar, you will invoke the wrath of the good Lord if you go on with this charade."

A moment passed as this choice morsel of regret left the lips of the raging Hollis, one in which Tolmaar found his voice, it having been momentarily stilled through bellicosity.

You have the gall to talk to me in those insulting tones. I'll have you know I was big in my time on earth. The great and powerful ruler and Emperor Phillus of Upper Gonderia and Tredo, conqueror of the mighty Vango, who inflicted such dire treatment of his subjects, promoted me to head of his imperial treasure holder, a position worthy of my power and note, until it was taken over by the ruling and domains of the man we are all at odds with, the Brighold.

"So it was a case of rank jealousy," Hollis blurted out before he could stop himself.

Tolmaar's voice was a shade rougher when he spoke of the man who had beaten him to riches.

You call it what you like, the Brighold deserved all he got. We both share our lives in the underworld together, but I managed to get the upper hand. I spent the last few years of my existence in the netherworld pleading for release from my torture. Thus I learned to talk to the dark angels and to converse with them in their scheme to end the domination of the people who dwell on the earth's surface.

"I happen to be one of those who live on the surface of the earth," Hollis grated. "I like the way we live and all mortal people who do the same things. We have existed for a thousand years and we hope to live forever."

Not with the plans I have in view for you. Tolmaar lifted up a snigger of amusement at this assessment of the situation. *I do assure you that the world is coming to an end. The emergence of man as a final force is at an end. Very soon, without any warning, a great catastrophe will overtake it and end the domination.*

"You speak of domination?" Hollis questioned. "Well, are

you not after the same thing, you and your dark angels?"

Tolmaar raised the temper of his voice.

You or your ilk will not understand the finer points of my argument. It will not suffice for you to know of what the conversation consists. If you think I will argue with you to maintain a conversation, you are very much mistaken. I have other things to do. My time is taken up with the myriad of tasks that I must do if I am to command the creatures on the upper plane.

Hollis scoffed at such a suggestion and said so.

"Who do you think you are? You are standing in the rightful place of the Lord God and it is blasphemous for you to do so."

So be it, my dubious friend. You talk of blasphemy and of my rightful place in the Creation. Who are you to question such differences? You know nothing of any value to me. You are as the dust in the air or the dew on the ground. You know not a single invective of any worth.

"That being so, I still desire to see the back of you. The world will be well rid of such undesirables such as you, so with God's help I'm starting the transition at once."

Oh you are, are you? Tolmaar sneered, in a voice that was rapidly nearing danger level. *And what do you propose to do about it?*

Hollis realised that if he was to effect the release of the boy and his friend, Meary, it was best if he was to humour the alchemist. He gathered in a breath of the fetid air and resolved to try another tack.

"Perhaps it is the Lord's wish if you were to try another way."

What do you mean?

"You could be a benefactor..."

I will be the benefactor when I rid the world of such insects as you.

"You will not benefit from your stubbornness. You have only yourself to blame if other things happen to deter you from your nefarious ways."

Hollis was in full cry when he was preaching and was in his element now the alchemist had seen fit to deny him his moment of glory.

"If you persist in your attitude then other forces will combat you. They will ensure you will comply, even if they condemn your immortal soul."

Tolmaar was unconcerned with the threat, and disclaimed it as trivial.

The threat is no concern of mine. It will all end in the final deliverance of the divine emperor. I will be his right-hand man, I can assure you.

Hollis blew a gust of air to show his annoyance. The alchemist was proving to be a handful and no kidding. Tolmaar was no fool and it was appearing as though he was getting the upper hand in the battle of what could only described as the war of the ultimate will. Hollis was despairing of getting a satisfactory ending to the argument and sighed in desperation.

"Tolmaar, can I plead to you for the soul of the two people? They are just an ordinary couple of people who live ordinary lives, especially the boy of tender age and consent. He never harmed a living soul and did not intend to. The older man, Meary, a man who has the heart of a lamb and the disposition of a saint, has never harmed anyone—"

He despoiled the grave of the Brighold, Tolmaar broke in. *He and others of his kind forced their way into the resting place of the dead man and removed him to another place.*

"Regretfully that is so," Hollis mumbled, trying to pacify the alchemist. "They had no right, I realise so, but they were doing it in the name of science." Hollis took another big breath and continued. "The corpse was removed because man was born with an inherent curiosity to delve into the unknown. The several men who were concerned had no conscious desire to disturb the rest of the Brighold. In their estimation they were doing a service to mankind and others to make available such knowledge to the world."

Nevertheless, the sleep of the Brighold was disturbed. They broke into the tomb and carried it away to the outside world, causing him to awake and wreak such mayhem as he did.

"Come on now, Tolmaar," Hollis scoffed. "You yourself said you were in command of the Brighold. If so, you are just as responsible for the murder and turmoil of the Brighold as the stone man himself."

I will not be dictated to, the alchemist roared.

"I'm not dictating," Hollis protested.

The alchemist appeared as a bright picture on the rock walls and suddenly materialised to the cowering man.

You will do as I command, he raged.

"I'm not at your command," Hollis protested.

The bright image turned into a man who glided towards the frightened mortal, bearing down on the man with a rapidly flowing outer garment glistening like flaming crystal. It took on a different glow as it flared into red fire that reflected on the rock backed sedimentation of the formation.

Hollis backed away as the apparition drew nearer. His heart was a hammer that threatened to tear his chest apart. He stepped into the dust heap and it wrapped itself around his feet like a writhing snake. He shook off the coils and felt the dust wriggle like a live animal. He stamped to extricate himself and it replied by issuing further coils that twined around his ankles like knotted rope. Hollis fought it. He kicked it and twisted it and even jumped on it, but it was unabashed by the ill-treatment. Hollis was losing the battle and he knew it. With every jump and crunching kick he administered the dust came back with more far reaching moves that had him gasping for breath.

Tolmaar, tired of his curious attempt at amusement and intoning a strange lot of peculiar words, caused the one-sided contest to come to an end. With the words he performed a series of strange circulations with his triangular shaped hands and without any warning the dust ceased its hideous convolutions.

You can see what power I hold at my fingertips, Tolmaar said, with assuredness. *The animals in the field, big or small, tooth and claw, come to my rescue. Even the dust aids me.*

"That *you* manufacture," Hollis said, getting rid of the dust particles that were still sticking to his shoes.

Yes, I'll answer to that charge, the alchemist said, softening his loud voice to a lesser tone.

Hollis was getting used to the wizard. In the inner workings of the soothsayer and sorcerer that was Tolmaar it ill bereft any unfortunate person who had the misfortune to meet him in single combat. He dusted himself down with a nervous hand, eyeing the apparition emblazoned on the wall with renewed vigour. He noted the alchemist and all his aliases was standing with his eyes closed, as if in prayer. Hollis seriously doubted whether he had ever earnestly prayed. The wizard maintained he had prayed in his time in the chamber, but Hollis doubted whether he had been openly praying to the Lord and no other presence. More likely the Devil, Hollis enthused with a half-smile crossing his face.

He was grinning, but he had never felt less like grinning. The pain in his ankles was so severe it was well nigh unbearable. The attentions of the dust had aroused in his legs an ache that threatened to last for the best part of the next few hours. Although Hollis was strong, he went to enormous lengths to appear so. He hated pain and all it brought with it. He dreaded pain because not only was it inconvenient, but it hurt as well. He decided to ignore it until it went away of its own accord.

As for the evil dust, it was a force in its own right, but with Tolmaar's instigation, and it was difficult to imagine how such a force was being harnessed. He knew the force was manifest in the wizard himself, but how did Tolmaar exercise such enormous power over it? It did everything it was told to do. What of the dust indeed, and its latent power? He could still feel the vicious coils winding around his legs and lower body. The feeling brought a cold sweat to his brow.

Tolmaar appeared to reawaken from his slumber and was gaining substance fast. He studied Hollis with wide open eyes that had no expression in the fiery glances. He stepped from his place at the rock wall with a gradual glide that had no visible motion, but rather a transition of events that reminded Hollis of slow motion film that was out of synchronisation.

Suddenly Tolmaar spoke, startling the silent Hollis.

You can see that I need the boy more than ever now to fulfil my rightful destinies, he uttered, still emitting the glow that illuminated the chamber.

"What destinies are those?" Hollis questioned as he rubbed hard at his ankles whilst treating the dust pile to looks of extreme hatred.

You know he is vital to my plans for entering the earth plane.

"So you have been at pains to point out," Hollis said, straightening to his full height, "but I have just tried to explain why I do not wish it. He has his own life to lead and you have no justifiable right to deprive him of it."

No right, no right? Tolmaar spluttered with the force of his convictions. *I have every right to expect an underling to comply with my commands.*

Hollis shot out an expletive at this juncture, directing the words at the blazing alchemist.

"Once and for all, the answer is a positive *no*. You are not listening to me, Tolmaar, or you would not push me so."

The wizard, endowed with the rage of centuries of frustration, thundered an instant reply.

I asked so you will understand the need for an assistant whom I can trust to aid me in my work, in my desire for help. Others more powerful to the extreme will ensure it is done without your consent. You will regret this ruling. They who desire it will force you to obey whether you like it or not. The boy will desire as well, for I will instil such a thought into his very being that will be impossible to remove.

The shrewd Hollis thought for a moment, mulling over in his mind what Tolmaar had said. He knew he was right, but another spectre reared its ugly head as he replied to the indignant wizard.

"You mentioned other interested parties, Tolmaar. What other interested parties do you speak of?"

Why do you wish to know? The matters in hand are the many tasks handed to the boy. He will decide —

"Will you answer my question?" Hollis demanded, spitting such venom he surprised even himself.

Tolmaar stopped emitting coloured sparks and regarded the vehement man with surprise.

Why do you want to know who is interested in the boy?

Hollis spluttered with the intensity of his demand.

"Not the boy, not this time, I repeat, who is the central figure in the desire? Who in fact is your master?"

This time Tolmaar was lost for the right words and remained silent. After awhile he muttered in a low key that was nowhere near the extent of loudness he had recently registered.

I have a master that is true, and he gave me all the powers that have been invested in me. He is in all respects, my benefactor, so I will not have any detractor such as you showing such disrespect to him.

Hollis had never meant to show disrespect and thought so, but he was dismayed by the partial admission of the alchemist to having other interested forces as well. All along he had suspected there were others involved, but the idea seemed not to lodge in his interest until now! He decided to pursue the subject without remorse.

"Who is your master?" he insisted in a voice that bordered on the demand. "Who is this person pulling the strings?"

Tolmaar tried to evade the question with a series of popping sparks that shot into the fetid air of the chamber in a crescendo of colour and noise. Hollis, although scared by the display, had the added knowledge that the wizard was once again using delaying tactics. He smiled in understanding, waiting for the firework display to cease, watching the show with renewed interest now he knew the wizard and understood why he did it. For several minutes it progressed. First the shower of red sparks with a deluge of incandescent light shafts that had tiers of circular motions running off in every direction then the slow film extract with the accompanying pop and bang, echoing around the chamber, to be followed by a squealing and squeaking of the animal kingdom set in a sing-song of mindless howls and scratchings.

Slowly it began to subside. The sounds died away to nothingness and a gradual silence descended on the chamber. Apart from the figures of Tolmaar and the silent Hollis, their immediate surroundings were empty of any other soul, although something seemed to be happening on the wall behind the alchemist. Hollis watched with interest, noting the features of the boy taking shape on the rocky backdrop. The dear face of the youth was superimposed before his very eyes, taking shape and substance as the time progressed, shining through cracks and scars, each indentation and ripple showing through the image. Behind the suppressed Tolmaar the silence spread through the chamber, gathering the gloom to itself, while the glittering picture of Bill winked in and out with rapid intensity. The alchemist seemed to be unaware of it, choosing to ignore its presence if he was.

Hollis sighed with the effort of standing in one position too long. He had no idea how long he had been in the chamber, but he knew or little cared about time because time seemed to be suspended in the half-light, a curious effect with the changing light and echoing noise. Hollis sensed the silence needed breaking and coughed to ease the need. The sound descended into quietness, adding a new dimension to the silence. The noise had the effect of rousing the wizard, who looked behind him as though he had just noticed the image.

A pretty picture? he growled to Hollis, who stood in front of him.

Hollis just grinned to himself and resolved to try Tolmaar with the same enquiry.

"Are you going to answer my question or not?" he said gruffly, neither wanting nor expecting an answer.

The wizard answered in the affirmative, which surprised Hollis.

If I do will you promise never to reveal the answer to another living soul?

Hollis was a man of his word, but the promise was beyond him. In this case he could see no sense of justice in it, so he shook his head in denial, remarking:

"I have a duty to my colleagues to report all that happens down here. I cannot make that promise. I must be true to myself and other people. You must understand my desire to tell the world what I know."

Tolmaar received his refusal in abject silence, mentally going through his words and passing it to his mind, gauging and measuring each and every item until the last drop had been wrung from it before answering.

Then I cannot reveal to you the identity of my master.

Hollis smiled to himself. He inwardly congratulated himself. He suspected the alchemist was glad not tell him the name, mainly because of its gigantic proportions. Hollis was also aware of its overtones because he thought he knew the name outright. Tolmaar mulled over the desire of reveal the name, but decided against it in the interest of his own personal safety. Hollis would have to wait until the time was right.

Now the youth was gaining substance, his body showing through the flowing robe, losing its transparency with the physique of the boy showing through the garment. Bill was different. His eyes stared blank and lifeless from the sockets, not the usual shine of eyes that exhibited boyish charm and appeal. Gone was the pleasant boy who took such pleasure out of ordinary life it was a joy to behold, who enjoyed each day to the maximum. He loved anybody, and anything that had anything to do with his chosen life no matter how small or trivial.

The boy who remained was just a shell of the human being who evinced such a manner. It showed through the facade with glaring falseness that did very little to dispel the effect. In full measure the wizard was responsible for the manifestation, with his ceaseless desire for the secrets of the universe and his tireless yearning to learn other things that did not concern him. The boy was in danger of entering the netherworld, being lost to the human race and all things connected to it.

Now this other thing had emerged; the name that Tolmaar has refused to mention at any cost. The divulgement of the name might help all three; the boy, Meary and the world in general. Hollis ran through the thoughts and realised the tremendous consequences of the knowledge was resting squarely on his shoulders. These conditions would cause an impact on the world that would set it back a thousand years. He realised it would take a force so powerful and magical that the extremes it reached made it difficult to imagine the result. He knew someone with that amount of power did exist. He only realised it was not he, but the boy. What had Tolmaar in store for him? In time the alchemist could build him up into a gigantic force that could possibly rival the Devil. At the moment it was difficult to see if the alchemist had these nefarious plans, plans that might include the youth.

Hollis resolved to scotch the schemes. He started by addressing the boy in a tone that spoke of his previous life.

"Bill, your mother will be distressed to learn of your refusal to speak with her. She is after all your natural mother and you owe her the right to have some discourse with her. You must leave this dark and dreary place for the bright and cheery world from which you recently came. Come with me to the daylight of the upper world, change your life from this dank and gloomy existence to one of sunshine and happiness. I implore you, I beseech you to think again of your previous life and return to your mother, home and family."

For the fullness of a few seconds, the youth looked the crestfallen Hollis in the face with his troubled eyes, searching for pity and help, then the look changed as the alchemist took over and seized control of his mind, holding him in a grip of metal vice.

"I assure you I am happy here," he said in a flat voice.

"The darkness means nothing to me. It will pass as we emerge into the upper world. I must forget about my mother and the previous life I lived. Tolmaar has willed it so and I must obey his commands."

The booming laugh of the alchemist followed this little repartee.

I warned you, he enjoined with alacrity. *The boy will stay with me. He will accompany me in my search for everlasting life. He will benefit from the ruling as I have. This I have decreed and it will be as such. The things I have said will come to pass.*

Again the demented laughter rang through the chamber like the howling of a wolf. Hollis realised he was right – Tolmaar had won. The boy was his to do with as he saw fit. The battle for the soul of Bill seemed to be over. The sparks flickered brighter in their stream, the unseen animals imitated the howls of the alchemist, the mirror of darkest reflection turned around to mock the abject man and his moment of sadness, dancing to the tune played by the exuberant Tolmaar. The wizard, with the backing of the dark angel, called the tune to which they all danced. He was joining in the furore with all the bestiality he was able to muster, ignoring the crestfallen Hollis, who felt like slinking away like a whipped dog. The wizard was celebrating his victory by holding the boy's arm in his, still emitting shrills of delight, echoed by the youth, who giggled to emulate his now master.

Hollis was preparing for his emergence from the burial chamber when the Brighold made one of his untimely entrances, materialising with startling suddenness near the horrified Hollis. The huge bulk of the stone man towered over him and the alchemist like some enormous edifice, waiting for the command to issue from the wizard.

Tolmaar was planning another phase in the destiny of the earth, and ignored the Brighold. This was reflected by the stone man, who appeared like some monstrous animal beside the quaking Hollis. The Brighold seemed to ignore him, which was to his liking, still waiting for a command from the alchemist. This was also to Hollis's liking because of the Brighold's nearness to him. The huge apparition beside him waited patiently for word to come from the lips of Tolmaar, standing and biding his time in stilled silence, his hands still stained with the blood of his victims, flexing and unflexing his fingers with uncontrolled rapidity.

Hollis had a feeling of utter revulsion for the figure standing beside him and stepped back into the shadows to avoid him. Tolmaar was talking again, so Hollis listened to the voice ranting and raving.

This then is the ultimate solution for the world. Destruction on a large scale is planned. The total annihilation of its many peoples is envisaged. The plan will be brought into fruition without any delay, starting with further destruction and killing by the Brighold.

His threat was echoed by the vast assemblage of hideous creatures that were hidden by the gloom of the burial chamber. Hundreds of bats skittered frenziedly overhead, while monstrosities scaled the walls, slithering their slimy scaly bodies over the rock face, their horrible mucous oozing down to the rock floor.

In reply, Hollis was violently sick, retching with the smell and the sight, but Tolmaar seemed to revel in the disgusting spectacle, joining in the howls of delight with howls of his own. The phalanx of sickening animals that crawled and slithered was joined by others that scuttled. Black rats, brown rats and others crawled, scurried and jumped over the shoes of the sickened man. Unmentionable snails and hustling snakes dodged in and out of his legs, hissing and slithering. The spiders came then, hairy and frightening, scuttling up the walls and hanging from silver threads that somehow bore their jiggling weight. Other slimy creatures crawled and dangled in his vision, gesticulating and waving in a show of horror and fear.

In his utter panic and sickness at the sight before him, Hollis was vaguely aware that the show was for him to see. The animals seemed to know this, for they crept around him and not the Brighold. The revelation came to Hollis, but it was lost in the desire to get away from the exhibition as soon as his legs were able to carry him. He edged towards the dangling chair, skirting the now dormant dust on the way, but then a new worry clouded his mind. The chair had no means of operating by itself, so he was doomed to stay there if the operator was absent. He swung into the vacant chair, daring not to call for assistance, but desperately needing the help.

The chair began to rise. Hollis was startled by the unseen hand until he realised it was the work of the wizard. He was exercising his power by reason of property. He had entered the burial chamber by the will of Tolmaar and now he was returning the same way. The ropes squealed through the blocks sending it on its way back to the entrance, taking with it the heartfelt sighs and wishes of the man who hoped and prayed it would continue on its journey upwards

Slowly the fetid air changed and was replaced by fresh

air that poured through the hole, enjoyed to the full by the delighted Hollis as he sniffed at the coming air and revelled in it. The chair swung through the cavern hole, scraping on the rugged sides as it met the roughness of the rock and earthen entrance, emerging into the daylight with a final bang.

Hollis heaved a huge sigh of relief and climbed out of the harness, leaving the swinging chair to its own devices as he looked all around for the portly figure of his colleague, Meary. The site was deserted. Meary had vanished and had not left any trace of to where he had gone. Hollis, full of his own experiences, was agog with excitement and wanted to relay it to his friend without delay. He climbed over the mound of earth that circled the hole, sliding down the tumbling soil as he did so. He felt the solitary rope engine, running it through his fingers thoughtfully, a worried frown etching a deep line on his forehead.

He trod the well traversed trail to the shed and found him. He was standing upright, clutching a shovel handle to his waist, holding it tightly with fingers that wound around the wood in a tight grip. Hollis regarded his colleague with an anxious gaze and made his feelings known with all sincerity.

"So, there you are. I was beginning to wonder what happened to you since I entered the chamber." He peered at the scientist with narrowed eyes, adding with concern, "Are you sure you are all right, you look a little strange to me?"

Meary shook his head to clear it, closing his eyes until they watered.

"It was like dream," he muttered. "There I was in the chamber talking to the alchemist. The next thing I remember is you waking me in the shed." He shook his head again, turned to Hollis and said, "Did you go down to the burial chamber?"

Hollis relayed all that had transpired down in the chamber to the astonished Meary, ending with a considered opinion that he, Meary, must have been hypnotised by the wizard.

"Well, I'll be jiggered," Meary said, shaking his head. "The man was talking to me in a strange way, so that must have been when I fell under his spell."

Hollis led the way out of the shed, followed by the scientist, both of them treading the track to the grave. They were standing at the graveside when the dust decided to erupt again.

"Oho," moaned Meary, "here it comes again."

The dust whirled atop the hole and the giant shape of the Brighold rose into sight. Without preamble he walked away from the graveside, making for the gates of the cemetery.

CHAPTER FOURTEEN

Tolmaar gnashed his teeth together in rage. When Hollis vacated the tomb chamber his schemes for world domination had suffered a severe jolt and his master was getting impatient with his constant delays. Tolmaar was in the ultimate phase of deep regret over releasing Hollis. The constant battle in the cosmos, between the Devil and Divine Entity was clouding the issue. Tolmaar waxed uncertain. He had deliberately sent the Brighold on one of his rampages to pacify the Devil.

The Devil himself, hungry for more human souls to add to his already overblown collection, demanded more with each passing aeon, rivalling the high God who had the concept of natural life in his inheritance. The Devil envisaged procuring this gift by buying the immortal souls of the damned with promises of great reward. The concept was rapidly taken up by those who desired reward, so much so that the thought was beginning to bear fruit.

Tolmaar, impatient and ever ready to do his master's bidding, called up the humpbacked dwarf and as this hideous midget materialised ordered him to follow in the footsteps of the scientist and his friend, Hollis. Speaking to him in the guttural speech of his kind, Tolmaar told him what had happened in the vault, relating to him all that had transpired recently. He introduced all that had emerged in the process, with all the embellishments and trivia imaginable. This was all delivered with the thunder and fire of his raucous voice, which worked overtime in its delivery and intent.

The monstrous features of Tillus the dwarf worked in a tortuous twist, leering at the words of fire, but grinning inwardly as he heard that Lucifer was involved. In the language of the dwarf, Tolmaar outlined the plans the Devil had for the earth. The dwarf's evil grin widened with each guttural syllable uttered by the alchemist. A hideous glance replaced the grin when Tolmaar spoke of his reward for doing as he was bidden.

The people will be enslaved, raged Lucifer. *They will do my bidding without argument. I will rule the earth as I was meant to. I will win the battle for the minds of the human beings. I will win the contest with the Lord.*

Tolmaar was mouthing the words of the arch demon with all the will he possessed, swearing each juicy morsel with the malignant vile he was capable of mustering. Tillus lurched with the onslaught, bending under the tirade as each piece spat from the twisted mouth with each passing moment, bearing the shower of virulent empathy with some fortitude, shutting his hideous eyes as each shaft on the misery of the damned possibly struck home in the mind of the missing scientist, Meary.

The dwarf listened, but was not really bothered who won, although, he mused, the Devil *did* wake a feeling of anxiety in him with each passing second. The alchemist then brought forth his time machine, which existed in the mind of the beholder and did not conjure up any mechanical contrivance in the eye of the user. The wizard favoured this premise, but its use was denied him because of its divine properties, which is why he had not used it before. In all other values it was better designed, it could be emphasised, in casting any entity in all directions, past, present and future, with all the properties if necessary. The subject would be transported to any part of the universe.

Tolmaar was well aware of his 'infinite limitations'. He also had the feeling the Devil was aware of them too, but Old Nick had the inbuilt desire for eternal domination and was using the wizard to achieve his ends. This was what Tolmaar suspected, but he did not have enough power to refuse the Devil his ambitions. Tolmaar earnestly desired universal domination, but the world would do for starters.

The dwarf, under Tolmaar's direction, was summoned to carry out the sorcerer's orders. Tolmaar used his fantastic brain to transpose the hideous creature into the atmosphere. He used the medium of the time machine to do that necessary trick. Tillus hovered between composition and decomposition, waiting patiently for the very high properties to emerge and assert control.

Gradually the innermost workings of the dwarf materialised in the chamber. Fine nervous strings showed through then arteries full of coursing red blood, red and white cells swimming in the flow. Transposing essentials full of teeming life rose into being, as did various vital organs, the kidney and the liver all pulsing life and performing their respective tasks. The muscles and their associated tendons appeared in line with each area view.

Slowly he vanished, and when he had gone the boy stood before Tolmaar, ready for his assimilation into the realms of the underworld. It would be a long and costly business, Tolmaar knew. Bill was imbued with the constrictions of the upper world, so he would be indoctrinated with the will of the alchemist. This part of the ceremony was the most dangerous as it impaired almost all Tolmaar's will with its far-reaching quantities. It left him open to all kinds of devilry, even though Tolmaar was prepared in part for some kind of deception.

Bill was dressed in black and white. The gown swept the rock-filled chamber floor, flowing over the now dormant dust, which seemed to embrace each motion. The boy neither saw nor felt the motion. He was transfixed by the eyes of the sorcerer, which appeared to slowly turn. Black irises held the boy in a gaze of intense concentration. Like the dwarf before him, the boy was held in the spell of the alchemist, completely under its influence. The skin of the boy showed a pallor of red brown, which contrasted strangely with the shine of his eyes, something Tolmaar seemed to sense, but not control.

The incantations droned on. The hours were interminable, but the boy and Tolmaar did not seem to notice the passage of time.

The Brighold had long gone, slamming the cemetery gates shut after his great bulk passed through, intent upon his errand of death and destruction.

The two scientists, Meary and Hollis, waited with great

patience for Bill to reappear. Strangely the hours were minutes on the earth plane surface. They were not aware of the happenings taking place in the tomb. They kept vigil for Bill, who had not emerged from the chamber for several hours. The Brighold had unnerved them for a time, but the minutes ticked by and their respective anxieties gradually faded to nothing. The chair swung back and forth on its blocks, but less now that it had not been used for awhile.

A gentle rain was falling, wetting the piles of chalky earth into a mud-encrusted avenue of approach to the grave. Meary was in the act of coiling up the muddy guide ropes, turning the twists around the central arm of the chair supports. Hollis was inspecting other graves for some sort of connection to the central grave. He drew Meary's attention to another rent in the surface of the grave by pointing to the ground. Another grave had partially collapsed into itself and parts of the memorial stone appeared to have sunk down into the earth covering.

"It looks like this one is sinking too," he observed dryly, clearing the heel of his shoe on the stone surround and banging it hard on the memorial stone to rid it of the clinging mud.

Meary shook his head.

"I would hardly think there would two entrances to the burial chamber. It's probably a natural phenomenon. The ground is sinking by the looks of it and no wonder with all the goings-on perpetrated down below." He looked at the big footprints of the Brighold disappearing into the light mist and rubbed at his glasses with a bit of rag. "I wonder where the Brighold is haring off to?" he said. "He looked in a great hurry."

Hollis sniffed in the rain and brushed off a drip that had become attached to his eyebrows.

"To do an errand for the alchemist no doubt," he answered. "He has a rod of iron attachment over the Brighold, and never lets go of the driving reins no matter what happens."

"Because *he* is the cause of the Brighold being here, *he* is the reason why the Brighold is or was entombed in the chamber, *he* started the process of the stone man and no other man can be held responsible."

Hollis mused over these words before answering.

"The king is also to blame. He sentenced him in the beginning, so he must bear some of the responsibility."

"Yes, of course. In the beginning the king *was* to blame, but Tolmaar administered the mixture,"

Meary grated. "It so condemned him to his misery that he is, or was, left with a life of extreme unhappiness and distress. He is equally to blame for the Brighold's deadly actions."

Hollis kept his council by not arguing with his compatriot any further and fell silent. His mind still raced in confusion. Meary was also confused, but not about the Brighold's fate, rather his mind was still in turmoil with the events that had taken place when he was last in the chamber. He tried to remember, but a lot of the time in the vault was a perplexing blur. He tried to remember and drew his brows together in concentration. He tried to focus, but drew a blank as the blackout of his entry slipped into place. The bit of which he was aware though, shone through. He was arguing with the alchemist for the boy's life, but there were patches where his memory failed him. He suspected Tolmaar had something

226

to do with his failure to remember, and Bill did not call for any assistance in his dealing with the alchemist, but merely acted as his extension and spoke the sorcerer's words when he wanted to say something to Meary.

The silence seemed to affect Hollis. He was striding around the various gravesides looking for other holes that might have opened up with another greater hole. The cemetery had upwards of eighty other graves and it took him several minutes to circle the decrepit looking gravestones that composed the graveyard, before arriving at the grave with the enormous hole in the bottom.

The abyss of the chamber still yawned at them and as usual it still presented silence in its make-up.

The dust was still absent, but that was to be expected. There was no other entity now that the Brighold was missing, so the dust had no one to guard or to answer to. That is what they could make out. The dust attacked anybody who spelled danger to the Bighold or Tolmaar. It had its failings as well; when it got wet its ability was impaired, that they knew for certain.

About the time the two scientists were inspecting the chamber and the surrounding graveyard an army truck pulled into the main square of the village and squealed to a stop. Khaki-clad soldiers jumped down from the truck and formed two lines at the side of the road. An officer marched up and down the ranks inspecting the soldiers and barking several orders to a corporal, who followed him in his inspection. The corporal spoke with two of the men and waited as they went over to the truck and threw back the canvas cover. They urged and shoved a canvas covered item from the back of the truck and between them lowered the big object to the asphalt roadway. The officer stepped over to it and pulled the canvas cover away, running a hand over what lay beneath. A gleaming anti-tank gun was revealed by the officer, who waved to the corporal to inspect the ordinance. The corporal worked the mechanism of the gun and stood back with his arms akimbo. He turned to the officer and grinned.

"Let's see the monster argue with this sort of gun," he said.

The officer, a lieutenant, leered at the thought.

"He may be eight feet tall, but this thing will shift a thirty-ton tank, so I'm sure it will make short work of a stone man."

Their laughter was echoed by the lines of soldiers, who grinned with their superiors and smiled at the thought of a lowly man, fresh from his grave, who had the temerity to oppose the British Army.

"We'll teach the upstart a lesson he won't forget," rang through the ranks. "It'll be like slicing butter apart."

They were still laughing when the Brighold topped the crest of the hill leading into the village When the soldiers first noticed the stone man he was two or three hundred yards away. All they saw for a while was a figure striding forwards. It was when he drew closer that they got the shock of their lives when they saw his immense size. There was a general rush for the anti-tank gun, and the turmoil it caused! The chaos heightened as the officer bellowed out orders that no one was about to obey. The soldiers were running in panic at the size of the Brighold, but the huge legs covered the distance between them with surprising speed. He did not appear to notice them, but as the spellbound soldiers suddenly stood rooted to the spot the stone man was among them, striking out.

The first soldier lost his head, literally. The head lifted easily from the body of a small fat soldier and vanished from sight under the massive feet of the Brighold. The next to try his luck was the officer. His act of bravado, in front of his men, lasted just five seconds before the massive arms hugged him to death. The rest of the squad hared for the safety of the public house where they cowered in terror when the Brighold stopped to get his directions.

The corporal, bleeding from the nose, cast about him to get his bearings and to think of what had happened. What remained of the squad were scattered behind the various shops and businesses on the village green. He was not a brave man by nature and in normal circumstances would not have imagined being violent, but these were not normal conditions and the situation did not call for normal things to happen. He saw that the officer had been torn limb from limb and lay in a great pool of glistening blood.

The corporal watched the Brighold standing in the carnage with great stone legs spread amid the bits of several men who had perished at his hands. They lay scattered in heaps at the feet of the huge stone monster with the anti-tank lying forgotten and abandoned close by. Two or three men were crying with fright, and huddled together for comfort, afraid to even look at the apparition who had decimated their ranks with such force.

Satisfied, the Brighold began to move off, treading through the torn flesh and rapidly coagulating blood. The corporal gathered himself together and did a brave act. He crossed himself and shot out of his hiding place with all the speed of which he was capable, making for the anti-tank rocket launcher. The Brighold, through the medium of the sorcerer, heard the warning in his thoughts and turned to see the corporal single-handedly load the launcher. The heavy strides of the Brighold brought him around just as the corporal trained the gun on the gigantic figure. He fired the launcher and missed by a wide margin. The Brighold, with the voice of Tolmaar in his head, bore down on the man, great stone hands ready to tear him apart. Suddenly the corporal's nerve left him and he abandoned the rocket launcher to its fate, speeding down the road as fast as his legs would carry him. The stone man, confused by the explosion of the rocket and Tolmaar's instructions, took it out on the rocket launcher. He lifted one massive foot and bent the barrel with his great weight.

No one but the wind witnessed the great carnage. The breeze blew a soft breath over the scene and whipped up a newspaper from the road. The page of newsprint scudded in the breeze and settled in the widening pool of red blood that told of the massacre.

The massive figure plodded away then, driven by the desires of the alchemist and the Devil, Lucifer, thumping on the tarmac with naked feet of stone, shuffling through blood-soaked khaki and bits of torn human flesh. The thoughts came to him as though in a dream. He had a never-ending vision that this was wrong, and the dream filtering into the stone brain of the Brighold, through a tirade of abuse, was the work of the alchemist. He was urged on his missions by Tomaar and Lucifer, which, without fail, confused his desires, but the uncertainty always added to the Brighold's overloaded brain cells and compounded the issue.

The Brighold wanted out, but he wanted it in his own way. He dearly wanted to return to the life he was used to, but he suspected this had gone. It was in another era; his time had rolled by. He neither knew nor cared about people or the little lives they led. He was not sure about what he was doing. The blood spilled by him was of little concern, but Tolmaar the master had willed it this way. Tolmaar's voice cut into his stone brain with increasing rapidity. The Brighold wanted others to talk to him, but the alchemist demanded constant obedience without question.

The voices were becoming more frequent since he had been awakened from his dream. The man who came to him after his awakening had disturbed his long sleep. He had vanished after the dust absorbed him. He and the other man were eaten by the friend of the Brighold – the dust. The stone man liked friends. The dust looked after him, driving away his enemies and, with its properties, scaring away the people who were going to harm him. The king had enemies and so had Tolmaar, but the king showed no mercy to him, the Brighold, or to any of the stone man's wives or friends. He took him away for a few years, but it was the alchemist who drove him under his spell.

Thinking was usually impossible for the Brighold, but these particular thoughts would not go away. He sensed rather than thought about anything. The voices never ceased, even since his awakening, but now they were demanding, ordering him to his trail of destruction. They were relentless and insisted he did as he was told, pounding it into his stone soul with their persistent demands.

The feeling of being comfortable in his coffin came back to him. Over the years of his long sleep he had become used to it, and missed its company and its surroundings in the chamber. No one had disturbed his sleep until the first man came. Ah yes, he sensed, I have enemies. Those who sent me to the long death in the chamber must have hated me enough to do it. He knew they existed in history now. They were a figment of a bygone age and it no longer mattered any more.

Now the voices echoed through his senses, still demanding and insisting, but with an increase in the urgency of the tone. The commands came through, describing each obstacle to overcome or to avoid. The demands crackled in his senses, but steered him clear of many objects when they were presented, many dangerous to the stone man, like projections that reached out to do him great harm, or holes into which he could fall, but most of all any fires that might swiftly reduce him to a cinder. His skin might resist fire, but they could not be certain.

Now the Brighold was in motion again. His naked stone feet thudded on the hard surface of the tarmac, but where it was pure earth and likely to be soft, he made deep footprints in the surface of the mud and regularly slewed each step. The great weight of him drove hard into the ground and crushed all stones deeper into it. Any small animals in his way were immediately obliterated or unknowingly pushed into nothingness beneath the stone feet.

Slowly the village fell back and the countryside took over. With Tolmaar's insistent tone of command resounding like a tolling bell in the Brighold's senses, the mighty giant tramped up a weed-infested hill and vanished into a belt of misty forest.

Tillus the humpbacked dwarf materialised in the graveyard just as the two scientists were leaving, crashing the two gates together in their wake. Meary, realising he was hungry, had suggested breaking for a quick meal, something that had escaped Hollis with all the excitement taking place down below. He also realised he was ravenous and wholeheartedly concurred as they headed for the dining room.

Ever hopeful, Tillus, with the ability to vanish at will, shadowed the two men grinning evilly as he recalled his master's orders to report wherever they went. The two men finished up in the dining room of the hotel where they stayed. Both were ravenous after finding their appetites and at once tucked into their plates of steaming food.

Ever ready to please his master, the dwarf appeared in view in the main street of the village. A little girl passed him by and gazed at his hump with apprehension. She eyed the dwarf and gave him a half-hearted smile. The child was about the same height as the dwarf, but the hump seemed to bother her. She had never seen one before, but it seemed to add to the child's fascination. The attraction was so great it urged the girl to speak.

"Why are you staring at the hotel window, mister?"

The dwarf decided to ignore her and continue his vigil at the hotel window. The child persisted. "What's your name? You look funny."

The dwarf replied in his language. A crowd was beginning to form about them, attracted by the guttural utterances of the dwarf, and his goatee beard.

"Who are you, mister, what are you doing with this child? What are you looking into the window for? You look like you're something to do with the monster terrorising the village,' a man said.

Tillus regarded the man and answered in the only way available to him – he began to vanish. The bearded man stepped back in amazement, pulling the child away from the dwarf in fright. The crowd was getting bigger; it was also getting uglier. As the dwarf went through the phases of vanishing, two or three people grabbed the child with outstretched fingers, pulling her away from the dwarf in the process. Before their astonished eyes the humpbacked dwarf, in the disappearance stage, was held by the first man, who grabbed him and held a part of Tillus that had gone. The struggled with something, but he held almost nothing. The dwarf was in the forth dimension, but held in the third dimension by the man.

Tillus shoved and pulled, but it was proving to be hopeless. He was lost in the cosmos, anchored by the restraining clutches of the bearded man. However, this was soon added to as other members of the crowd helped the man out by grabbing hold of the remains of the devolvement and hanging on tight. Now the young girl, the object of their anger, was shoved to the rear, forgotten in the general turmoil of the incident.

Hollis speared a juicy sausage on the end of his fork and delicately cut off the end. They were in the front dining room of the hotel and were able to hear the cries of alarm of the crowd as they tussled with the dwarf.

Meary and Hollis appeared, curious to locate the cause of the hubbub. They saw what amounted to a pack of hysterical people trying to hold on to the vanishing dwarf. The sudden apparition disturbed the tenacity of the crowd, so they let go and, consequently, the humpbacked dwarf finished what he had been doing and completed the disappearing act.

For their part, the scientists heard what had happened, but seriously doubted what the crowd was saying, and returned to their meal. Tillus was relieved by the opportune diversion of the two men and, hiding behind the cloak of invisibility, skulked in a nearby alleyway. Meary and Hollis were not aware of the dwarf because of their ignorance of what had previously transpired in the chamber. They would not have eaten so heartily had they known of the dwarf and his closeness to them. Finally they pushed their plates away as their hunger was assuaged.

"A fine meal," Hollis remarked, giving a gentle burp behind closed fingers and smiling at the older man.

Meary returned the smile and spooned sugar into his cup. The younger man broached the subject of the Brighold.

"I wonder where he is now at this very minute," he said, not knowing of the incident with the rocket launcher.

"No doubt causing some sort of mayhem, I suppose," returned Meary, stirring his tea. "We must involve the military, more so now. We must use its expertise in fighting the Brighold and his friends down below. This must be our first priority."

"But it must be remembered where it all began," Hollis interjected, speaking softly. "The king at the time was to blame for all the things that befell the stone man."

"Yes, I agree that we must not forget where it all began; with the instigation of the king. He must bear the initial responsibility, but the cause of most of the woe and misery must lie at the door of the alchemist, Tolmaar. He must be responsible for the Brighold and his killing of the people."

Some time later Hollis arose from the table to have a shave, and while he was absent Meary contacted the police by phone.

"I suppose you don't know of the incident with the military?"

Meary confessed his ignorance of the skirmish and was appalled to hear of the soldiers' fate.

"It is getting more serious by the day," he said, "but what can we do to fight back? Every time we try something Tolmaar gets around it by using the Brighold's violence or his own cunning contrivance."

Inspector Harding was not convinced.

"Can't we do something like filling the chamber with water or something similar to flush him out?"

Meary laughed at the policeman's ignorance.

"You can't flush out witchcraft like you would a drainpipe. The forces of the Devil will soon overcome your puny efforts to fight him. The chamber must be preserved even for the fact that it is a burial place for the stone man and his master, Tolmaar."

"You are advocating disaster on a grand scale," Harding exploded, breathing hard into the phone. "He is homicidal and dangerous. If we don't stop the Brighold he will finish us all. Right now we all know what kind of evil Tolmaar is planning, what sort of mayhem he has in store for the stone giant to perpetrate. He is a public menace and must be stopped before it is too late. We must stop him while he is out of his bolt-hole."

"You have no idea what kind of monster is unleashed,"

Meary stormed. "It is not some sort of King Kong running riot, but a ghost of the past, a stone man that looks like it is supernatural and possessed with enormous powers of strength and durability that will make the average male pall. You are right he *will* destroy us all if he is not brought to book."

"And pray tell me how we are going to beat this monster?" enquired the inspector sarcastically.

"If he is supernatural and out of the past, he will be invincible because he no longer exists. If he no longer lives he is dead to the world, in a manner of speaking. He should by rights have died out in the region and time into which he was born, but by a quirk of nature or fate, or even the supernatural, he survived to terrorise the people of the village." Meary, puffed with the effort of explaining, added, "And now he is here to do the bidding of a greater catastrophe to hit the human race than has ever been imagined. Tolmaar, the master sorcerer under Lucifer, the major wizard alchemist and enchanter, has jurisdiction over his former victim. That much I do know because he told me so. He outlined his ambitions to rule the world and the human race. He is very serious in what he wants and with the help of Lucifer will do as he says he will."

"Lucifer indeed," sneered the inspector. "You expect me to believe all this tomfoolery? It's probably a madman on the rampage, ready to kill and do as much damage as possible before he is caught. I'll admit he is a *huge* maniac with the amount of damage he has caused to the military, but in the end he will be caught or restrained and locked up securely."

Meary put down the receiver with a sigh and shook his head at it, remarking:

"If it is left to you we will soon be dead"

Within a few minutes Hollis returned and joined Meary at the table.

"I have been talking to the inspector of police," Meary said, with a slight smile on his face. "It seems he does not share our belief in the Brighold's fate. I tried to convince him otherwise, but you know what the police are for having their own way." He sighed and showed his teeth in a broader smile. "I was going to tell him about the session I had with Tolmaar when I argued with him to save Bill. It was then I saw something in the chamber that really startled me."

Hollis was following the older man's words with baited breath.

"What did you see there?" he questioned.

"You are not going to believe this, Hollis, I can hardly believe it myself. Tolmaar was cast in the light of his own making. The fiend was well lit, but to my dying day I will be able to swear he had no shadow!"

CHAPTER FIFTEEN

Outside in the alleyway the dwarf paced up and down in his undetectable state, gnashing a set of stunted teeth as he did so. He wanted urgently to follow his master's orders, but even with the cloak of invisibility he was finding the going hard. The little girl and the crowd had seriously undermined his personal capability and it rankled his determination to succeed for the master and Lucifer. He was determined to follow orders to the letter to shadow the two scientists to the best of his ability, which is why he waited for them to emerge from the hotel.

Tillus had to wait for another two hours for this to happen, still invisible and impatient to be off. He was glad he waited when he heard of the mode of conduct the pair of scientists were planning.

Meary consulted a colleague of his who had rented a building in the village. Very soon the two men were outside the premises knocking and banging on the oaken door.

"Hello Brian," Meary greeted the newcomer.

Brian Dunne, an expert in the ancient art of black magic, led the way into his neat lounge and after pouring out a few drinks addressed Meary.

"Well, I was waiting for you to come and see me before I continued with my experiments."

Hollis sipped the Scotch and water, and listened to the exchange of compliments and well-wishing the friends were making, then things became serious as the conversation got around to the question in hand.

"If I can explain," Dunne said, addressing the two men. "Yes, I have always been interested in the occult and all things concerning it. That is why I have been working hard to perfect an invention that I'm sure will have a big impact on your work in the burial chamber."

"Yes, I did hear of your invention, but the description was a bit hazy."

"Can you give us some idea what the invention is capable of?" Meary questioned.

"Come with me, gentlemen," Dunne said, rising from his chair.

They followed him into his front parlour where he stood before something hidden beneath a blanket. He whipped the covering away to reveal the object and the invention, pressing a lever on the machine. It glowed with a yellow light that intensified with each passing second. Dunne fiddled further with more knobs, and the light grew brighter and became a red one that he trained on the opposite wall, getting brighter as it grew stronger.

As they watched, the wall began to peel away and transpose into the outside street and all that was going on there. Passing people, some on bikes, flew by as did cars and other assorted vehicles. Some were just walking past in pursuit of their daily lives, while a trio of talking and laughing women lounged at the corner of the street. All this was viewed through the wall, which the machine was faithfully reproducing in detail, colour and content.

Meary could hardly believe his eyes or ears and turned to Dunne with all the enthusiasm he was experiencing, shaking his hand with a degree of warmth he was hardly able to conceal.

"Capital, Brian, you have outshone your place at school with your timely invention. As usual you have brought forth something that will not only aid us in our fight against evil, but ensure that we see what is happening in the chamber as it unfolds."

Hollis was astounded by the invention and could not fully see how the machine was capable of penetrating bricks and mortar, but with the evidence his eyes brought to bear the invention showed it was fully workable and capable of doing the job.

"A wonderful invention indeed," he enthused, shaking the delighted Dunne by the hand and smiling happily. "I must endorse what my colleague said and congratulate you on your invention. It will help us enormously in our fight against the madman, Tolmaar."

The ears of the dwarf nearly fell off in surprise. He was listening, hidden by his invisibility, and saw the demonstration of the machine and its far-reaching qualities. He was appalled by the magnitude of its potential and vowed to tell his master.

The inventor was switching off the machine and the light beam was beginning to fail. The wall returned to normality and the picture faded. Before they left, the two scientists spoke of the enormous help they were expecting from the invention and would be delighted if Dunne would use his machine in helping them achieve their aim. To their joy he accepted the invitation and agreed to use it in the fight against the alchemist and his ally, Lucifer.

The humpbacked dwarf heard and saw all that had taken place and was in a quandary as to what to do. He had two choices; to go back to Tolmaar and report his discovery, or continue following the two scientists. He chose the latter a little way from them.

Inspector Harding was again entering his office with the intention of bringing the Brighold episode to a close. The facts of life aired by the scientist, Meary, had a prickle of self-inadequacy in their meaning. That meaning had been directed at him. It hurt after all those years of service to the community, notwithstanding the fact that he was well paid for his services. He had a grand house on the edge of the village and all the accoutrements befitting his position. He had a young and healthy wife who had given him two lovely children. What had he to do with running all over the village to apprehend a monster? Leave it to his underlings to deal with, let them earn their pay by capturing the stone man.

He slid into his state financed car and let in the clutch. He was looking forward to a leisurely drive home and the usual kiss and cuddle with his wife. Slow but sure was his motto. He applied this criterion to most of the things he did.

The house came into view as it always did and he throttled back to take it all in. He edged the car to a step at the gateway, vaguely disturbed by the unusual silence of the house and the lack of activity in the garden. He pulled on the handbrake, switching off the engine–then it began; a nagging fear that started in the pit of his stomach and slowly radiated to his brain. The fear was like a spider of alarm that spun a web of dread through his vitals and into his nervous system.

He opened the front door and fell over a half-full clothes basket. The clothes were stained with coagulated blood and lacerated skin. Harding yelled at the sight and, bracing himself, ran into the front room. He screamed at the sight of the dismembered body of his wife lying in a huge pool of drying blood. He was spared any more shocks because he dropped to the floor.

Detective Inspector Horace Lee was informed of the murder of his chief's wife and immediately suspected the Brighold. The stone man had been seen in the vicinity by four frightened neighbours, who had barricaded themselves into their houses and would not come out.

The army, after its mauling at the hands of the Brighold, ringed the village with a wall of armoured cars and rifle-carrying soldiers, but now a colonel commanded the unit and a machine gun equipped captain was the second in command. Lee tried to convince the colonel that the Brighold was responsible and would be long gone if he knew anything about the monster. The army refused to acknowledge it was the work of just one man, but the work of maniacs high on drugs. Lee shook his head at the obstinacy of the pair of khaki-clad officers and, after arguing for a full hour, left them to it.

Lee departed the scene at the house with lips tightly drawn, and went back to the station. He downed a couple of cups of tepid coffee and opened two letters before he noticed the leather bag resting on his desk. The bag was accompanied by a brown envelope containing a note. The note described an assortment of ashes and powders as an elixir for which the Brighold was searching. The note said it was found by the murdered man, Lund. The letter continued that Meary had further said Lund had been experimenting on them and had found one strange element that had unusual properties when mixed with other ingredients.

Lee read the letter and put it in a drawer. He immediately forgot about it and turned to other more important issues. Uppermost in his mind was the Brighold and his fight against the community. Lee doubted whether he knew he was doing these terrible things without instruction. If he was responsible he must be brought to book without further delay, but how do you reign in a monster? Where do you start? Lee wondered vaguely. What resources do you need and how much will it all cost? The queries seemed to mount up as he thought. The question of prophesying where he would strike next occupied his mind, but the Devil himself, where was he placed in the order of things? What were the astronomical odds in beating him?

Lee was only too well aware of his own limitations against the power unleashed by the nefarious subterranean duo pulling the strings. It will be a case of gritting your teeth and doing your job, Lee said to himself.

"The monster will be caught and jailed," he mumbled out loud to convince himself. "Today will be the exception. I'll finish him for good if its the last thing I do. No one is above the law because the law is order and *must* be maintained."

The tea lady with her tea urn and cups and saucers gave him a look of curiosity as the detective mumbled to himself. She gave him another look after her enquiry as to if he wanted sugar.

"You slimming or something?"

"No thanks, I've got to watch my figure, try one of the others."

As she moved away he watched her serve other people with their wants. He picked up a charge sheet and sat there, tapping the rolled end on the edge of his desk. He was thinking furiously, crossing from one thought to another trying to push several ideas into one and getting nowhere. He was in the throes of indecision when a knock sounded on the glass door, interrupting his chain of thought.

"Come in," he said, dropping the sheet onto the desk.

The door opened to admit Meary and Hollis. The two scientists stood there awkwardly until the older man spoke.

"Are you the detective in charge?" he enquired, eyeing the policeman. "Did you get my note?"

"What note is that, what note are you talking about?"

Meary drew in a deep lungful of air before answering.

"The bag with the ashes and the powders, I left it on the sergeant's desk. I was hoping he gave it to you to look after."

Lee pulled open the desk drawer and plumped the bag onto the desk before him.

"What's it all about?" he asked, nodding at the bag.

"What have all these ashes and powders to do with the Brighold?"

Meary inhaled another big gasp.

"It may hold the key to why he was incarcerated in the tomb."

"I heard he was buried because the alchemist made a mistake," the policeman said dryly.

Meary eyed his companion standing beside him.

"There were a lot of mistakes made," he said slowly. "From his king to his master, Tolmaar, who both underestimated fate. They were both wrong about the sickness that eventually killed them both."

In his invisible guise, Tillus, the humpbacked dwarf, heard everything that was being said. He understood the English language, although not being able to speak it. He saw everything as well. His eyes gleamed as he caught sight of the bag. He noticed from where the detective had brought forth the bag and the letter. The master will be pleased with my success with his orders to follow the two scientists, he thought in a grim inner voice.

The elder of the two men was speaking again.

"My friend, Lund, was conducting an experiment on the compound in the bag. He found something unusual in the make-up, but we cannot find his notes. Until we do, it will just be an incomplete experiment."

Lee placed the bag and the note back into the drawer, relocking it. He put the key back into his pocket.

"I'll take care of it until there is some sort of conclusion to the experiment," he said.

The dwarf watched the two scientists exit through the glass doorway. He was still eyeing the drawer until he remembered his master's ruling to follow them at all times, so dutifully complied with his wish.

Tolmaar watched the progress of the dwarf with satisfaction. The dream of conquering the world was well on course. Domination will soon be mine, he mused. Those interfering scientists will be no more. He laughed in the face of failure, cursing them for their meddling, which was obstructing his dreams for the earth. The human race will die out, he raged to himself. Every single trace of its influence on the earth will cease. Everything it achieved or did not do will be forgotten. The memory of its existence will be removed from the people's brains, until the fateful day when it will eventually and entirely end.

That day, that eventful day, would come if he, Tolmaar, had anything to do with it. The world would be peopled by his animals, from the lowly slug to the wriggling worm. The earth would be dominated by the netherworld and its occupants. Vicious snakes, hissing and venomous, would slither over hill and dale in their millions. Creeping spiders, armed with deadly bites and stings, would populate the world, while sadistic scorpions with deathly stabs would scuttle and scurry after the human beings, who would eventually be gone forever.

Tolmaar relished ultimate power. His dreams of dominance did not include the Devil, although he had played a part in getting it for Tolmaar. He was just a pawn in the grand design of the master wizard, which did not include any other part. Most of all, the alchemist would vacate the netherworld and its limitations. He had had his fill in pandering to Lucifer and his world of goblins and hideous imps. He wanted more – he wanted the universe with all its wonders and desires. The enslavement of the human race was just a beginning of his wish for self-importance, although it was a start. He was aware it was the ultimate of what he was seeking, for he meant to take over the role of supreme being, not for him the second place taken by Satan and his specialist devices. He wanted Heaven and all it contained.

He knew it was a dangerous game he was playing, but during his years of incarceration he vowed it was the work of the Lord who put him where he was. The Devil had hardly a role in the outcome, but he was responsible in a small way though. In the end he did provide scope for the Lord to act in his demise and, being Tolmaar, he was unable to forgive and forget the incident.

Tolmaar liked being a wizard. He had all the privileges designed for his rank and none of its disadvantages. He was at liberty to cause mayhem and misery on the earth plane, if only he was able to get there. Lucifer was free to roam the entire planet at will, but he was put off by the Lord, who allowed him to wander at will. Lucifer was being contained and he was aware of it, but it seemed to satisfy him. Not so Tolmaar, he was another matter entirely. Although hundreds of years old, they were as fleeting as the morning mist and hardly there for all eternity, he was able to outwit divine providence and present a different slant on the situation, inasmuch as he was overlooked in the general run of things.

He was in the bowels of the earth and ever ready and willing to do things his way, but was never called on by the Lord to deliver a verdict of any kind.

Now Tolmaar wanted his due. He was tired of waiting for eternity and a day, and wanted a change without delay. He was sick of waiting for his eventual emergence and tired of marking time for his due. He wanted action, and action without delay. That is when the gravedigger shook him out of his fantasy and into doing something of which he had been dreaming for the past hundreds of years. The episode with the Brighold was unfortunate for the stone man, but fortunate for him. He used him to procure his fulfilment of his rightful place in destiny. It was ill fated for the Brighold to be included in his big dream, but good luck in his realisation of his ultimate place. He, Tolmaar, needed someone to battle the human race for existence and the Brighold fitted the bill. His murderous ways were the ideal foil to outfox the humans and keep them busy, providing a red herring to enable him to escape the police or the military.

Tolmaar was troubled by them. As he watched the play of things happening to the Brighold and the dwarf, he saw things were not as they seemed to be. He was only able to partially see the invention that Dunne had brought forth, but it eluded his senses to understand how it worked, and that worried him. The years in the chamber were having an effect on his powers and observation, and that troubled him too.

He yearned for freedom and the choice of the upper world or the chamber. He really wondered what the humans saw in the lightness of the sky each day. Although he wanted the world it would include night and day, and if it also encompassed perpetual night he would be more than delighted. Not for him the green grass of summer or the white coldness of a snowy day in deep winter. The cold dark of the chamber suited his purpose and design for now. It would be another thing to experience the thunder and lightning that were becoming the norm since the opening of the entrance to the tomb.

In his mind's eye he watched the movements of the dwarf and read his thoughts. The little man was running the events of the day through his mind. The machine that Dunne had invented was occupying his mind. He ran through the sequence of events until it got to the scene where the wall peeled away. It was easy to assume Tillus did not understand how the machine worked. He was at odds to see how a section of the wall could be missing. It further confused him that he was able to see living and talking people through bricks and mortar. The brain of the dwarf could not take it all in and mentally shut it out of his mind and vision, simply by closing his eyes.

Tillus was still following the two men and listening to their conversation as they walked along. They were unaware of his presence due to his invisibility, thinking they were alone. The dwarf thought Tolmaar had his interests at heart, and he had, but not in the way the dwarf envisaged. Tillus had great faith in the wizard and trusted him to make things right for him. Of course anything done by Tolmaar had strings attached. The wizard, entirely selfish, had a plan, but it would succeed if the dwarf's note if it was carried out to the letter. Tillus laughed to himself to disguise his nervousness. He needed someone with Tolmaar's determination to win the day. Under the wizard he had all the will to win, in fact he wanted the sorcerer to win in all circumstances, at all stages, not in part, but every time.

Tillus stepped on a pebble and stumbled in mid-stride. Hollis heard the sound and looked back. He had a funny feeling they were being followed, but saw nobody. The two men were on their way back to the graveyard.

Tolmaar, with his powers, saw everything. He controlled the dwarf and in turn, the Brighold, but they were both busy. The wizard was interested in the two men, and spoke into the ear of the dwarf.

"Watch them, watch them well, especially the older man. I do not trust him to make the right moves. He will conform one minute and then move at a tangent. He is not to be depended on, so watch him very closely."

The dwarf listened to the voice as it continued.

"Trust not the young one, the one called Hollis. He has not the knowledge of Meary, the older man, but he has courage enough to call on if needed."

After the incident with the pebble, the dwarf hung well back, walking twenty yards or so to the rear, just enough to avoid being found out, but sufficient to dispel their fears of being overheard. Meary deeply regretted not having a car being made available to him, but in doing so relished in the freedom the walk gave him. Within minutes the gates of the cemetery drew close.

"Wonder what has been happening," Meary said, looking for anything that might alter the scope of his recollection of the graveyard, and getting nothing.

"All is quiet as far as I can see," Hollis had to agree.

The graveyard was as before and showed no changes that they could ascertain. The collection of leaning gravestones was still leaning, the gates still emitted their customary whine of protest at their entry and it still showed its customary air of solitude and suspense.

Tolmaar was aware of their return. He was also aware of the dwarf's proximity to them. He wanted to hear of the little man's version of events, and waited as he drew himself up and appeared before him.

What did you discover about the humans? he demanded.

Tillus managed to break into a thin laugh.

"About them, very little," he answered, "but I saw the effect the invention of the man known as Dunne had on them."

Tolmaar pooh-poohed the effect it was having on the little man by scoffing at the idea.

It's silly and needs to be thoroughly tested by the inventor.

Tillus kept his silence about the importance of the invention and instead decided to humour the wizard.

"Oh, master, they had a leather bag containing the Brighold's release ashes. It is in the policeman's drawer. I was tempted to steal it, but I waited for your orders."

Tolmaar walked up and down, deep in thought. He was in quandary about searching for the solution to the Brighold's salvation. He had no doubt he could find a cure, but if he did this he was without an ally. The Brighold, with his murderous ways, provided a cover and foil to frustrate his enemies. Tolmaar was very aware that the humans would fight back. Even now the military was in the process of making life difficult for the Brighold. They were shadowing him in his forays, while making it harder for him to do his speciality – plain murder.

Tolmaar depended on him if he was to rule the universe.

You did well, Tillus. The invention that the man Dunne, used must be destroyed. You will find it and eradicate it. That is your task, Tillus. Go now, find it and destroy it, is that clear?

The dwarf nodded in agreement. He clearly wanted to please his master and looked for ways to agree with him.

"I will obey, oh master. I will find it and destroy the machine."

Do not harm the man Dunne, for he will help my overall plan for world domination. I will use him to think up greater machines for me. Now go!

The dwarf, cringing before the wizard, uttered a cry of alarm and vanished into invisibility. Behind him, Tolmaar was wearing a smile of satisfaction at the way events were shaping. He would eventually welcome world and universal domination, but he must not get complacent and expect too much of his servants; their extinction would come soon enough. Right now he must control everything. He concentrated and brought the figure of the Brighold into focus.

The stone giant was there immobile in a flock of sheep, hands clasped to his sides, dripping with blood. He had just killed a lamb and with legs slightly apart, straddled the corpse. In the stone man's mind the wizard saw he was undecided what to do with the dead body. Tolmaar also saw another side to his nature as well. He saw unwanted compassion for the animal. Tolmaar did not want the pity and whispered into the stone brain to disregard his alien feelings and do as he was ordered. The wizard urged him to go on, but still he hesitated. The Brighold heard the commands, but still did not respond to the power.

Tolmaar raised the timbre of his commands and waited for the Brighold to comply. Slowly, reluctantly, the stone man's mini revolt was over and he strode away, hands clenched to his sides. However, when Tolmaar repeated his commands in the thoughts of the stone man he was immediately glad to see the immense figure swing into action. The frightened sheep scattered out of his path, bleating with terror as he began to walk towards them.

The big figure splashed through a small stream that coursed through his big fingers, washing the lamb's blood from his dangling digits, which, mixing with the bits of gore, was washed away on the flow. In the pathways of chemicals that passed for arteries in the make-up of the Brighold, a slight tremor of compassion awakened in his breast and filled him with a new feeling of remorse and pity. Tolmaar now sensed revolt. The giant was showing defiance and that spelled disaster in the eyes of the wizard. He wanted immediate response and conformity from the Brighold, not dissent. He wanted blind obedience to every demand directed at him.

Tolmaar loved orderly things, where his underlings did everything they were ordered to do without question. He was in command, and woe betide the entity that tried to usurp his authority, for it would feel his wrath whenever it occurred. Tolmaar never understood pity. It just amounted to animosity of the highest order, a non-conformist, a traitor to the extreme.

He watched the Brighold tramping through a thick hedge, pushing the dense growth away with massive hands that bent the thorns aside as matchwood. He ripped up the loaded branches with the greatest of ease, his great footprints filling with muddy water whenever he walked through small streams.

The great legs and arms carved a path through deep water, sometimes even enveloping the huge figure as the depth proved to be too much for his immense bulk. In doing so he emerged from the deepest stream, dark water running from his enormous head and streaming down his naked body.

Lucifer regarded the wizard with narrowed eyes. He viewed the content of the man with deep suspicion. The netherworld was filled with others of his calibre. They all harboured some sort of ambition to get back to the upper world where they all, without exception, wanted some sort of hold over the main occupants, the humans. Until now they had all ended with the usual failure to his name.

Tolmaar was another matter entirely, for he had help with his ambition. The Brighold was his slave and did his bidding. He was currently engaged in clearing the village of humans by murdering them. Anyone or anything he met he killed, but even with this it would take years for him to make even a dent in the enormous human population with the vastness of its growth since the dawn of man's inception on the earth plane. They were that numerous. That suited Lucifer, for he had forever to succeed, and waited for the wizard to end his self-endowed destiny.

The wizard gathered his friends around him. Now he had the constrained friendship of the humpbacked dwarf on which to rely, but Tillus had been used against his will and was proving unreliable due to his fright of the wizard. The little man would only be genuine if the wizard was watching. The dwarf was afraid Tolmaar had some unknown and unseen end for him if he refused him anything. He was terrified of him and of what dark ends he could produce if pushed.

Lucifer gazed into his crystal ball and wondered if the wizard really thought he was good enough to inherit the earth, never mind the universe. To show his contempt, the divine power neither interfered in his manifestations nor showed any interest if he was aware of it. Lucifer laughed at his omissions of events. Tolmaar took everything for granted and thought the best was yet to come. He had a great desire to take what the world had to offer with nothing in return. If he thought it was so, the awakening would be astounding to say the least.

Nearby, a crestfallen dwarf was filled with dread. The two scientists and the inventor, Dunne, were in the act of setting up the invention. Hollis was listening to the insistent Dunne, who was determined the machine must be used properly.

"It must be used in *this* way if you want the best out of it," he said, tapping a series of glass tubes with the stem of his pipe to emphasise his point. "The idea of looking into the cavern is to reveal what it contains. All that goes on below will be made known to you if you use it the right way."

The dwarf looked on in dismay, not sure of executing the orders that Tolmaar had given him, and undecided about how the actual destruction of the machine would be carried out. He was also fuming because the men had managed to bring the machine to the cemetery so quickly. He was also wracking his brain to think of what he was going to do to destroy the thing. Now they were in the act of plugging in an electric line to fuel the invention. Tillus had visions of turning off the current, if he knew how. He seemed to imagine the cable was a pipe in the manner of a water pipe, having no knowledge of electricity or its potential. He dare not return to Tolmaar and report failure. He had strict orders to stop it by destroying it.

Tillus watched the three men. The machine with all its different coloured wires and glass tubes glowed with green incandescent light, emitting a series of spitting sparks and shooting power streaks that squeaked with a loud hum and squeal. Other squeals were pitched from high to low in rapid succession. The dwarf suddenly saw the muddy spade that had been used recently. He resolved to stop the machine in the only way of which he was capable and, approaching the spade, gripped it in his invisible state.

He waited for the men to be fully immersed in what they were doing, crept up behind them and raised the spade high into the air, waiting for an opportunity and trying not to arouse them too much at the interruption. The three men were standing with their backs towards him and did not see or hear the heavy, mud-encrusted implement lift of its own accord. Tillus held the spade away from their combined gaze and at the same time brought it down on the cable with a heavy thump. Immediately the screen of the machine went black and emitted a blinding flash. The electric current travelled up the handle of the metal spade and entered the flesh of the dwarf. Tillus gave a howl of agony and let the spade fall, dropping his invisibility with the severity of the shock.

Before their captured gaze, the humpbacked dwarf was revealed in all of his glory, writhing on the ground with all the agony electric power can muster. With a look of unified horror on their faces they saw all that had taken place. The humped back of the dwarf was evident, as were the smouldering blackened hands of the little man, with the distressing cries of the dwarf echoing through the graveyard, calling their full attention to his plight.

"What in hell have we got here?" asked the surprised Hollis.

The dwarf, seeing his disguise was discovered and in agony at the results of the electricity burns, gazed in mortification at the trio while rubbing his hands together in acute pain The older scientist, Meary, after the initial shock caused by the flash of electricity, gazed in dismay as the screen faded into black and he heard Dunne bemoaning the fact that the dwarf had caused untold damage to the machine.

"He has *ruined* it! It will be weeks before I can repair the damage to it."

The three men, goggle eyed and gobsmacked at the intervention of the dwarf, stared at the apparition lying on the ground in dismay, causing Meary to cry out in wonder.

"Where on earth did he come from?"

The dwarf, seeing the lie of the land and how the shape of things were progressing, wrung both hands together, trying to rub the life back into them. He was calling on their sympathy, hoping they would view his actions as merely a prank. He concentrated, trying to invoke the invisibility shield. He breathed in closing his eyes then opened them again to see three pairs of eyes still regarding him with a mixture of horror and amazement.

"Tolmaar's work, I'll be bound," grated Hollis. "What is this thing that's lying on the ground?"

He stepped forwards to get a better view. The dwarf, with hideous hump exposed, jumped back in fright, uttering vile threats. Dunne made a grab for him and picked up the spade to arm himself. The scene began to take on a threatening attitude as the three men surrounded the fallen dwarf, preventing him from producing any alternative course, then Tolmaar came to the rescue. Billowing green dust poured from the cavern and covered the cringing figure of the dwarf, only this time the central figure who seemed to be controlling it was the white-frocked Bill.

"I will protect Tillus from harm," he intoned. "You must not do him any injury. The master has the power to wish you great harm should you do otherwise. You must release his servant and let him return to his rightful place in the cavern."

The dwarf regained his feet and stood beside the figure of the boy. They waited at the cavern's entrance, wreathed in green dust that swirled and eddied in a vortex of whirling wind.

"So Tolmaar has beaten us again," rasped Meary, his voice heavy with emotion. "Bill is certainly in that devil's grasp. It will take a miracle to wrest him from the wizard's clutches." He turned to the downcast Dunne. "Can you not get the machine working again to see if you can help the boy?"

Dunne shook his head after giving it a cursory inspection.

"I cannot see what has happened," he said in a crestfallen voice. "The surge of power that shot through the coils has caused a serious short in the valve system. It might be crucial or superficial, only time will tell. That is all I can say."

Meary inhaled a big gasp of air to show his displeasure.

"Back to square one again," he said. "Tolmaar forestalls us at every turn. It looks like we are cursed with bad luck no matter how we turn," he said quietly.

Hollis creased a frown on his forehead and followed the progress of the green cloud that was enveloping Bill and the dwarf.

Tolmaar saw the whole scene as it unfolded and laughed out loud. Everything was falling into place as he had predicted. Soon the ultimate would happen and the earth would open to admit the wizard, then the world would his to do with as he liked, but he would be satisfied with the enslavement of the human race – for starters. The universe would come later, but it would come, no matter whom it hurt. He must be patient and cool his ardour, now and forever, if he was to net the results he wanted. He was hungry for Heaven's secrets, so much so he was feeling magnanimous towards the dwarf and struck him from his thoughts of revenge.

The magnitude of his aspirations never ceased to amaze the watching Tillus. After the episode with the invention he was quaking in his boots, waiting for the eventual punishment to be administered. He hoped the new boy, Bill, would be able to convince the wizard his failure to destroy the invention was none of his making, but just a part fate had in taking a share of the blame.

The boy had hopes as well. He had only helped the dwarf on the wizard's orders and only in a half-hearted way, for he was still an apprentice and under the spell of the master, who worked great magic and did such wondrous things. Bill's memory of events in the earth plane was fading fast. The snatches of remembrance that intermittently occurred in his memory barely registered at all now. The words of the wizard were gaining ascension with each passing day. Tolmaar had done his work well and the blotting out of all recognition of his life on earth was done, but even so, snapshots of his mother still vaguely came into his mind. It was difficult to imagine her voice with any assurance. Bill was almost sure the voice of his natural mother was the voice of Tolmaar. He was too confused to recall it. The memory of his mother's voice and that of Tolmaar seemed to fuse into one in the boy's mind, further adding to the discord in his overtaxed brain. Now Bill turned more and more to the commands that echoed increasingly through his head until any vestige of his mother's memory gradually faded into the background.

Meary was a different matter though. He was associated with the chamber and what had taken place there. The memory of the youth was alive with happenings between the older man and himself. Tolmaar won each argument with the magnitude and power of his vocal chords and various tricks that had the effect of unnerving Meary until he was unsure of himself.

Tolmaar was master of all he produced in the chamber, but he had yet to fully understand the mind of man. Meary was the product of countless aeons of human imitations that had been repeated, without exception, in the same mould since the inception of humanity. He had millions of years on which to fall back, all in the same vein and the same mind to control his make-up. Tolmaar had none of these feelings because his service to the ages beneath the surface of the earth was without precedent, therefore, he was without knowledge of what had transpired during the years of his incarceration in the chamber. He had no idea of what the ordinary human beings felt or of what they were composed.

Lucifer was different. With his recognition of human failings as normal, he was able to grasp more than the wizard was able or capable of. Tolmaar's inherent failure was that he did not understand humanity, or want to. It was a major failing to fall ignorance to, and one he should correct if he wished to realise his ambitions. In some small measure he was hoping to assimilate the human side of the youth to do this part of nature and conform. He was aware the boy had no knowledge of his intention to use him as a foil to achieve his nefarious ends, but at his tender age it meant very little for him to fully understand that his meaning was threatened. He was unaware of Tolmaar's plan for his future life in the cavern.

The stone man was nearing the encampment just as daylight arrived. The circle of tents that encompassed the military line inwardly surrounded the motor pool, shielding them from attack, should it come. All was relatively quiet as the soldiers slept, the only sounds to be heard being a stray cat that had decided to add its cries to the sound of snores that came from various tents.

A solitary guard, half-asleep himself, heard the approach of the Brighold, but was unable to fully appreciate his death when the huge figure of the stone man sliced off his head with one vicious swipe of his massive arm.

CHAPTER SIXTEEN

For the space of one minute the stone monster paused, the voice of Tolmaar ringing in his subconscious. Standing there, uncertain of what he was doing, a form of unconscious pity welled up in his stone mind.

He looked down at the headless body, still jerking with the life that would soon be extinct, and regarded the head. The blood still coursed slowly from ruptured arteries, and congealed in the morning air, steaming and rapidly cooling as it coagulated. The hardening blood hung in drips and dried into thick black strings before him.

The Brighold was matted with old blood that pitted his fingernails and stained his hands to a dirty brown. The new blood further added to the stain, giving him a look of extreme horror. In his mind's eye he saw the new redness, trying to gauge the full implication of the fresh blood and failing to understand why it should be so. Within himself he was sure that spilling blood was wrong, but he just became confused when he saw the result. Other factors came and went. The tones of the wizard shot around his stone mind, further compounding the confusion and adding to it when he thought the Brighold did something unintentionally.

Tolmaar really doubted whether the stone man had the ability to defy him, but he was not going to chance it ever happening. He resolved to test the giant while he was able, and whispered a command into his head. The Brighold stood stock still, bent over with his hands hanging before him, unmoving and regarding the guard's body. Tolmaar sensed another revolt, which were getting more frequent with each successive day. The strength needed to control him increased with intensity every day. It called for more energy from the wizard, which had the effect of draining it away. He knew he was in danger of losing control of the Brighold, his closest ally. He must not do that.

Tolmaar tried again and received a partial response. He was relieved when the stone man moved half-heartedly, then he tried again and spoke with authority. The giant straightened up, listening to his master's compelling voice, trying to do as he was ordered. The alchemist edged his words with firmness. He kept his temper so that he did not confuse him. He spoke softly, trying to instil a sense of loyalty between them by suggesting it would all be over soon and the rewards for them both would be never-ending and enduring. He laughed softly at the thought of the Brighold believing he was destined to be anything else but a stumbling stone shell with the likelihood of ever being anything other than a hideous stone gargantuan.

Tolmaar sneered at the thought and, as other things came into his mind, he drove into sight that the stone man would do as he was told and nothing more.

Now you do nothing more than you are told to do, he breathed into the Brighold's ear. *You will hear nothing but my voice. You will follow my dictate no matter what you hear.*

He waited for the words to sink in and watched the giant regain his height by straightening up. The stone man headed for the nearest tent and barged through the opening and the restraints by tearing them with his enormous legs and trampling them into the soft earth. He waded through sleeping men and a welter of blankets and other paraphernalia, trailing dying men and human parts that gathered around his stone legs in pools of gleaming gore.

The screams of the dying and mortally wounded soldiers shot into the early morning air. For awhile, as the massacre proceeded, the camp shook itself awake and listened to the howls of agony, then pandemonium was let loose and the camp became alive with wondering men, all in their pyjamas and listening to the screams.

The killing continued. The huge legs tramped through men like so many matchsticks. The weight of the stone giant trod men and equipment into the ground, the bloody imprint of his feet trailing clothing and other crushed objects, walking through the mixture of men and materials and out the other side.

Now some semblance of order was being gathered. Authority in the shape of non-commissioned officers rapidly began to take command. Bellowing sergeants screamed orders to the confused men and waited to follow what the officers had to do. Bleary eyed brass, in all sorts of undress, watched the second tent collapse under the weight of the giant. Crying men, mixed in the muddle of tent parts, puzzled them until the cause of their suffering became only too real.

The Brighold, running with blood and gore, came into sight. The hideous figure was bedecked with clothing tatters and came into their horrified gaze with alarming suddenness. The gigantic stone man stood there until he sensed their presence. He waited until Tolmaar saw them, and spoke into his mind. He was aware the leaders were the big men of the company of military men. Tolmaar urged the Brighold forwards and was pleased to see him respond to his orders.

The officers blanched and fell back, frightened of the stone figure and falling over each other to get away. The nearest, a tall captain who had managed to don his jacket with three metal pips on the shoulder, was the first to muster some sort of resistance, and died because of it. To his credit, he stood up to the immense figure, pulling his revolver and blazing at him until he ran out of bullets. He cursed as he triggered an empty chamber, and threw the gun at him. He might just as well have had a toy gun for all the good it brought him, for the heavy bullets just bounced off the thick stone coating of the giant and wheed into space

In answer to his attack on him, the stone man lifted him high into the morning air and threw him twenty feet or more, into a knot of gaping soldiers. The screaming waxed louder then, as terrified men fought to get out of the way of the monster, fighting and kicking to put some distance between themselves and the Brighold. He ignored them though. His trampling toes and great legs were already heading for the motor pool, shuffling through the remnants of the tents and scuttling soldiers as they desperately tried to avoid him. The din was growing louder with each passing minute. Howling men leaped over dead and dying comrades in their haste to get out of the way of the maniac.

Tolmaar listened to the tumult and guided him on to his next job. He tore the canvas canopies from various lorries and dropped them onto the grass. He lifted smaller vehicles from their axles and, using his massive strength, tipped them over onto their roofs, where they lay enmeshed into each other, wheels spinning with the force of the effort, crashing and grinding echoing around the village green.

Suddenly, amid all the screaming and cursing of the dead and dying, an unannounced lull came into being and the carnage came to a temporary halt. The stone man was waiting for Tolmaar to speak into his ear again, but the wizard was listening to the youth, Bill. The young man was gazing at the cavern wall, watching the amount of damage being enacted with great interest, and had seen the devastation of which the stone man was capable.

"Oh, great and powerful one," he gushed, "I have seen astonishing, terrible things happening today and I have wondered where I might get the power to do mighty things like this?"

Tolmaar, realising his ultimate wish was bearing fruit was sure, at long last, the youth was beginning to have faith in his ambition and would follow his ruling. The wizard had one more string to his bow with the assimilation of the boy to his way of thinking. Now his time to take his place in the order of things was coming to pass. His joy knew no bounds. His was the ambition that had no equal, nowhere in the universe yes, even Heaven with its final resting place for the human soul. Tolmaar had visions of usurping the divine power, but not yet, not just yet, but with the help of the youth who knew where fortune finally lay with its fickle ways and meandering luck?

Tolmaar saw something in the boy's face that drew him to try and induct him into his ways. It was obvious to the sorcerer from the outset. The boy had ways that needed to be drawn out and nurtured.

He had no known knowledge of the occult or of any of its magical properties, and it was extremely doubtful if he brooked any interest in the subject or had even thought it existed. Well, I will be his burning ambition now, thought Tolmaar. In his journey into the unknown he will be schooled without question. It will be hard and merit a lifetime of dedication for the boy, but it will be worth the hardship, for the rewards will be immeasurable. Yes, the boy will be useful to me, he mused, but it must start right away. The youth's observation recently was the fillip needed to fully assure his assimilation in its entirety.

I'm now sure you are beginning to see things more clearly, the wizard said to the wondering youth. *In the future you will see much more that will astound you further. You will see a lot more than you will understand.*

He turned around to view the Brighold and noted that he was in the same spot where he had stopped his killing, hands trailing drying blood, still dormant with the wreckage surrounding him. The funny thing about him was the entire lack of any other person. He was alone and left to his silence without any movement of another soul. Tolmaar whispered into his conscience and was rewarded by an upwards surge in the movement of the man, who slowly shook himself and reared up to full height. The wizard directed him, telling him what to do, and the man dutifully turned in the direction of the remainder of the camp, sloshing through the wreckage entirely alone and unmolested.

From a safe distance the army, what remained of it, watched him march through other deserted tents and tear them from their posts, trampling through the canvas and equipment. The wizard followed the proceedings with much interest. He saw the fear imprinted on the faces of the soldiers as they huddled together, well out of range of the monster, trying to gain some sort of comfort from each other by talking in whispers. They somehow thought noise might rouse him from his silence and repeat his murderous action to their detriment.

The Brighold ignored them, however, and decimated the rest of the encampment. He came to the last tent and ripped it asunder, kicking the poles down and splintering them to matchwood. His attention was then distracted by the crowd of soldiers. He was regarding them with some thought, as if trying to weigh up whether they were mustering an attack on him. They stood out of range, ready for instant flight if he made for them. Instead, he came to a halt and dropped his arms to indicate he had done what was meant of him.

The wizard began to urge him forwards by crying:

Now! Attack the soldiers, kill them now!

The stone man just stood there swaying, with his massive hands hanging down, but this time the wizard noticed that he was wet under his eyes, and realised he was crying. He was weeping with frustration about the bloodletting he was causing and did not want any more.

Kill them at once, do you hear? the wizard roared.

The Brighold had a conscience of sorts and was weeping because he did not want to kill the humans. Years of hopelessness had come to the fore and how he had been condemned to his living death in the chamber. He was in the stage of forgiveness, something the wizard could not allow if he was to play his part in the order of things. Tolmaar resolved to use the stone man to his greater advantage by not pressing him to do what he thought was wrong. He could play it to the full if it appeared right. The Brighold might have a change of heart and continue in the same vein, he might act as though it was his own idea. The thought spun out of sight, for he chose not to insist in the killing of the soldiers, and let the matter drop.

Follow my directions and I will guide you to your next task, he said, hoping the placation was enough.

Now the subject had changed from spilling blood it seemed to affect the stone giant's attitude, and caused him to comply with the wizard's demands. He stopped showing emotion and ceased crying. Tolmaar was relieved and shrugged to shake off the disappointment of not using him to further his cause, but let him not repeat his revolt lest the consequences be catastrophic for the Brighold, he promised himself. He must not think he is getting away from his allotted task because he has a few qualms about bloodletting.

In the end, the wizard decided he had the necessary qualifications to take on the army and win. That was the only object he desired of the Brighold, and the only thing of which he was capable.

Tillus the humpbacked dwarf was bored with watching the inventor, Dunne. He spent hours studying him and his paraphernalia of many different components that littered his workbench. Dunne, as usual, was engrossed in his work and never thought to look up and think others might be observing him or show any interest in what he was doing. Tillus showed a little interest in what he was going to show the master, but could not muster any curiosity about the thing that lay on the bench He knew full well the master would be angry if he did not do as he was ordered and get the full facts about the machine, which is what prompted the dwarf to show a little interest in it. That is why he was waiting for Dunne to leave the machine and do something else.

Tillus was in a quandary. He was in two minds whether to steal it or destroy it, but he was waiting for Dunne to give him a chance to do either one. The inventor lovingly cared for the machine and worked to ensure the damage inflicted by the dwarf was quickly and skilfully repaired. Fitting other new parts to repair the breaks in the system was taking much of his time and needed his full concentration. He ate very little and devoted all his remaining time to mending the machine.

He was currently soldering a length of copper wire to the chassis to produce an earth, thereby ensuring that all charges were grounded. If he was to really look, the magnetic surrounds of the invisible dwarf could be seen in the bright light, but Dunne neither saw nor realised anything was amiss, being so engrossed in his work. Tillus smothered a yawn and settled down to watch the inventor. He had finished soldering and put the iron down to cool. He wiped his hands on a square of soiled rag and surveyed the machine, smiling and muttering himself.

"Now for the important part of the operation."

He was just going to fit a new replacement to the damaged machine when a knock sounded on the front door. He covered his prized possession with a nearby cloth and opened the door to admit Meary and Hollis.

"Well, well, gentlemen," he enthused, leading them into the workshop and uncovering the invention, "nice to see you both again. I have made a start on the repairs as you can see. I have worked non-stop to repair the damage, so you can see I have not been idle. The damage was excessive, but I have it under control."

"Can you say with certainty when the invention will be repaired?" Meary questioned, eyeing Hollis.

Dunne turned to it and gave it a cursory inspection.

"I would say in about three days. The intricate part is over, it is just sweat and toil from now on. Come back in about a couple of days and it will be ready."

Tillus, resting against the far wall of the room, ground his brown stumps of teeth together in frustration. Hearing what had been said further added worry to his outlook. He had a choice of whether to destroy the machine now or carry it away. He could not be sure what the master had ordered him to do because of his notoriously bad memory. The thought of doing something against his master's wishes filled him with dread, for the consequences of such an action were too dire to think about. He must gain some sort of control over the machine, but what? Steal it or destroy it? He had an alternative, but his recent tangle with the machine only caused him to fear its capabilities. He still had the scars on his hands to remind him of its awesome power. The master had insisted, but *what* had he insisted? If only he could remember. He must destroy it to be on the safe side, but the memory of the last lot was too painful to risk it. He eventually decided the thing must be destroyed by fire.

He had watched Dunne at work soldering the thing together and noted how hot the iron had become. It glowed with fire after he had switched it on, emitting heat. He felt the red tip and burned himself when he touched it. It set fire to all it touched. He grinned gleefully and made his plans.

Things were happening in the chamber. Tolmaar had decided to enter the earth plane. The realisation of his dream was coming to fruition. The days of frustration and hopelessness were at an end. He did not know whether to tell Lucifer of his decision. He would have some sort of contempt for his plans, so he decided against it.

Well, let him, he fumed, *he already controls darker space and rivals the living God. Well, that too will end as soon as I enter the earth plane, then the battle for the supremacy, but first things first. I will use him to fulfil my ambitions.*

The excitement of his potential primary foray into the upper world thrilled through his being. The Brighold would keep the humans busy. They would not know what they were doing until it was too late. I will control the actions of the stone man, Tolmaar thought. He will keep them occupied while decimating their ranks. As soon as the light of day enters the atmosphere, I will emerge from my underworld prison and walk the land of the humans. He giggled, and startled the humpbacked dwarf, who had only just

273

materialised in the chamber.

"Oh, master," Tillus fawned. "I have found a way of stopping the scientists, I will burn the invention and stop them looking into the chamber."

Tolmaar regarded the dwarf with scepticism. He had never really trusted him, and now that the realisation of his dream was nearing its end his trust in the dwarf was diminishing further.

Never mind about the invention, he rasped, *I have changed my mind. I will not need it now. I have decided to enter the upper world at first light on the morrow. You will follow me and, using your invisibility, will watch for any intrusion into my affair.*

"Yes, master," said the cowering dwarf, "just as you say, master."

Tolmaar hardly heard the dwarf's reply, for he was filled with the exhilaration of the joy of self-achievement. He was in another world altogether. He wanted to cross swords with the best the humans would provide. He was sure of his supremacy.

All through the dark hours Tolmaar waited, the humpbacked Tillus at his side. He only moved once to gaze at the grey light of morning as it crept through the cavern opening.

He floated through the fetid atmosphere and swum into a shaft of daylight, briefly hesitating before emerging into it. For an instant the weak sunshine rays blinded him. He waited, getting used to the unusual daylight. Suddenly his breath throbbed in realisation, bathing in the new found feeling of excitement, delight. He relished the feeling and inwardly cursed himself for the life giving qualities that were unreachable to him from the earth plane. Inwardly he cursed Lucifer for his failure to explain about the light and sunshine that bathed the whole country with brightness and illumination.

Unused to the light, Tolmaar shifted uneasily in the sunshine. The sun felt warm on his skin and it was not unpleasant. He floated down to the mud-encrusted earth, feeling a surge of pleasure that he had never experienced before.

Well, well, he enthused to the now visible dwarf, *do you feel the warmth of the sun on your skin? The humans were loath to talk of it. It is something they never discuss.*

The dwarf was uncertain of his new role as the companion to the wizard.

"Master," he said, cringing, "perhaps if I lead the way you can avoid the mud."

It was only a suggestion so he winced as the wizard scolded him.

I will manage myself. I am your master, and I will walk the way I like. You will lead the way only if I say so. That is my ruling, you understand?

The humpbacked dwarf inwardly wilted under the words and made himself as dutiful as possible by cowering down before the wizard. Tolmaar ignored him and strode forwards determinedly, intent in seeing everything, leading the way out of the cemetery followed by the disconsolate Tillus.

Tolmaar was sure he had done everything to ensure his transmission into the supreme being he so ardently wished to be. To achieve this he needed the help of the Brighold, something vital to his aims. That was for where he was heading. In his mind he was already the leader and would tolerate no interference with his plans.

He thought he should fall in with the local people and dress as they would. He quickly changed his attire for the clothes they would wear by imposing a long coat that reached down to his knees. He tucked his long flowing beard out of sight beneath a deep collar, buttoning the coat tightly up to his throat. The change of garb hid most of his tall figure. He replaced his wizard's hat with a cloth cap. He waited for the dwarf to acclaim his appearance, but Tillus just sniggered behind his hand at the apparition.

Tolmaar ignored him and led the way out of the cemetery. In his mind the key figure in his plans was the Brighold. The huge man was a major part in his desire for world domination. After that, what happened to him was of no concern to him. The stone man was destined to go as far as Tolmaar would allow and no farther. The sorcerer had no feeling for him now. His ambitions entirely consumed him, filling him with all the thoughts he was able to muster.

The Brighold slipped from Tolmaar's mind as the gates clanged shut behind him. Tillus, in his minor role, followed dutifully behind, undecided whether to be visible or not, ducking in and out of invisibility, but still trying to remember what the master had willed him to do.

Meary spooned sugar into his teacup and sipped his drink delicately. It was hot and he blew gently on the amber liquid. The two scientists had left Dunne to his own devices after he had assured them the machine would be available for them to use within a couple of days. He was dying to see what it would reveal of the burial chamber and how Tolmaar would react when he found out he was being watched. He confided his hope to Hollis when he ventured to speculate what he was hoping for in its first use.

"It will be something of a surprise for the fiend to find out he is being watched by us. He might do something to surprise us when he does. He is full of tricks as you have seen and has a few nasty surprises up his sleeve in retaliation."

"Perhaps we are giving him too much credit," Hollis said. "He will have a reaction, that is understandable, but he cannot read minds or predict what we have in store for him."

Meary sipped his tea in silence, thinking about Tolmaar. He had no way of knowing the wizard was out of his tomb and heading for the Brighold. He was also unaware that the cavern was empty of its occupant. Meary was about to remark on the invention when the phone rang. The caller was Detective Inspector Lee. Meary listened intently as the policeman spoke, uttering little ahs as the man related all that had taken place at the army camp.

Replacing the phone he regarded Hollis with concern on his face.

"That was Lee," he said in a quiet voice. "The Brighold is up to his old tricks again. He went on up to a company of well-seasoned troops and routed them. He trounced four hundred men and decimated them. He brought them to a shuddering halt with his great strength. He killed seventy-five men and wounded scores. He subjected several vehicles to wholesale damage after tearing the men's tents to shreds. The equipment was torn to pieces and afterwards he set fire to the remains."

CHAPTER SEVENTEEN

After the Brighold had come to rest the troops heaved a collective sigh of relief. The cries of the dying could still be heard, but quieter now the carnage appeared to be at an end. The still figure of the stone man still dominated the site, but there was silence as well. He stood still, outstretched hands dripping with coagulating blood. His eyes were tight shut, seemingly trying to shut out the sight of so much spilt blood. His stone face showed traces of pain now that the agony was over and finished. His audience watched fearfully lest the carnage would be repeated. They watched from a distance, unsure of their actions, but hoping he had finished. The boldest of them trained all sorts of weapons on the huge figure, but were afraid to wake him in case the recent actions were to be repeated.

The words of Tolmaar echoed in the Brighold's senses. His reaction seemed to meet some sort of obstacle in his stone mind, a kind of blockage in his desire to end it all. Even with the block, the curt demands of Tolmaar held sway, and with his will the wizard demanded that he listen and obey. The fettered stone brain of the Brighold fought to throw off the yoke of the demands, but was yielding the fight. The stone man knew it, but yet was still in there amid the fray. Bit by bit the Brighold was losing the fight. He twisted and twirled to break free of the voice and almost succeeded in his endeavour to overcome it, but the commands were too strong or he was too weak.

His bid to straighten up was seen as a sign of his return to his recent slaughter. The watchers waited, ready to flee should he make any attempt to limber up for another onslaught on the camp or its occupants.

The Brighold was just waiting though. He knew the battle to defeat the wizard was finished. Through all the vitals of the Brighold, the churning gut wrenching unfairness of the man who held sway on his desires to quit was there. He earnestly wanted an end to it all. All he yearned for was a rest from all the tribulations that troubled him, to sleep forever in his coffin, never more to wake into the world, the world that just did not care about his welfare.

The wizard snarled as he stepped up his commands.

You must hear my voice at all times. You must listen to me and not to other thoughts that run through your mind. You must forget other things. You must obey at all times. I will guide you and keep you safe from all harm.

The continual drone had the effect of mesmerising the Brighold's senses and holding him in its spell. The constant repetition of the voice's demands was controlling him. He moved forwards once more, intent on doing what was wanted, moving like some lumbering animal, naked as the day he was born, then it happened. An enterprising corporal, under the command of Lieutenant Carstairs, espied a large hole dug by a road digger and, seeing it was in the direct route of the advancing stone man, feverishly covered it with a large square of netting. The result caused the Brighold to experience his first failure by plunging down the twenty feet deep hole in the road.

For a brief while, Tolmaar forgot his invisible cloak and appeared on the rim of the hole, staring at the huge figure. Now the Brighold was forestalled, and pawed at the sides of the hole in desperation, trying to walk through the clay wall. The wizard was faced with a major hitch to his plans until he found a solution, which he set out to accomplish by materialising an army of rats that burrowed into the pit sides.

From a safe distance the corporal with the officer at his side watched the scene with goggling eyes.

Scores of scurrying rats covered in earth and grass, bored through the sides of the pit, intent on creating a pathway for the Brighold. The rats, screaming and hissing, fought to get at the clay barrier, scrambling over each other in their desire to do the wizard's bidding.

The two men watched the excitement of the scene, until the NCO espied a barrel of fuel oil lying on the edge of the hole. The big black barrel, lying in a pool of oil oozing from its bunghole, caused an idea to form in his mind. He quickly ran to the barrel and twisted the cork free. He kicked it away from its wooden wedge stay and pushed it to the edge of the hole as it spouted black oil. The fuel oil poured out of the barrel and covered the rats. The corporal dropped a lighted match to the fluid and the fire whooshed up, enveloping the creatures.

At last man was making an impression on Tolmaar. His features were hideous as he recognised the victory of the humans. The rats had done enough though, to enable the stone man to limp out of the hole, but he was suffering. The heat from the fire had sapped his strength and affected his gait. He was no longer the man he used to be. The flames had also affected his vision. He was wandering as he walked, and barged into several obstacles.

Although the sorcerer did not fear humans, he was depending on the stone man to use his strength to battle the humans, but judging by the shape of things it seemed the Brighold was losing his ability to terrorise the villagers, especially now that he had some reluctance to carry out his programme of killing.

It was vital he continued his campaign against the people, putting fear into them without end. Tolmaar was afraid the giant man no longer had the same fear that had previously been instilled into him. Now the grim truth looked him in the face and he did not like it. Determinedly, he vowed to carry on with his ambition regardless. He must use all his resources. It was vital he found something to replace the fear of the Brighold, but what? The dust? One good thunderstorm and the dust would be nullified. The humpbacked dwarf? His laugh was hollow with a tinge of hypocrisy. The boy who had shown such promise? Yes, that was it, the boy, Bill. The humans would listen to someone of their own kind.

As Tolmaar watched, the huge man blundered into a stone wall and was sinking to his knees. He adopted a sitting attitude and looked ahead of him with a face filled with misery and dejection. He was plagued with eyes that saw through a mist, evidence of the damage the flames had caused.

Tolmaar now had to call on the boy. He was in the chamber and readily answered his call.

"I hear you, master," he intoned without question, seeing the seeming end of the Brighold. "I will negotiate with the humans. They will listen to me."

He appeared beside the wizard and confronted a crowd of villagers and soldiers. For awhile the scene looked decidedly ugly. Both the villagers and the soldiers booed them until a burly individual with a bushy moustache shook a stick to them, shouting and mouthing obscenities.

"You murdering pair of swine, you deserve hanging!" he yelled.

Bill held up his hand to indicate silence.

"I must apologise for the murders," he said as the crowd quietened. "Tolmaar does not wish to harm anyone. He will take over the running of our government. He will be the new president of this land. He will be the new president and will govern wisely and fairly. I promise you that he will."

The burly man shook his stick, and, turning to the rest of the crowd, shouted:

"We don't want a president. We don't need another man to tell us what to do. We want peace. We want an end to the murders..." He twisted around to face them again. "We don't need you or your master to take over anything."

"The stone man did the murders and he will pay, I assure you," protested Bill feebly.

The burly man was not to be pacified. He shouted above the cry of the youth.

"They and the giant caused the murders, the monster

should be strung up from the nearest tree."

These words were echoed by a soldier with a bandage around his forehead.

"I'm for hanging 'em right away," he yelled. "I'll get the rope."

Bill could see it was useless talking to them, so stepped back to confer with Tolmaar.

"Master, they will not listen to me, I fear for your life if you will not go."

Tolmaar resorted to invisibility and hid from sight. He had never imagined such a thing happening, and swore to be avenged. He was in no danger though, because of his cloak. He resolved to enlist the help of Lucifer, and returned to the cemetery, leaving the distraught figure of the Brighold to his fate.

After his rest, the stone man climbed onto shaky legs and tottered forwards. He had decided to return to his place in the chamber and yearned for its comfort. He tramped through the village streets, followed by a few daring people. They sensed he was in some sort of difficulty and needed help of some kind. He did need help, Tolmaar the master's kind of help. He followed the same tortuous path he had trod to do his murdering, stumbling and barging into obstacles without end, fearful lest another hidden hole would come. His senses jumped higher with recognition of the way home. He was where the chamber was. He was going home.

As he drew nearer the graveyard the crowd grew thicker until it developed into a mob. Children were pushed to the background and hefty men with a variety of weapons took the foreground. The crowd was led by a sprinkling of soldiers and policemen who trailed behind him less than fifty yards away. After walking into a tree, the Brighold paused to rest, leaning on it. The crowd stopped too, dawdling and ready for instant flight should he turn on them.

The giant man pulled in a huge breath and sat down. In his senses he could feel their presence near him, but he could bear them no ill feeling. He wanted them to feel it and not hate him for his activities, for he had only been acting under the orders of his master, Tolmaar. An inner voice kept telling him that they were enemies and not to be trusted. The crowd mistrusted his move to rest and were afraid of him. They dared not approach him and hung back, ready for flight.

After about an hour he used the tree to pull himself upright. He was finding it more difficult every time he moved, experiencing extreme pain in his chest and head. The mist in front of his eyes was getting thicker and more pronounced. There was a nagging ache in his legs.

The cemetery was getting closer with each huge stride, the iron gates just that bit nearer. His great legs became slower and slower, fighting the desire to rest. He leaned against the stone wall of the cemetery and panted for breath, fighting against it. Now the crowd was nearer, hanging back less than thirty yards away, fearful should he turn on them, but he was in no mood to harm them, rather to the contrary. He ignored them and pushed through the gates with a squeal of unoiled hinges and a crash of iron bars. As he lurched through leaning gravestones and sloughed down into mud encrusted graves, the crowd streamed over the walls and trickled through the gravestones, marking time when the stone man stopped and rested for awhile.

The Brighold teetered on the brink of the hole waiting for Tomaar to pull him in.

Hours before the Brighold arrived Meary and Hollis looked into the chamber with the aid of the invention. Dunne twisted the controls and brought the chamber into full view. At his insistence the picture gained substance and colour, and emitted a sort of sound. Little by little he persisted and gradually got it almost perfect, swinging around to them and exclaiming:

"There, that should take care of the fiend now. He little knows he is being spied on."

The two scientists were delighted. They clapped him on the back and congratulated him for his achievement.

Down in the chamber the revelations were enormous and sickening as well. Everything, including the piles of stone supports where the Brighold slept was revealed in the image, as were the hideous monstrosities that frequented the cavern. There were creatures that scuttled up the walls and slithered rather than walked. There were sliding scurrying monsters that hurried into dark corners in the little light seeping through the vault opening. A myriad of spiders, dangling from countless webs, danced in the feeble breeze emanating from the hole. There were fantastic worms and other creations diving for cover at any opportunity, and hundreds of reptiles slithering over the rocky ground. Rats scampered around the snakes, hopping over and, in some cases, under the gliding creatures. Grey and brown rats, mixed in with the ginger variety, skipped and hopped in a medley of colourful motion.

Meary watched a huge black rat waylay a tiny mouse and swallow it with one swift gulp. Other unknown animals crawled and hid in the gloom, slinking in the half-light and waiting for an unfortunate victim to fall prey to their attentions. All the sights were revealed in detail before the goggling eyes of the three men. They were all gifted with strong stomachs, but the sight of the spectacle was too much for Hollis to bear; he was violently sick.

"My God, what a sight," Dunne said, turning his eyes away. "How can anybody live in such an awful place, it must be hell to even breathe in such filth?"

"For someone human, yes," said Meary, "but he's not human. He is dead, but undead, if you know what I mean."

Hollis wiped his mouth on his shirt and commented.

"The man is a devil. He is out to control the world by the actions of the Brighold, also with the help of that hideous dwarf who damaged the invention. Tolmaar will do it if he is allowed."

Dunne twisted a knob and brought the picture into sharp focus.

"It is what you said," he remarked, "you warned me and now I know. The fiend will take over if he is let alone." He pressed a switch and the picture faded to black. "The point is," he continued, "what is going to happen to us after he takes over the reins? He can be stopped, but it will take something spectacular to achieve it."

Meary thought about it and spoke to Hollis.

"The key to all this must be the Brighold. He is the one who is commanded by Tolmaar. The wizard must be out of his bolt-hole at present, so we should concentrate on the stone man."

Hollis, thin lipped because of his nausea, had to agree.

"We must agree to let science slide for awhile and bring him to book. The stone man must be killed before he murders us all."

Meary gave his colleague a worried look.

"Yes, we must forget about saving him for posterity and do away with him," he ventured. "He is a menace to society and deserves punishment for his crimes against humanity."

Dunne unhitched the machine from its supply of electricity and coiled up the cable. His stomach felt decidedly queasy from the sight down below. His eyes had seen what the other two had described, but the sighting was just awful. The horrible things he had seen in the chamber would be with him for the rest of his life. He lifted the invention into his car and waited for the other two to get in with him. The three men missed Tolmaar by two hours and the Brighold by three.

The military, backed up by the police, were told of the use of the invention and its inventor, Dunne. All eyes went to the inventor as if he was willing to confirm its use.

"This invention of yours, does it work?" asked the police in the shape of the commissioner of police.

Dunne repeated all he had seen in the chamber, describing it all in full detail, ending with:

"... all this without seeing any sign of the wizard."

The police commissioner listened in silence and only said a few ahs as every detail emerged.

"My machine produced excellent pictures of the chamber.

Horrible I know, but authentic. I repeat, Tolmaar was absent as was the young man, Bill. They were at another location."

The telephone shrilled on the desk and the commissioner answered it.

"Are you completely sure?" he enquired into the receiver, and waited as the agitated caller spoke into his ear.

He replaced the phone on its cradle and addressed the three men.

"That was a constable I have covering the proceedings. He said the Brighold has gone back to the cemetery." He spoke to them with some conviction when he added, "That means Tolmaar is back in the chamber after his brief foray into our world. We must use this opportunity to make sure he stays in his grave." The police chief was out of breath with the depth of his passion. "We *must* bring all this lawbreaking to a close by either jailing or killing him."

"We realise this," said Meary, eyeing his friend and raising his eyebrows. "We are all responsible citizens, so we say the Brighold must be destroyed or detained in such a way that he will never menace the public again."

The commissioner needed to indicate he was listening and nodded in agreement.

"I don't think there is a prison safe enough to hold him," he said slowly. "If we *do* succeed in holding him, there's no guarantee he will not break out, no, if we get the chance of destroying him we must do it." He nodded to the general of military intelligence, standing by and said in addition, "What say you, Douglas?"

In reply the general looked up from the paper he was studying.

"I fully endorse what the commissioner is saying," he said, folding the paper and sliding it into a breast pocket. "He is literally getting away with murder each time he wins. We must lock him up and throw away the key. The only alternative is to kill him. There's no other solution."

Meary and Hollis exchanged meaningful looks. Their dream of studying the Brighold was fast becoming exactly that, a dream. All the work of the Lund and Dunne association was as for nothing.

"Is there no way we can do anything but destruction?" questioned Hollis, looking at the two government men. "We worked so very hard to achieve what we set out to do. Can't we use some sort of drug to quieten him?" He looked at Meary, hoping for his support. "What about the powders and the ashes that Tolmaar concocted, cannot they be used to affect some sort of change to his condition?"

Meary looked at his colleague with some sort of sympathy.

"The powders and ashes are of little value to us now. Lund was mistaken in his analysis of them. The wizard has generated a situation where he has created a cause, but no remedy."

The phone rang again and the commissioner answered it.

"What is it? I thought I said we were not to be disturbed?"

He listened for the space of about two minutes as the voice rasped into his ear, before speaking in a soft tone.

"That was the constable again. He said the cemetery is now nearly occupied by the military and the police. The place is crawling with the public, who all say the Brighold has disappeared down his hole." The commissioner continued with feeling. "Now is the time for us to act. The rats are back in their lair and ripe for extinction. We must use the time to bring to a close the episode of the Brighold." The commissioner reiterated very slowly as they listened. "The Brighold *must* be destroyed before he has another go at us."

The general agreed and went out to arrange a meeting with his senior brass. Meary consulted his two friends, Hollis and Dunne.

"It was a nice try, but the odds were stacked against us from the start. Tolmaar in his lust for power went down the wrong road. It must lead to perdition as all his kind find out in the long run."

A little way away from him, Tillus the humpbacked dwarf, lounged against the far wall and, in his invisible state, heard all that was being said and wondered what was intended for him now. Tolmaar once again was in the chamber, right back from where he started. Tillus considered what he must do. The tables were being turned with a vengeance. What should he do? Go back to the chamber or stay on his own? He wished he could remember what the wizard had ordered him to do. He tried to follow the run of conversation, but it was too deep for him. He fell into a lethargic state and decided not to bother any more.

Lucifer eyed the disconsolate Tolmaar and wondered why he had ever concluded that the wizard was more than a failed alchemist. He professed airs of greatness and required his underlings to treat him as such, but Lucifer, with his proven gift of feeble enlightenment, listened to him and his complaints, and was surprised he had ever thought of him as anything more than a jumped up dreamer.

They had the affront to hold me responsible for the murder of their citizens, he was complaining bitterly. *Me, who was going to bring magnitude to their world with my born leadership.*

Tolmaar's face was a mask of humiliation and defeat, and radiated contempt in the eyes of Lucifer.

Knowing full well what had transpired, Lucifer lied about his knowledge of it by asking:

"What happened, Tolmaar?"

The wizard outlined what had taken place and complained about those who rejected him, with a tirade of abuse that had the advocate of evil covering his ears.

They will be the losers in the long run. My time in office will make them all rich and powerful.

And yourself, no doubt, thought Lucifer with a smile. Out loud he sympathised with the disconsolate man by agreeing with him.

"They just don't know when they are well off, so typical of the human race. I have many who are just the same. Do not recognise sincerity when it hits them full in the face."

Lucifer was uncertain where the next move of the wizard was going to be and, curious, posed a question.

"What do you propose to do now?" he asked with baited breath, waiting for an answer.

The wizard waited for awhile before answering.

They won't get rid of me that easily, he grated, with teeth gritted and lips in a firm line. *I will wait awhile and then give it another try, only this time it will be worse. The murders of the stone man will be more pronounced, more horrible to witness. I will include children, even babes in their mother's arms. I'll teach them to reject me. The Brighold will support me in my campaign. He will show them a lesson they will never forget.*

Lucifer smiled to himself and promised to remember on whose side the wizard was supposed to be.

Tolmaar looked at the Brighold standing in his usual fashion, limp hands falling from relaxed arms, fingers outstretched so that dirty brown stains were evident. He eyed the naked man and wondered whether he was over his attempt to rebel. He had no real way of communicating with him and realised he had not even been glad of his support. He was after all just an animal like the rest of the lowly monstrosities that frequented the chamber.

In the space that represented his brain the stone man watched the wizard with not a little apprehension, inwardly expecting him to insist on his help, but not demanding it like he had done at the outset. His make-up was such that born within him was the desire to end his murder of the villagers. It was a new found feeling and something he wished to preserve. The opposing force of the wizard wanted it otherwise, that is where the two men disagreed. Deep within himself he had the feeling that the wizard wanted it to be different and would insist on his help, which is where he was determined to resist his demands and refuse!

In his past years, leading up to his incarceration, his imprisonment in the chamber was, to the king, justified, but the Brighold was not in total agreement with the result of the trial and wanted final recognition as such. He cursed the progress of the years in reducing his chances of redress. In his heart he little wondered whether he had any chance of seeing any change in the outcome. In the mind of the stone man too much water had passed under the bridge for it to make a difference, but the thing that did make a difference was the trial and its result. Even now after all the years had passed he wanted justice, and in full measure. He demanded it. The Brighold only had his past life in the chamber to make comparisons, so anything that had happened in recent years was unknown to him, but that was enough. The imposition of later years was far too much for him to consider, so he simply chose to ignore it. He had had too many things to think about since then. His senses clawed at the fragmentation of happy years, but ignored the sad ones.

He had very little recall of his previous life during the reign of the king who had imprisoned him, but he chose to disregard it as of little consequence. Ancient scenes of happiness ran through his head and coursed through his stone veins in a constant stream. The pictures flowed through his brain and filled him with remorse, causing him to recall his murderous ways – in contrast to the wizard and his devices to continue them.

The wizard ended his study of the Brighold and returned to his other thoughts. Since his return to the chamber he had been filled with revenge towards the humans, and plotted vengeance. Now with every urge of his body he desired to even the score. He constantly harped on the cause and the result. He strode around in anger, returning without end to the same dark thoughts, running through it again and again. He chose the same theme and touched it constantly. He wanted to beat the human race in its desire to outlast him, but lacked the qualifications of endurance. Tolmaar mused on his thoughts and came to a decision. He would return to the upper world and try again. How he was going to do it he was in no way sure, but he must try if he was to succeed.

His gaze took in the Brighold with the same degree of decision circling his mind. There had been something uneven about his attitude since his return to the chamber, as if he was no longer his old self and projected a softer and milder image. The difference disturbed him for awhile and he vaguely wondered if he was the same man. To add to his discomfort he remembered the attempt at rebellion by the stone man. It was most important that he complied with every command if the wizard was to realise his ambitions. Tolmaar needed the Brighold's strength and murderous ways if he was to overcome the humans. He could never match his enormous energy no matter what he did.

Through eyes that no longer had their previous intensity, the Brighold saw the object of his domination and cursed him for it. Regardless of his great size, he knew he would surrender in the end. He was a prisoner of the wizard as surely as the prison he had relinquished in the chamber.

Meary and Hollis first espied the Brighold from a great distance. He was limping on a wounded leg and used a sword as a crutch. He looked so formidable they hesitated in mid-stride, gazing at the naked man in horror.

The two scientists were in the van of a crowd of soldiers and policemen. On seeing the stone man, the crowd dispersed to the shelter of the rock-strewn woods. The two men gazed at the huge figure from behind a rock, watching him swing his sword, cutting a branch with one enormous sweep of his hand. His actions were accompanied by a limp that seemed to add to the fearsome gait of the huge figure.

As they stared at him they were aware of the hideous lacerations to his skin, caused by the fire. His stone skin was hanging in tatters around his body and his face was blotched with open sores that showed advanced infection. He staggered with a zigzag to his walk, holding on to nearby trees for support. The two men could see his agony.

"He looks all in," Hollis said, watching him. "Now is the time to get him while he is injured."

"He is still dangerous," Meary said, peering around the rock.

A single man decided to risk it and stepped into view less than twenty-five yards from the Brighold.

Immediately the hidden people held a collective sigh of horror and watched the stone man for his reaction, but there was no answer from the Brighold. He just looked at the man and dropped his head, closing his leathery eyes in abject misery. Bit by bit other men appeared from the woods and stood at the edge of the trees, ready to flee should he attack them.

Time progressed and there was no action from the Brighold. He dropped the sword from relaxed fingers and ran an enormous hand around the wreck of his jaw, fingering the lacerations with questioning fingers. Gradually the nervous crowd left the shelter of the trees and slowly filtered down to the road. A policeman sat on a rock and wiped his brow with a coloured handkerchief. His face was wet with sweat and he fanned it with the square of cloth.

The knots of people stopped away from the stone man and would not approach him, standing in groups less than fifty feet from the huge apparition. The Brighold ignored them and went on fingering his face. He squinted around him, looking at the people. The fire had damaged his eyesight and he constantly rubbed his smarting eyes. His big features turned to and fro, trying to make out the crowd and how it was formed.

Suddenly, in an explosion of red tinted fire, the wizard appeared beside the Brighold and stood there regarding him. He addressed the crowd and shouted at the massed ranks.

See what you have done to the poor man, he said with waving hands. *Through your refusal to accept me as your soul saviour, you have put him in mortal jeopardy.* He waved his hand to encompass the crowd. *I will be a fair and honest leader and will listen to all complaints. You will not regret regarding me as your protector. I will rule the earth and cast out all who disobey me. I will—*

"We don't need a leader. We don't need *you* to tell us how to lead our lives," the policeman interrupted as he finished wiping at his face. He turned around to regard the rest of the crowd. "Who is he to tell us what to do? Where does he come from, who is he? Who or what is he to lord it over us?" He turned back to face the wizard and yelled, "Go back to where you come from, we don't want you and we don't need you. Go while you are able."

The stone man will back me up, yelled the wizard, backing away, his face visibly blanching with fear.

The crowd surged forwards, clutching a variety of weapons. Tolmaar retreated, hiding behind the crouching figure of the Brighold. He could not understand why the people would not accept him, but he was not about to risk their anger. With one wave he vanished in a puff of smoke.

The stone man levered himself upwards as the wizard

vanished. He threw the sword high into the air and limped forwards, back along the road he had just travelled. Deep within his breast was anger towards the wizard. He somehow knew the cause of his resentment lay with him. He headed for the cemetery and home.

The remnants of the crowd followed him, still not trusting the huge figure and hanging back, seeing where he was going and following at a safe distance. The two scientists were drawn along with the crowd, surging along with them and joining in the general hubbub.

Bit by bit, the countryside returned to normal. The birds returned to the trees and twittered in the branches. The squirrels scampered amongst the leaves and ate the acorns, sitting on their haunches, a far cry from the silence of the grave and its recently returned occupants.

The wizard was fuming in anger to Lucifer and ranted about the reception of the crowd.

They rejected me, he said incredulously. *I was prepared to give them the benefit of my expertise, but they rebuffed my advances.*

Lucifer smiled. He was glad it had turned out this way and delighted it had happened to the wizard.

"You cannot trust the humans to do the right thing," he said. "I should know because I have been dealing with them for years."

But they rejected me, Tolmaar insisted. *The Brighold was there and did not support me in my bid. He is a failure.*

"The very man," Lucifer declared. "The stone man has entered the gates of the cemetery."

CHAPTER SEVENTEEN

A transformation seemed to be happening in the mind of the youth, Bill. Confused thoughts ran through his brain with alarming regularity. His mother played a major role in them and appeared without end in most of them. Meary also played a significant part by surfacing, but in a lesser role. Bill tried to find a connection with the two, but could not manage it. The wizard was there as well, but he presented an entirely different picture to his other friends, more of an afterthought, but with vague recollection. Bill's mother came through as a soft option and so did the older scientist, but the wizard showed a stern side and brought forth the lad's recriminations.

It was easy to see whom the boy preferred and he was beginning to show it. In the boy's mind Tolmaar was the master and always presented himself as such, but there were other things more wholesome and homely. His mother stood for security and comfort, and always had. The wizard showed a harder side, and constantly exhibited it by his actions.

Bill met the two scientists in the lane near the cemetery

and managed to produce a shy smile. It was evident the boy was back to normal, for it showed in his attitude. Hollis was first to notice the difference and welcomed his return to his recent self by exclaiming:

"Bill, lad, welcome back to the land of the living. We were concerned for your safety, so it's doubly welcome to see you are free from the clutches of that fiend underground."

Meary joined in the celebrations by slapping him on the back.

"Glad to see you back to normal, Bill. Your mother will be pleased to see you once more. She has been so worried about you. The influence of the wizard was something she could not understand."

The baying throng yelled loud cries designed to force the wizard into doing something about the murders perpetrated by the Brighold. The bravest of the crowd reached the walls and scaled the rocky surface. They trailed through the leaning gravestones and finished up at the grave in question, staring at the black void and shouting down into the pit.

The two scientists and Bill stood watching them from outside the graveyard walls, staring as they swung on the ropes of the rope hoist and pushed the chair around in tight circles.

The Brighold confronted the wizard and stood gazing at him with eyes that threatened to fail. He squinted at his master and realised his entire life in the chamber was wrapped up in his disposition. His very existence was due to the ambitions and designs of the figure standing before him. All the way it was the wizard who pulled the strings and he was just the puppet who danced to the tune. The stone man was aware it was Tolmaar who operated him to his satisfaction and never ceased in his desire to cause him unrest. The stone man relaxed in his willingness to do the same to the alchemist as he did to others who fought back–kill him! He dropped his crooked fingers and let his butchered stone arms fall to his sides. He was beaten and the wizard was free to cause havoc on the earth willy-nilly.

The wizard sensed the indecision and rejoiced inside. He had won the war against the Brighold and was aware of it. The Brighold was a beated hulk and he knew it.

Outside the graveyard the trio was added to by the appearance of the inventor, Dunne, who eyed the crowds.

"Quite an assembly, I'm thinking. They will not do any harm to the equipment will they?"

Meary followed his eyes and noted his concern.

"There's not much left anyway, I have managed to save the important items— What on God's earth was that?"

The interruption by the expletive heralded a small tremor in the ground that ran in the earth beneath their feet and died away. The quick flash of shock caused a disturbance in the topsoil, which led it to shed the topmost layer of dust covering the earthen tracks left by the crowd.

"It is some sort of seismic shock," Dunne said in small voice, laden with awe. "I have never experienced it before and it worries me."

The people in the graveyard also felt the ground move beneath their feet and after a few questing faces looked at each other with glances of concern, began to retrace their steps. Now the topic was the shift of the earth under their many feet and what it meant. The gradual shift to the gates became a torrent of people, all with precaution in mind and their safety if necessary.

The cemetery returned to normal with the remaining people. The hubbub continued now the danger appeared to be at an end.

"Was I imagining things?" Hollis asked the other three. "There definitely was a movement in the ground."

"It might be the beginning of something extremely serious," Meary volunteered, in a voice barely above a whisper, exchanging glances with Hollis as he spoke. "We all felt it, so it is no trick of the imagination."

"There was a shock," Dunne said, looking at the others.

They beheld the sight of a few nervous people leaving the cemetery.

"Looks like they felt it too," Hollis remarked. "I wonder if it is also worrying them."

They watched the slow process of the returning people climbing over the walls and trickling through the iron gateway.

Lucifer faintly felt the ground move beneath his feet and decided to vacate the chamber. It was the first time he had experienced a seismic shift and the sensation was worrying him. It was almost unrecognisable as a shock wave and could be mistaken for a normal earth displacement by movement of the land, but he was going to watch points and if necessary change his abode for one that promised safety. He eyed Tolmaar and the Brighold, but they did not seem to have noticed anything untoward.

The Brighold began to move, returning to the place

where the coffin had rested. He squatted on the stone floor of the chamber and sat there squinting at the standing figure of the wizard. His stone flesh was in the final stages of rank decomposition and hung down in huge shreds. The red weals caused by the flames glinted evilly in the half-light, running from his massive shoulders to his huge pelvis. His bony knees, folded beneath his skeleton, showed deep incisions in the hard structure, which threatened to open up again.

He sat on hard rock piles, head hung low and deep on his chest, What remained of his face was hidden beneath bunches of hairy flesh that weeped a continuous flow of suppurating liquid. He put his brown stained hands to his forehead and rubbed at his sore head, transferring his hand to his eyes, which ached without remission. He blinked endlessly and rubbed at them continually, enjoying the brief relief from the pain and irritation. He shook his head in desperation, trying to rid himself of the squint. Finally he shook his head in abject misery when he was aware that his fingers were having no effect.

From his place in the chamber the wizard studied the movements of the stone man. He was still thinking about his recent altercation with the crowd, remembering the last part when he had decided to leave them to it. To say he was furious with the Brighold's behaviour was an understatement – he was livid. The Brighold was realising the joy of freedom from killing others and now openly defied him to issue another order. This will not do, he fumed. He was the master and all orders must be obeyed without question.

In his rebellion, the Brighold was trying to refuse his orders to return to killing. It was this last denial that shook the wizard into doing something alien to his nature. He must enlist the help of the Devil incarnate, Lucifer, and offer him a share of his kingdom in the earth plane. Not too much, but a small part. He felt a partial rock tremor beneath his feet, but ignored the vibration. What is a spasm in the earth compared to my future ambitions? I will rule the earth so with it comes all conditions, he thought.

"The Brighold seems to be on his last legs," Lucifer said, noting the state of his skin "He will not last much longer, so I will use him to further your cause before it is too late."

As much as I dislike Lucifer I have to use him to gain my own ends, the wizard mused. He had to show him he was willing to sacrifice a little of his protracted domination. He had to allay his fears if he was to gain the initiative.

I do not think he has a liking for the programme I have mapped out for him. He is showing a dislike for killing by his rebellion. I have offered him a major job in the future, but I do not think he will be able to handle it.

Lucifer had his own idea of who should do what and when if the tasks were to be meted out. His dislike of the wizard was masked by his continual denial of the worth of the Brighold. He decided to question him by means of artfulness.

"I do not think he has the moral fibre to hold down an important job," he ventured, watching the wizard with narrowed eyes. "He has shown nothing that I can say gives him eligibility for any major assignment I can mention."

I suppose that is rightly said, Tolmaar returned. *I need someone such as yourself to do it.*

Tolmaar held his breath and waited for the expected reaction to his proposal.

"Me?" echoed Lucifer. "I don't think I will have the time."

It will enhance your standing in the world of the humans, the wizard said, giving a weak smile.

"I will think it over," Lucifer replied.

Perhaps you can provide somebody if you cannot do it?

"I said I will think it over," Lucifer said, a little perturbed by the question.

The wizard spoke then, more like a constant influx of continual information rather than a mild discourse between two opposing factions.

I studied under the Great Grattu for my wizardry, as you know. I entered the Grand Division containing the special school of advanced demonology. I passed with honours. The school provided a special medal to commemorate the occasion.

Lucifer was waiting for the invitation, noting it was on cue. He had been expecting the wizard to make him an offer of this magnitude for a long time, but what of the long-term view? He already had the expectation of the world and its prospects. This was said as signed and sealed, but what of the greater rewards to which the wizard was hinting? What of the final recompense? That is what the archangel was interested in – the ultimate reward.

The wizard was into his final discourse. As if alone, he uttered a monotone of words delivered in a loud whisper.

I was the young man with the most promise. I had the world at my feet and showed the highest of expectation. The world will not see the like of me again, and all I get is a quick ending in a dungeon, which I no longer want or need.

"It was not your fault you became sick and died," Lucifer

said, matching his whisper. "There were millions like you who suffered the same fate. Look at the Brighold, see how he was treated by the king."

Tolmaar ignored the remark and steered the conversation back to the subject he liked most.

I had dreams of running the world. I would set a standard for my subjects and dare them to exceed it. No matter what they did I would give them a tiny fraction and take a huge portion for myself.

The words of the wizard echoed around the chamber and bounced off the rock walls.

Up above in the cemetery the clouds gathered and waited as the deluge began. The thunder ran through the darkened sky, lit by the occasional snapshots of lightning that forked through the heavens. A thunderous roar following each brilliant flash, reverberating around the graveyard in a rending crash that had the effect of bouncing off the tombstones.

The second stage had begun. The rain poured down and ran through the graves in a rising flood. It soon turned to hailstones and repeatedly drummed on the stones. The dark came and bathed the scene with a gloom that almost resembled night-time.

The cemetery was deserted of people, the remainder of the crowd having long since gone. The four friends had also departed, taking with them the knowledge that they had seen the results of the partial collapse of the graveyard. Before they left they each satisfied themselves that the subsidence was at an end and no longer threatened to escalate, but unknown to them the storm was a danger to the place and was in the process of destroying their cosy expectations.

Meary looked at the sky and cast doubt on whether the storm would abate.

"This will delay any more operations at the cemetery now. It is up to the military to take it from here."

"I am sure they will do all they can to bring it to a suitable conclusion," Dunne said, eyeing the sombre nature of the sky. "It is set in for the night. I don't like the look of all this rain, and how dark it is becoming."

"How does Tolmaar see the fact that you are once again your old self?" Hollis asked Bill.

"He won't like it," Bill replied, smiling. "I know him and he will be furious. I was his star pupil and he had such promise for me."

Meary sniffed to show his derision.

"*Forced* star pupil! Someone who is under a spell is not a pupil, but a virtual prisoner. I do not call that a star pupil."

The dinner gong sounded and ended their conversation. They trooped into the dining room and tucked into a steak and kidney pie. The steaming plates were piled high with the delicious food and they waded in with huge appetites as the rain turned to hail and beat a rapid tattoo on the glass window. They looked at the falling hail then looked at each other.

"A dirty night ahead," remarked Hollis with a half-smile. "I wonder if it will affect the ground of the cemetery?"

"It might," said Meary pensively, rubbing his ear with a thumb. "We saw the results of the ground shifting, we felt it move beneath our feet."

"Yes," Dunne said, dismissing the comparison with a wave of his hand, "but that is no criterion. It was just a minor disturbance of the topsoil and may not mean anything."

"*May not* is right," Hollis said, lifting a fork full of pie to his mouth, "but with all this weather affecting it we might see a different picture."

Bill raised a piece of pie to his mouth and chewed delicately. It was the first he had had of any type of food and Meary said so with a puzzled expression on his face.

"What did you eat while you were in the chamber?"

The boy furrowed his brow to show his attention to the question.

"You are wondering and so am I! I ate nothing that I can recall, but I never felt hunger like I do today." The youth shook his head to emphasise his inner feeling, and added, "It is so good to feel hungry again, I forgot what it was to taste normal food," with a nervous giggle that had the rest of them joining in.

Outside the hail danced on the window and beat at the walls. The storm was increasing in severity and the dark threatened to plunge them into gloom. The waitress flicked on the light and drew the heavy curtains. For a few minutes, silence reigned and the only sound was the constant scrape of dinner plates.

Meary burped behind his hand.

"An excellent meal," he said to the waitress. "Something I have been looking ahead to these past few hours."

These words were heartily agreed by the rest of the diners, who raised their voices in chorus. The drinks came in then and the usual toasts were uttered.

The time marched on to ten, the boy said goodnight to all and made his exit, bound for his bed. The wind smashed at the hotel, driving the hail in a series of buffeting blows. The curtains lifted in the draught, a testament to the force of the wind outside. Dunne remarked at the lifting of the curtains with a hoarse laugh that echoed around the dinner table.

"It's not predicted in the weather forecast," he said, producing a newspaper. "Not on such a scale as tonight. There will be a lot of damage to property, I'm thinking."

As if to emphasise his statement the wind hit the window with a heavy thump that lifted the curtain into the air. The blast of howling wind rattled the glass against the wooden frames and threatened to dislodge the heavy windowpane.

The whisky had reacted with his dinner and caused a pain in the stomach of the older scientist. He tossed from side to side trying to ease it, but it persisted. He got up from his bed and searched his pockets for something to allay the pain, but found nothing. With the expectation of suffering further pain he went in search of relief.

He knocked on the bedroom door of his compatriot, Hollis, and waited as he heard the sound of slippers approaching the door

"Have you got such a thing as a couple of aspirins? I have a pain in my stomach and it is excruciating."

Hollis obliged and watched as Meary swallowed the tablets.

Meary was just about to retire when the phone rang. He looked at his pocket watch and noted the time as close on midnight. The person on the other end of the wire was the police inspector. He apologised for the lateness of the call and spoke in a voice heavy with alarm.

"We have had calls about the severe weather conditions and of the effect it is having on the cemetery."

Tolmaar was still ranting on about the stars and their order in the scheme of things in the past. He was saying that everything had their rank from the beginning until the end of time.

The stars and worlds infinite were created to hold the countless animals and plant growth that existed from time immemorial. They each, after dying and leaving this earth, travelled to infinity until reaching their allotted goal. The stars, created after the big bang, split into countless worlds where each entity now resides.

"And you believe they still live, roaming their particular piece of the galaxy in a mortal state until the final end," remarked Lucifer, preparing to leave the chamber. "It is my belief they died in their time on earth and nothing will revive them after their death."

Don't you believe it, scoffed the wizard. *Nothing really dies, that is why I am waiting for my call to take over the reins.*

"You still think they will stand for your recall after the way they rejected you?"

They will do as they are instructed. They are after all my servants and will do as servants do.

Lucifer gave a bitter laugh.

"You expect them to come to heel just like a lowly dog? My instincts don't match yours in the final summing up. They are all born with the will to survive and with it a degree of humility. They will never surrender it while they live."

Tolmaar echoed the laughter of the Devil.

Then they will not survive. Without me to guide them they

are lost, he said derisively.

Lucifer kept his temper and his council. He was at a loss to make the wizard understand that since man's conception into the supreme dynasty it had been ever such.

"They will not like it," he vowed in a whisper. Out loud he said, "Most have this common factor, *modesty,* with the abiding sense of fair play, plus a liberal sprinkling of courage to go with it."

That will avow them nothing. I have the greatest say when it comes to strength of purpose. I will overcome their puny efforts of resistance to my ideals.

Nearby the Brighold awoke from his torpor and watched the rats jump over his legs. He felt no pain from his ordeal, rather the opposite. He had no idea what sleep was and just closed his eyes to protect them from danger. His leathery eyelids were burned and swollen, and showed red weals where the fire had reached them. He had no eyebrows and he very seldom sweated. Now his deeply pitted forehead was running with the same sort of watery substance emitted from the rest of his body. He neither cared nor felt the soft scratches of the rats scampering over his stone feet. He had long since done nothing to discourage their desires.

Owing to his failure to talk, he was never asked anything or to say anything. On countless occasions he had felt the desire to say something as it reached his lips, but he never said anything other than uttering a cry of agony as a hurt registered. Now a new factor had emerged; the feeling of pity. He had never imagined he would feel anything for the victim, but nevertheless the desire was still there.

The fire had not affected his hearing, so in himself he heard his two masters discussing him and his fate.

He will not survive his injuries, the wizard was just saying. *The fire has affected his judgement and his resolve. He will die in the chamber. The potions and powders that I produced do not have the effect I wanted. If I find something to help him overcome his entombment, I will try to undo his final days in the chamber with the result."*

Lucifer was incanting a set of words to precede his departure from the chamber. The cavern echoed with his weird words that were designed to produce the right atmosphere to take him on his ride to infinity.

So, are you not going to help me in my ambitions? the wizard questioned.

"There is little time left to us," Lucifer argued. "Did you not notice the earth tremor a little while ago?"

Surely you are not afraid of a little shift of the earth? Tolmaar said, answering a question with his own query.

"It's never happened before, not in all the years we have been together, and that is since we have known each other."

Friendships do not last forever, the wizard said,

"Friendships indeed," the Devil said, pursuing his previous thought by smiling in sympathy.

The storm showed no sign of abating. The darkness increased until it was just like night. Torches flared constantly from a line of policemen walking down the cemetery lane. They trudged along an avenue ankle deep in rainwater and mud, sloshing through puddles and miniature rivers that threatened to block their passage. The lights carved a waving line of reflected illumination in the water pools they encountered on their walk

Detective Inspector Lee, heavily fortified against the slanting rain, dug his chin deeper into his raincoat and inwardly cursed the rain and the freezing cold that seemed to accompany it.

"Just my luck to be called out on such a night," he muttered to himself, looking for a non-existent pile of rocks that some eager person had reported had erupted.

He stepped over a deep pool of rainwater and felt the cold water in his wellingtons. He shivered as it sloshed in his boots and travelled up to his calves in a numbing agony of cold despair. One man slipped to his knees, falling over a hidden rock that lay just beneath the surface of a large puddle. Several men pulled him out, and as he recovered he uttered curses at the pool, and the weather in particular.

The pile of rocks that constituted the fall was a rain-soaked mass that somehow seemed to have happened in the vicinity of the graveyard. It covered an area fifteen feet or more across the lane and in the gloom looked an imposing three feet deep. Lee called his men together and shouted above the sound of the rain.

"We've got to clear it. The commissioner will be here shortly so look sharp."

A sleek black police car pulled up beside the rock pile and the commissioner got out. He was dressed in oilskins and a sou'wester buttoned tightly beneath his chin.

"I know it's not the night for clearing it away, but it must be done and as soon as possible."

To set an example he grabbed a large rock and heaved it over to the side of the road and dropped it down. One by one the policemen copied his action and soon they were all carrying bits of rock and ferrying them to the side of the lane.

Overhead the rain teemed down and was joined by the lightning that flashed to light up the scene. The thunder rolled, crashing and echoing among the many gravestones. Rainwater poured off the graves in a stream and ran away down the central grave hole. Despite the intensity of the bad weather, the men were sweating with the work and added to the water with perspiration.

Little by little the pile lessened and, as the hours increased and the pile decreased, the lines of working men ate into the rock pile. To his credit, the commissioner did his share of labouring and only paused to tip the water out of his wellingtons. Gradually the rocks in the middle of the lane were transferred to the edge of the road, where they lay soaked with the force of the deluge.

It stopped raining and the wind lessened, giving the workers some respite. Lee copied the commissioner and emptied his boots. He climbed into the welcome relief of the police car and basked in the heat radiating from the heater. The commissioner clicked open the passenger door of the car and joined him.

"What a terrible job for the men to do in all this weather," he said to the commissioner. "I hope the powers that be are satisfied with this night's work."

The commissioner grunted to show he was listening to him, and relaxed against the cushions of the car.

"It had to be done," he said, still blowing with the exertion of the work now over. "Trouble is it was left for us to do." He looked out of the car window and gazed at cemetery wall. "I only hope that this business of the Brighold and the others will come to a satisfactory conclusion."

Lee sniffed in derision. Some hopes, he thought, judging by the stories he had heard. Tolmaar could not be relied on to do something he had no desire to do. According to the talk going around the village he wanted to be president or something.

"He is a complete idiot if he thinks he will be accepted without a national cry of foul. The likelihood of our leaders standing down and letting him take over is preposterous. They'll never do it, especially without a general election."

The commissioner laughed at the idea and spoke with some finality.

"Imagine the prime minister cow-towing to this upstart. He'll have him put in prison."

He watched the lines of policemen come to attention and answer their roll-call. The lights were flicked on to see where they were marching and the policemen waded through deep puddles and large pools of stagnant water as they went. The two men followed in the car, skirting the numerous pools of rainwater and threading a tortuous path between them.

Behind them the cemetery relaxed into silence. The only sound to be heard was the steady drip of falling drops. The rows between the graves still showed ankle deep water, but it was lessening all the time as it drained away. There was an unearthly silence overall, and this was added to by the end of the storm.

The world waited with baited breath for something to happen.

The Brighold was rubbing his forehead again. The weals

were looking angry now and stretched from eye socket to temple in an eye watering line of pain and misery. His arms still bore the red marks of the fire. His stone skin was still displaying big sores that were emitting green pus with every flex of his mighty muscles. The rats smelled putridity and sniffed at the massive frame of the giant.

The huge man played with the dust by trickling it through his fingers and out between his outstretched legs. He could feel the friendship of the dust and amused himself with it whenever he could. It filled him with affection and kindness towards it whenever he felt the fine particles run through his outstretched hands.

The wizard saw him playing with the dust and wondered what it was that amused him so. He had no idea of the bond that existed between the two entities. He was alone now. Lucifer had long since departed and was now on the journey to where time began. Tolmaar sniggered at the idea and wished him success in his travels. It will little serve him, he thought, to avoid life's little pitfalls. The shifting of the earth was just one of these little obstacles. I myself am used to such obstructions and leap over them with infinite ease. I have that capacity to overcome all known troubles, such trivialities as the Brighold playing with the dust are beneath contempt for one with my intellect.

He dodged a hanging spider spinning its web and realised he was alone. He was friendless in the entire world and called no man his ally, but it was ever such. Since his interment beneath the surface of the earth he had had other things to occupy his mind, with little time to call his own. His main occupation was fulfilling his destiny, and he had no interest in other affairs. He was invested with pride for his devotion to ambition and would not allow any other thing to deter him.

A thousand years of denial would never alter his aspiration to soar above his rivals, not that he had any now. The years and man's inability to rise above little things had set out to kill him, like the parasites that live in the body. It was those that put an end to him. He was filled with a burning desire to be as simple as the thing that played with the dust. He still picked it up and let it filter through his fingers. It was difficult to see what the Brighold felt when he did it, but he was getting a certain degree of pleasure from the action, like a human child playing with a toy.

Tolmaar was making comparisons more and more, using the human being as a simile. He resolved to use something else with which to relate other than those. He had no use for time. It was not on his side that he could recall. Through the years that had come and gone he had little desire to remember any particular occasion that he had held dear.

With an enormous heave the Brighold pulled himself upright. The exertion cost him dearly as it pulled open a number of fissures that spilled liquid. Every movement caused extreme agony and shot through him with the pain of mortal despair. He limped badly and only moved now he had a purpose to fulfil. He was going to kill the wizard.

The water seeped through the ground and into the crevices that surrounded them. The rain was adding to the weakening of the ground by its continual fall. A deluge of rainwater struck the ground with some force, removed the topsoil from the graves and deposited it in the rivers of water that washed off the surface. As each torrent ran away another stream built up and disgorged its watery load into the central grave pit.

It was just two hours later when the final shock hit the area, displacing a further amount of soil that dribbled away. The water, marked with bubbles of floating earth, surged in its urgency and rushed pell-mell to the central grave that acted as a drain.

The second seismic shock was much bigger than the previous one. It radiated through the cemetery and trembled through the leaning headstones with a degree of violence that had them sinking farther into the mire. The shed was almost the first to go. It suffered by shattering the superstructure, which split and let the wooden planking of the rotten roof slide down into an abyss of sliding mud. At the base of the shed the hard cinder that packed the composed surface of the floor heaved and reared up in an agony of tortured ashes and stones.

Amid all this confusion, the chair with the ropes entangled around the central uprights slid into the hole without a murmur or sound, slipping into it with comparative ease. Several stones, already sunk, slipped down to a newer level. The gravestones, old and new, slid into the void created by the shifting earth. The occupants, old and new, vanished with the remains of their coffins into the void opened up by the upheaval, hurtling down with their possessions to the cavern below.

Gradually everything changed. The walls encircling the cemetery slowly sank into the void, settling down into the mud encrusted ground with effortless ease and disappearing into the sodden earth with hardly a gulp. Strangely the gates remained upright to the last before silently sinking into the mud. The angel with uplifted fingers clenched in prayer vanished into a watery grave as did the name of the cemetery inscribed on the iron railings of the gate.

Of the series of shocks suffered by the graveyard the last one was the most severe. The hidden rocks, sharp and precipitous, rose into existence, displaying knife edges of keenness that spoke of razor sharp edges. Above the turmoil other larger boulders emerged. These were the final layer of flinty stone that heaved up from the deep fissures of the earth and made a sudden appearance in the cemetery. This showed a penetration to the upper limit of the cavern. The rock face encircling the chamber parted from its core base so that its skin of gravity was affected. The resultant urge was to throw off the gravity, resulting in anti-matter that shook off its pull on the earth.

The huge roar accompanying this change in the aspect of the cemetery rang through it interminably. The sound batted from one rock to another in an avalanche of reverberating echoes. The rain ceased, but the seismic agitation continued. The earth shook with it and trembled as the earth dipped crazily in a violent display of earthen disorder.

In its entirety the disturbance lasted for a number of hours. The shocks were felt as far away as the village. People feeling the disruption and hearing the roaring came out of their houses to see the cause of the commotion. Of course they knew it had something to do with the cemetery, so they just as quickly went inside again.

A solitary policeman riding on a bicycle witnessed the end

of the transformation. He went back to the scene of his recent rock carrying job and saw the amount of devastation that was happening to the graveyard. He was amazed when he saw the amount of damage. He pulled his notebook and pencil out of his breast pocket and took down a few notes. He especially noted the change regarding the amount of rocks present, the absence of the graves and the familiar headstones that accompanied them. He licked his pencil to make it appear stronger and drew a small sketch to itemise the change.

It was then he felt a few aftershocks and decided to exercise caution by curtailing his inspection. He did up his bicycle clips and, muttering about caution being the better part of valour, got on his bicycle and peddled away to the village and the police station.

He met the two scientists, Meary and Hollis, as they emerged from the police station, and wished them a cheery good morning. The two men were just off to inspect the cemetery and the noises they had been told about that had been heard during the night. The elderly scientist was curious about the noises and wanted to see what had caused them.

"I think the noise is something to do with the wizard," Meary said, fishing in his pocket to find his spectacles. "Now he is alone in the chamber I will see what his reaction is."

"What do you mean, reaction?"

"Well, now he is without the youth, Bill, to console him."

"He will probably find another one on which to unload his troubles," Hollis said with a forced smile.

Meary polished his spectacles whilst walking, and finished by wiping them on his trousers. The puddles of rainwater hampered their way along the lane, making them skirt the really deep pools by walking in a wide circle around them. The pavement showed dangerous subsidence that was repeated every so often by the appearance of small rock falls, which further prevented them from walking with their constant assembly. After a particularly heavy fall of rock was blocking their passage they both felt the need to have a rest.

Meary sat on a big slab of rock and expelled a large blow of air.

"Look at all these piles of rock, there must have been something of a disaster to see such disturbance!" he exclaimed.

Slowly, fastidiously, they picked their way past the rain-filled holes and into the area surrounding the graveyard. The devastation was hardest around that area. The walls encircling the cemetery were flattened as if by a tornado. There were rocks and debris everywhere, and even the iron gates with the proud emblem of service by the council, were missing. The two men climbed over the piles of stone and saw the heap of splintered wood that had once been the shed. They trekked around the wood and associated tools lying near the demolished hut and ran smack up against the remains of the headstones.

They each threaded a tortuous path around each obstacle as they met it, climbing over huge boulders and rocks in their way. The devastation to the cemetery was appalling. Evidence of the catastrophe was everywhere and mind-boggling. Slowly they got nearer to the central grave for which they were searching.

The graveyard with its freshly dug soil and stone gravestones was entirely finished. Not a trace of it remained. There was not a single flower to be seen amidst the wreckage.

Meary stooped and picked up a piece of broken stone, squinting at the lettering. He had great difficulty deciphering the words, but he managed to read it.

"My beloved hus…," said Hollis, who was reading the words over his shoulder. "Obviously my beloved husband," he said. "There's not much else left of the cemetery."

Surprisingly they eventually stumbled upon the central grave without much difficulty. It was flanked by several large pieces of rock intermixed with pieces of the same design. Among them was a child's doll caught under a sharp piece of rock that prevented it from blowing away. Hollis retrieved the doll with some difficulty and stood there studying it.

"Probably left by one of the children in the crowd," Meary said, examining the scruffy clothing. "They were all here, all looking for something to see."

Hollis folded it up and put it into his pocket.

"You never know, she might come back for it. I will ask around to find out if someone is missing a little doll."

A weak sun decided to emerge then, its watery rays bathing the scene in a thin atmosphere. The damage was intense and far-reaching. It stretched for the entire length of the cemetery and not an iota further.

"Curious to say the least," remarked Meary with his customary suspicion of most things peculiar.

Hollis bent down, put his ear to the orifice of the central grave and listened. He straightened up with a curious expression on his face, calling Meary over to him. Meary stepped over to listen and put his ear to the hole.

From the grave came the sound of hideous demented laughter…